VANESSA IS NOT A VICTIM

GABRIELLE S. CLARKE

LIFESLICE MEDIA

Dedicated to my characters.
Sorry!
(Not really though)

AUTHOR'S NOTE + TRIGGER/CONTENT WARNING

Hey reader,

Trigger Warning/Content Warning things to note - instances or discussion of death, murder and family loss.

Also, there are dialect and grammar choices that are intentional and specific to the regions and cultures highlighted.

If you've found an editing error, please shoot the team an email: sbrent@lifeslicemedia.com

If you enjoy the story, please leave a review:
Amazon
GoodReads
And sign up to receive book news, updates and giveaway opportunities!
https://bit.ly/VanessaSignUp

PROLOGUE

To Whom It May Concern:

The first of the deaths was not our fault.

In fact, we didn't know about it until it hit the news. Or, more realistically, until it hit our notifs.

It was all very Stephen King. Or, R. L. Stine, maybe. Mack Van went missing, and two hikers found his body in Watercress Woods the next day. A singular stab wound to the chest, a red cloth napkin laid over his face, and he was Black, so… Super stereotypical. Very uninspired.

A tragedy, of course.

Mack was a good kid, even when he shouldn't have had to be. Unfortunately, his life ended for a convenient plot device.

The second death was not our fault, either. When Rosette Colton was found in the girl's bathroom at Logan High School a month later, it started the serial killer panic in our town. A dead, pretty, popular, blonde girl made the situation suddenly serious to Logan. Suddenly, people started caring about their lives (though the alcohol and tobacco markets did not crash), and parents suddenly started paying attention to their kids. It was all very new, exciting, and interesting. For once, we all had some conflict.

At first, we were bored, and (to one of us) the situation seemed like a good opportunity to fix that.

Then, it got personal.

Of course, the police weren't doing much of anything, but after further... investigating, it proved to be a bit more than the police could chew, anyway.

We, however, had the resources and the knowledge to stop the entire ordeal. At least, we believed we did, which was enough to make us jump into action. We are the very reason half this town wasn't dust by now, yet we were made into the bad guys?

That's a bit cruel.

We don't blame anyone for this misconception. In fact, we probably could have worked harder to make everything make sense to the rest of you. Unfortunately, no one except those who saw it happen would believe us.

We write this letter hoping someone out there might understand. We hope someone might recognize why we did all this and why you won't find us. To those who knew us, we are the most sorry.

To the rest of you useless jerks, thanks for nothing. And you're welcome.

Anyway, as we attempted to explain, and will continue to elaborate on in the near future - provided we live that long - no, we didn't start any of this mess.

But did we finish it?

Hell yes, we did.

Love,

The Sentient

OPENING CREDITS

I was bored. As usual.

I'd always been like that. I started things, got tired of them, and moved on to the next. I tried sports, art, academic rigor, delinquency, and an infinite number of fandoms.

Nothing stuck. There's not a single thing in the world I found interesting enough to commit to save for the occasional corny horror movie. I liked those.

So, after a while, I stopped trying. Now, I stuck to the average. Average daily routine, average school life, average eating habits, etc.

I kept my appearance simple. My hair was loc'd up, as it has been since I was six, and claw clipped out of the way, or tucked behind my ears. I didn't bother with makeup, and while I liked how I looked when I wore it, usually I was not motivated to go through the process of it all.

Most of my outfits consisted of whatever the other kids found popular at the time, toned way down for convenience. Following the trends wasn't difficult, though I didn't spend extensive funds on specific brands. I mismatched the miscellaneous pieces I already owned and made it work. I had an average-looking face and body, so I was relatively pleased with my looks. There was a time when I dwelled on them much more intensely, but *that* got boring.

Not much provoked an emotional reaction from me, so my facial expressions were minimal. Apparently, someone who never reacted nor showed interest in much of anything was not what most people looked for in friends. I didn't mind being alone most of the time, though I suspected it contributed to my boredom.

Of course, I had my elderly aunt with whom I stayed for several years now... So yeah, basically I had no one. It used to be a big concern to the adults around me, but a series of poorly planned, forced playdates revealed I was just not a people person. At least, that's what I stuck with for most of my life.

Essentially, my life was mundane. Finding a dead body under a stall in my school bathroom changed that.

I considered walking out, ignoring it, and allowing someone else to deal with the discovery later. That wouldn't look good on the school's cameras, so I thought again.

I considered screaming, curling into a ball in the corner, and waiting 'til curious passersby entered as I stared at the body petrified, their inquiry regarding my demeanor prompting me to extend a shaky finger to the fresh-ish cadaver. That was a bit dramatic, so I thought again.

Sighing a bit, I started with the simplest option, which was pulling out my phone and calling 911. I paused.

A red cloth napkin covered the body's face. I kept a clear distance from the body, not really keen on getting into a puddle of blood. But the napkin was... interesting. I remembered they found Mack with a napkin over his face, too. I couldn't remember if it was red cloth, or stained red from, well, the circumstances. Carefully, I stepped to the side of the puddle and set my backpack on the ground. I reached in, grabbed a pencil, and used the eraser end to hook and lift the cloth. Slowly, I uncovered the body's face, and realized something.

It wasn't a body, it was a person. A nice person. Rosette.

We weren't close. I wasn't close to anyone, but she was nice to me. She gave me a pen, once. I'm not a very empathetic person most of the time, but seeing her on the ground like that made me understand why God would want to wipe out humanity and start over a couple of times.

I dropped the napkin, stood, and tossed the pencil into the trash. I would feel weird about using it again, so... Scooping my bag up, I picked up my discarded phone and started to leave the bathroom. I paused for a second, turning to look at the napkin again.

There was something about the cloth that felt strange. Not just the fact that it was clearly the killer's signature, placed almost artistically over the face of someone who'd never done anything in her life to deserve such a display. It felt... familiar. Something about it seemed to reach out to me, and I didn't even notice I reached toward it until I felt the soft fabric under my fingers.

As soon as I touched it, something happened. The hum of the air conditioner turned into a thick, loud, and jarring buzzing sound, filling the air. The room felt different, and the lights above me seemed to pulse, as if the room was breathing. Alive.

It didn't feel like a place I should stay in, but for some reason, I couldn't leave the cloth. I picked it up and tucked it into a slightly hidden compartment within my backpack that usually only housed a few sticks of gum or lip balm. Straightening up again, I exited the bathroom and gazed down the hall.

Nearby was a teacher from the middle school, pacing the halls, looking for trouble. Teachers like her always bothered me. She was the sort who may have once enjoyed growing young minds, but at some point down the line lost that passion and rediscovered another in the form of a power trip. There was a part of me that wanted to tell her just to see the prideful look on her face melt off like butter, dripping from her chin like the blood off Rosette's.

The other part of me felt a bit bad as horror etched her brow. I wondered if maybe for someone else, someone like me, perhaps, such news wouldn't be such a traumatic blow. Clearly, the information I shared with her wasn't the trouble she expected on a Tuesday afternoon.

The next several hours were a blur, and I spoke to way more people than I ever had in one day. They pulled me into the police station for what felt like endless hours of questioning. Throughout, I became several different people in a short amount of time - a witness, a suspect, a witness again, a poor girl, an asset to the case, a slightly less helpful witness.

To my aunt, though, I was being a nuisance.

"Why're you causing trouble, Vanessa? I'm always telling you not to cause trouble, yet here you are standing in a police station over the death of a little white girl," my aunt fussed, shaking her head.

"How am I causing trouble? I didn't kill her, I just found her. I've been helpful today."

"Don't talk back to me."

Well, that's the end of that conversation.

Anything my aunt said after that, she really was just saying to herself.

The drive back to our house was silent, and I went straight up to my room. I didn't realize until I tossed my backpack onto the floor that the buzzing sound had stopped. Something about that fact was disappointing, but I couldn't tell you why. I pulled off my clothes, retrieving an only slightly dirty t-shirt from the floor, and some shorts from my dresser. After I was comfortable enough in my pajamas, I laid across my bed. The box springs creaked under my weight. My blankets were balled up at the foot of my bed, and I stretched them out before sliding under them. The whole day had been understandably exhausting, but for some odd reason, I couldn't sleep.

Now, I truly never struggled with insomnia. Being chronically bored made it easy for me to sleep at any given moment. Yet that day, every time I closed my eyes, I saw Rosette.

Pale, motionless, *lifeless*, right in front of me.

For most, that was the stuff of nightmares. Many would have developed PTSD that same day. But there was something about the sight of Rosette that was so... poignantly *not boring*.

The red cloth vivid as the puddle she laid in, the way the room came alive right in front of me. It was quite honestly the most interesting thing I'd ever come across. Which was why I wasn't annoyed when they dragged me off to the station for questioning. In fact, the whole thing had been poignantly *not annoying*!

I sat up straight with so much energy I probably looked like a madwoman to the dusty posters on my wall.

Rosette. A victim of the perfect, classic horror movie crime.

Horror movies were truly the only things I was consistently less than bored with. Most were stupid, illogical, cliche, and weirdly bigoted, but they begged the suspension of my disbelief, and I always willingly gave it.

And now it seemed real. I could truly indulge in something interesting.

I'm no high-school detective. I didn't want to solve or avenge Rosette's death. I wanted to *live* Rosette's death.

Think about it: how much closer could you get to being a part of the horror than to be the victim?

I practically fell out of my bed as I pushed the covers off of me. I dashed to the other side of my room, kneeled, and tugged the cloth from its compartment in my book bag. Once it was in my hand, my goal became permanent in my mind.

I'm gonna die.

No.

I'm going to be killed.

Better still.

That killer is going to kill me.

Something in the air changed. Something bigger than my

room, than my block, than the entire street, shifted. I could feel it. Something was suddenly very different in this town, and I intended to be at the front of it all.

CLEARLY, the universe hated me.

That was the only explanation I could come up with after a full two weeks of trying and utterly failing to become a victim. You'd think it would be the easiest thing in the world, but it absolutely was not.

I spent every evening by myself (which was not much of a deviation from my usual routine), with all the doors unlocked, lingering in my kitchen and staring at the outdated, almost useless home phone that sat on the counter. Any call with no caller ID that popped up would get a fast and enthusiastic answer from me, only for me to hang up as soon as I realized it was just another telemarketer targeting the elderly. After a few hours with no results, I'd give up for the night and go to sleep.

The next day, I started it all over again, adding a few more stupid decisions throughout the day for good measure. I investigated odd noises I heard, only to discover it was the group of weird kids who thought making stupid noises and faces equaled comedy. Or it was a couple under the stairwell who didn't understand the concept of, I dunno, waiting until they got home to get up to... whatever they were doing.

In their defense, no way was their shoddy and uncomfortably public relationship going to make it to the end of the school year, so they were probably just getting those nasty make-out sessions in while they still could.

I could respect that.

At one point, I followed a trail of what I thought and hoped was blood, but it ended up being an even more concerning liquid seeping from one of the school's air conditioners. I thought better than to further investigate that one.

Any and every time I heard a noise somewhere in my house, I called out and asked if someone was there. The only problem with this was that my aunt literally never left the house, so I'd get a very rude, "Of course I'm in here, lil girl!" yelled back at me every time.

Through all of these disappointments, I stayed more optimistic than I ever had been in my entire life. I just *knew* I'd become a victim sooner rather than later. The killer hadn't struck in days, and I was convinced I was going to be next.

I came to the conclusion I either had the best or worst luck in the universe when I saw him for the first time.

The killer.

Dressed head to toe in black, with a blank white mask covering his face, he hid whatever might have been visible beneath the shadow of his raincoat hood.

When I first saw him, I think I smiled. He was perfect, exactly as he was supposed to be. The relaxed yet intimidating stance. The anonymous, but distinct attire. How anyone on the street could easily tell he was a psycho, yet still never have the foresight or care to report him. He was a delightful mirror of the most stereotypical, comically one-dimensional killers of the small-town-high school-victims genre. I affectionately named him the most fitting title I could gift: Killer.

The problem with Killer was he seemed to want nothing to do with me. As soon as I saw him across the street from school two weeks after I found Rosette, I thought my chance had finally come. Unfortunately, he didn't seem to feel the same way. He walked away, and in a blink of an eye, he was gone.

That was fine, I thought. He couldn't make his move here, of course. There were too many people around. Giddy, I noticed the sun quickly setting - a gift from the changing season. I hung around the school for a couple more minutes, before setting off as slowly as possible toward my house.

I made sure to take all the quietest, longest routes, dipping into any and every alley I could manage. I was so certain my perfect death would come that evening I stopped in a convenience store and bought an iced tea to make sure my throat was well-hydrated so I could perform the perfect horror-movie scream at my end.

Looking back, the most embarrassing part was when I realized in the pitch-black darkness of an alley behind the movie theater, Killer wasn't coming. I had spent hours walking around my little town like an idiot waiting around for a flake.

I'd never been stood up on a date–I'd never even been asked on a date before–but in that moment, I understood why girls swore off men forever over it.

Honestly, all men do is lie, I joked to myself.

I wasn't completely out of hope, though. This was the first time in my life I was really motivated to do anything, so I wasn't about to give up yet.

There was one fact that made me certain I would be a target soon — the lurking guy I saw out of the corner of my eye.

I didn't know if he knew I could see him. Well, I couldn't really see him. Anytime I turned to look at him, he was gone. I could barely make him out in my peripheral, but I knew he was there.

Occasionally. No, not occasionally — when I held the cloth (which was more often than I cared to admit) he'd show up, I'd try to look at him, and he'd be gone. It was really freaky, actually. Back then, I assumed it was Killer, but when I started to see him in my empty room, I assumed instead that this "Person" was some sort of wishful hallucination.

In any case, I should have known it was something much, much more concerning, but more on that one later — you're not ready to hear that yet.

Back to the become-a-victim thing. I had one more trick up my sleeve: revisit where they found the last two bodies.

I decided I'd have a better shot at getting picked off in

Watercress Woods, where they found poor Mack. I'd have the best chance of death at night and the bathroom where I found Rosette had become a memorial, and there was no way I'd get into the school at night and getting arrested for trying would really throw a wrench in my plans.

So, I set off in the middle of the night, putting on an outfit I thought would look nice when the authorities found me. Can you imagine how embarrassing it would be to be literally caught dead looking crazy? No thanks.

Unfortunately, the first time I made a careful outfit choice turned out to be for naught, thanks to the whims of the idiots I encountered that night.

TIP FOR AN IDIOT #1: DON'T MAKE OUT IN MURDER-CRIME-SCENE FOREST

TIME AND TIME AGAIN, Kian proved to me that he was an absolute idiot.

So much so that I, someone who had been actively trying to be murdered by our town's serial killer, was in the same space as him, tucked into the trees of Watercress Woods, right where they found Mack Van a month ago.

Unlike me, he wasn't there because he wanted to be a target; he was there because he wanted to swap saliva with his third girlfriend of the year, Laine Meeks.

I couldn't imagine anything more stupid than bringing your date to the scene of a murder while the killer was still actively killing, but there he was. Saddled up in his Volvo, an arm snaked around Laine's shoulders. She giggled over whatever undeniably nasty thing he whispered into her ear, cooped up in my death spot. I mean, it was perfect. Two unsuspecting hot people in the middle of a dark forest, being idiots together. I would have tried to kill them too.

Pause.

Ignore that last part, I'm not Killer.

Play.

Anyway, I had two options: one, let them steal my death and go home, or two, make them move before Killer arrived. I wasn't about to give up yet another one of my victim moments, so I decided on the second option. By the time I had decided such, the buzzing from before started again. In the last two weeks, I forgot just how loud and annoying it was, and I didn't even think about why it suddenly started up again until later.

I started toward the car, but the Plot was quicker than I was. Killer made a noise from the trees just next to the car. Our resident genius, Kian, got out his car to investigate, because, of course, he did. The next few minutes played out just as they were supposed to.

Laine sat oblivious when Killer struck. I saw the glint of Killer's blade as he stepped from the trees - black raincoat, plain white mask and all - but Kian didn't see him until Killer was directly in front of him. Kian didn't even get the chance to scream before the sharp metal plunged into his abdomen. I crouched to the ground, feeling around for a heavy rock, a sharp stick, something. No way would I allow Kian Wilson to become a victim before me.

Killer pressed Kian against the driver's window in true villain fashion, allowing Laine to see his blood dripping down the glass. I could hear her scream from my hiding spot, and she stumbled out of the car, running toward me. As soon as she passed me, I stood again, tossing a rock up in my hand. Killer raised his arm above Kian, ready to strike again. I wound my arm and threw the rock as hard as I could in Killer's direction. Fortunately, a decent amount of training from my softball days lingered in my head. Enough for the rock to hit Kian's car. Not enough to hit Killer.

So, I missed.

But the noise was enough to make Killer pause in his tracks, allowing me to approach him, pick my trusty rock back up, and hit him over the head with it. I expected him to fall unconscious immediately, like in the movies, but he mostly just looked confused.

Confused enough to allow me to hit him again.

After three hits, I was pretty embarrassed at my lack of strength, but eventually he crumpled to the ground.

Kian leaned against his car door, eyes wide, as he watched the scene unfold. *What a helpful guy.*

I guess I couldn't blame him, he was losing blood pretty quickly.

"Take off your jacket," I said, catching my breath. Knocking a guy out was kind of tiring.

"What?"

"Your varsity jacket. Take it off, quick."

Kian blinked a bit, but complied, wincing as the cloth pulled away from his wound. He wore one of the school's white spirit wear t-shirts, our school's mascot now painted crimson. I took the jacket from him, lining it up with the wound.

"This is gonna hurt," I warned. I didn't know what I was doing, but I tied the jacket tightly around his waist, like a tourniquet. He yelped but stood still until I had fastened the jacket as best as I could. "Alright, make sure that doesn't fall off, okay?"

I looked up at him, and he was paler than ever, but he nodded. I wondered about his willingness to follow my directions so easily. I came really out of nowhere, yet he trusted me blindly. Something about it was endearing, but mostly it was a tribute to how frustratingly stupid he was.

Right, now I had to go get the other idiot. I glanced up, expecting her to be long gone. Somehow, by some insane idiot-logic, she'd barely passed the tree I had been hiding behind.

"How could she possibly be that close? She's been running for like, ten minutes," I muttered to myself. Kian made a noise and shifted against his car.

"She's no track star. And she's got heels on."

"Okay, but she's running from a serial killer. Why doesn't she just kick her shoes off?"

"I dunno, you're the woman. Shouldn't you know?"

"Please shut up. I'm starting to regret saving you." I opened his backseat door and motioned for him to get in. "Stay here, I'll go get her."

Kian's eyes widened, and he shook his head frantically. "No way. I don't want to be left here alone."

"She's literally twenty feet away."

"And the guy who just stabbed me is lying right there. He could wake up at any minute," Kian reasoned. I rolled my eyes harder than I probably ever had.

"Alright, fine." I put my arm under his and around his back, supporting his weight as best as I could. He leaned against me, and I could smell whatever unnecessarily expensive cologne he put on to impress Laine. It was oaky and overbearing, pretty fitting for the annoyingly heavy athlete I was supporting.

We shuffled after Laine, who was so caught up in running she didn't know we were behind her. Kian called her, albeit weakly, in an attempt to catch her attention. I don't know if she couldn't hear him or was just dead ignoring him. I couldn't blame her if it was the latter.

Dragging Kian along with me slowed me down significantly, so we were thirty feet behind Laine the whole time. She screamed as she ran, her movements oddly flouncy and not at all urgent. The real kicker, though, was in a display of predictable absurdity, she tripped.

Over nothing.

I swear on everything she tripped over air.

I had to stop dead in my tracks to keep from facepalming myself to oblivion. At least we had the opportunity to catch up to her, rather than, you know, standing, Laine had opted to crawl across the forest floor, still screaming.

"Laine. Stand up, let's go," I said from directly behind her.

"Somebody help me!" she screamed hysterically, thrashing her arms around. For someone whose life was in imminent danger, her demeanor was just lax enough to preserve her perfect appearance. Despite crawling on the ground, I don't remember seeing a speck of dust on her white blouse.

"I'm trying. Stand up, we need to leave."

"Anybody! Please!"

"Oh, my fu— Laine. You're fine. Get up. I'm not standing here for much longer."

Laine finally released herself from her trance and turned back to look at us.

"W-what? No, that guy was chasing us—"

"Handled it."

"But... I sprained my ankle—"

"No, you didn't."

"Oh."

A silence that was about as long as the situation... Ridiculous.

"C'mon, Lainey, I can feel my organs shutting down," Kian groaned, clutching his wound. Laine awkwardly rose to her feet, shifting on her broken heel. She rushed to my side, standing behind my shoulder as we turned to get back to the car. My hand slid into my pocket to check for my phone to call the police, when I felt the softness of the cloth.

I paused for a second before starting to walk back, noticing the Person in my peripheral again. I looked behind me, almost pointlessly, since I knew Person wouldn't be there when I checked. I needed to focus on getting the two idiots on my arms back to the car, but it took me another few seconds to move again. Before, Person had just felt like someone else's shadow following me around every once in a while, but in that moment, it felt much, much more sinister than that. Despite my desperation to become a second-rate horror movie victim, I didn't like the feeling Person gave me. It was different from Killer. Scarier.

It felt like a main-character problem, which was certainly not what I wanted to be. So, I snapped out of it, tugged my hand from my pocket, and led the idiots back to the car.

Laine's eyes widened when she saw the still-unconscious Killer on the ground by the Volvo.

"Is he... dead?" Laine whispered, and I could feel her shiver a bit against my arm.

"I hope not," I muttered. I ignored the looks Kian and Laine gave me and pulled open the driver's side door. "Gimme the keys."

Kian raised an eyebrow in hesitation. "Uh..."

"Don't argue with me over this. I won't crash your precious car, alright? I'm still actively saving your life, remember?" I said, my hand outstretched impatiently.

"Right." Kian patted his pockets and found the keys, then tossed them to me. "Sorry. You have a license, right?"

I chose not to answer that question. After a quick lesson on which controls were which, Kian instructed me to drive back to town while he leaned his seat back, his face contorted in pain. He had been trying to play it off, but we were getting to a critical point with his wound.

"Wait!" Laine cried suddenly. On instinct, I slammed on the brakes, and Kian made a sound as if he had just been stabbed again.

"What?" I whipped my head in Laine's direction.

"We shouldn't leave the guy there, right? Shouldn't we pick him up and take him to the police station? I mean, what if he's the serial killer everyone's been talking about? The police should have him—"

"Laine." I cut her off, giving a hard stare. "What year are we living in? Is it 1985?"

She blinked, shaking her head in confusion.

"That's right. It isn't. That means we don't have to bring the dangerous guy who just tried to kill us in the car with us. We have cell phones. *Just call the police.*"

"Oh," she murmured.

I couldn't blame her for not thinking straight. She didn't come here with the same expectations that I did. Because of that, I needed to think for the three of us. One silly move and they become victims with me. Which was not my plan.

I didn't have control over whatever happened to the town after I got killed, but until that happened, I would make sure only I got the opportunity. I didn't want Killer getting burnt out or caught before he got to me, and all the best kills were toward the beginning of the movie, anyway.

We drove off, Laine on the phone with the police next to me. Kian was in the backseat, making a small, wounded noise every time I turned a corner a bit too sharply. He didn't relax until we were clear of the woods, back on the main road. Considering the size of our town, it didn't take long to get to the hospital, and nurses rushed to our side as Laine and I carried Kian in. They quickly separated Kian from us, and we stood side by side as they rolled him away to who knows where. A few nurses came to talk to Laine and me, but I slipped away. I wasn't hurt, so there was no use in wasting time being doted on by a bunch of strangers. I needed to get back to the woods.

I didn't feel right taking Kian's car, and all the buses stopped running hours ago. It would take a while to walk, but that was the only option I had. I needed to make sure Killer was alive. Maybe, if I was lucky, I could get him to kill me then and there.

I didn't make it very far toward the woods before my aunt spotted me. It's not a large town, and someone from the hospital must have recognized me and called her. Whichever snitch was responsible earned me a long lecture on the short drive home.

"What did I tell you about causing trouble, Vanessa?" my aunt fussed.

"I didn't. I saved a kid today. Two, actually. I was being helpful. Again."

It was no use. I knew that same phrase would follow every time, no matter how I tried to defend myself.

"Don't talk back to me."

Convo over.

I went straight to my room as soon as I got out of the car. I glanced at the alarm clock on my nightstand, which flashed 1:30 a.m. I sighed as I tried to get comfortable, but I couldn't sleep. I grabbed the cloth from its hiding spot in the drawer of my nightstand and stared at it for a bit.

"Put it on," something said.

To this day, I don't know if that was my mind playing tricks on me, or if something had genuinely told me to put the cloth on. I also don't know why I obeyed, but I did. I laid on my back, took a little breath, and laid the cloth over my face, covering my eyes.

God, I must have looked so stupid.

It took me a second to remember that this same cloth had been laying over the face of a corpse a few weeks ago, but I felt stupid taking it off at that point. So, I sat there like an idiot for a few seconds, or minutes maybe, or it could have been hours, before things got quiet, and I'd fallen asleep.

My dream was strange, consisting simply of me walking through my town. Nothing was happening, and I don't mean that in a "this-town-is-lame-as-hell" way, as I normally would. Genuinely nothing was happening. No one on the streets moved. They stood still as if stuck in a trance. The only thing that moved was the sky, which had a weird, dark red tinge to it. Not like a sunset red, but red like the cloth.

Probably a trick of the light filtering into my bedroom, seeping into my dream.

That's what I thought, but somehow I knew I was lying to myself. No matter how far I walked, how many people I passed, no one moved. At some point, I found myself at school.

In the bathroom. Rosette was there, cold and unmoving, but not like the others. I recalled the state of her body well. It was like she had just been left there for weeks. I found the same thing when I wandered into the woods and saw Mack and I felt ill. That might have been what woke me up.

I ripped the cloth off my face, sitting up straight. My head pounded, and I felt like I was going to throw up.

"It was just a dream," I reminded myself, but I wasn't convinced. I had a weird feeling in my head that something had gone wrong when I saved Kian and Laine, and not being able to make sure Killer was still alive wasn't helping. I knew this was real life, not some movie, and our town's serial killer was probably just a crazy guy who got off on cutting down high school kids, yet I couldn't shake the nagging feeling that this was much, much different than just that.

Much weirder.

Much more interesting.

I'm rarely wrong.

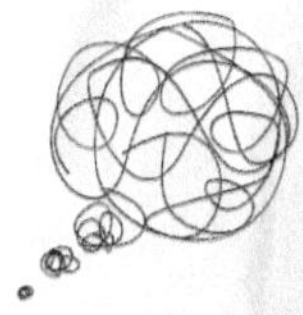

KIAN'S NOTE #1: RE: DON'T MAKE-OUT IN MURDER-CRIME-SCENE FOREST

FOR THE RECORD, we weren't making out.

Was that the goal? Maybe. But at the time I was stabbed, we really were just talking.

Funny enough, my memories of the first encounter with Killer drift in and out of my mind. I don't remember getting out of the car, I don't remember the mask Killer wore, I don't even remember feeling the blade plunge into my stomach. The one thing I remember consistently is her.

Vanessa.

I remember seeing her duck from between the trees in the woods, and the disappointed expression on her face when she missed with the rock. I might have been going into shock a little bit at the time, but I could have sworn the moon cast a halo of light above her locs, and her eyes flashed solid white. I couldn't take my eyes off her, nor her swift and determined movements. I watched in complete awe as she bashed a guy's head with a rock. This girl, who I'd only ever seen drifting by herself through the school halls or taking naps in the library was now another being, something both not human and more human than anything. The school's hermit now looked like a mythical hero, descending from the heavens in all her glory to save me.

In other words, she looked freaking awesome.

I don't think she noticed me staring at her as she drove us to the hospital, and if she did, she probably assumed I was staying hyper-vigilant of her treatment of my car. I won't pretend I didn't die a little inside every time she hit the brakes a bit too hard, or ignored the very nature of a speed bump, but none of that could really pull my attention from her. There was something about her I couldn't really place, but I chalked it up to the admiration anyone would hold for someone who saves their life. Right then and there, in that car, I vowed everything to her. It didn't mean very much at the time, but I was deter-mined to be there for her unconditionally as she had been for me.

What I didn't know was how little she wanted me around her. I asked about her constantly after I they stitched me up, and the doctors informed me repeatedly she had left. I didn't let up, however, until my father arrived in my room.

It's hard for me not to tense up around my dad. Maybe it's his nature as the town's sheriff, but anytime he looked at me I got an uncomfortable feeling that I had done something wrong. That I was doing something wrong. That *everything I did* was wrong. I don't know if it was fair of me to think like that, it wasn't like my father ever insinuated his disappointment in me, but I felt it there regardless. But now, I must have looked really messed up, because he started to cry. It was... uncom-fortable. He wasn't, like, sobbing or anything, but he was crying. It was kind of annoying, actually. Like, I'm the one who was stabbed, what are you crying for?

I sat there awkwardly until he wiped his eyes.

"Dad, I'm fine.. Chill," I muttered as he stepped to me.

My dad was a bit younger than most of my friends' parents. He and my mom had gotten married young and wasted no time in having me. I don't have a lot of memories with my father when I was younger, considering he'd had a lot less vacation time as a lower-level officer before he became sheriff. I never really understood why he insisted on working so much. My mother's inheritance from my grandfather ensured that we had a very comfortable life, but my father worked anyway. It was more annoying as a kid than it was now. Back then, I knew what I had. Our house was bigger than all of my friends' houses, I had more toys, more clothes, and I was rarely denied anything I asked for as a kid. So why was Dad working so much? Why was he a stupid police officer when he didn't need to be? Why was he gone so much when he had the choice to be with me?

As I got older, I figured it out. Some people can't stay idle. Some men can't stand the prospect of not being the breadwinner. Some people were restless. And some people didn't want the option to stay with their kids. What I hadn't figured out yet was what kind of person my father was.

It didn't become any clearer as he sat next to my hospital bed. He struggled a bit to speak, opening his mouth and then closing it a few times. He finally settles on what to say.

"Are you alright?" His voice was small, careful, and I hate him. I don't know why, but I hate him for such a stupid question.

"Yeah, they stitched me up or whatever," I mumbled. I want him to leave. I want him to leave, and I want to go see Vanessa. I need to thank her.

"I need to thank that girl who saved you," My dad said, and I think he read my mind for a second. "Laine told me what happened while they had you in surgery. That girl, Vanessa? Do you know her well?"

I shook my head. "She's in a few of my classes, but we aren't close or anything." My dad frowned.

"Do you know where she lives? I want to find her, I need to thank her and make sure her parents are informed. I should probably take her to the station as well, so we can get her statement. I've got guys looking in the woods for the man who attacked you, but they haven't found anything so far. Based off of Laine's description, there's a good chance this is the guy we've been looking for—"

"Dad, please, shut up," I heard my voice say. I didn't mean to say something like that, it just blurted out. I hated when my dad talked about the station, and right now I hated the sound of his voice. "I just want to sleep for a bit, alright?"

My dad recoiled a bit, then nodded. "Right. Sorry, son. Ah, your mother wanted me to video call her so she could see you..I'll just do that when I come back in the morning. I have to go back to the station, so—"

"Yeah. I know."

My dad nods again, shifting uncomfortably. "Right, well. Goodnight, son. I'm glad you're alright." I didn't reply, and didn't exhale until he left the room. I took a second to calm down, before reaching to the bedside table to grab my phone. It was cracked, a result of dropping in on the rocky ground when Killer got me. I tapped it so it lit up, and through the cracks appeared an abundance of messages. My best friend, Marco, asked if I was alright, and promptly made a gross joke about my new wound. My mom asked me to call her. Laine was checking in, and there were a whole bunch of other texts from a variety of people. I ignored most of them, only replying to Laine:

do you have Vanessa's number?

She replied quickly:

nah i didn't get it before she dipped. you
okay?

I sighed at her answer, texting back without much urgency:

oh okay. yeah im good. you?

It took a bit for her to reply, and I watched the three dots disappear and reappear at least twice:

yeah.

Another pause…

shaken up, i guess. but fine thanks to vanessa

I clicked my phone off and set it back on the bedside table. There was no use in going all detective right now anyway, chances are she was as shaken as Laine was. The doctor had said I couldn't be discharged for at least another two days, which was frustrating, but I doubted I'd have been able to find Vanessa over the weekend anyways. My best bet was to wait 'til school on Monday and find her there.

For now, I closed my eyes, the action of the day combined with the pain meds they doped me up made me extremely exhausted, and I shifted a bit so I was slightly more comfortable to sleep. Sleep, however, would prove to be much less comfortable than simply staying up.

As soon as I closed my eyes, I was back in the woods. Back in the Volvo, right next to Laine. The trees were twisted around the car, yet the whole space felt so uncomfortably vast. I turned to confide in Laine, but she was gone. Replacing her was Killer, face shrouded in the shadow cast by the hood of his jacket. It was as if he didn't have a face at all, but he was looking at me. I just knew he was. I could feel it. I began to panic, tumbling out of the car and starting to run. I didn't get far before crashing to the ground, and I screamed out at a tree root impaled my side upon my fall. The root didn't stop upon colliding with my flesh, only digging in further and further, as if growing between my intestines only to sprout a small tree as it broke from my other side. I was stuck, trapped in the tree's claustrophobic roots, and I knew Killer was close. I knew it was the end for me, and I couldn't do a single thing about it. I found myself doing the only thing I thought could save me.

I screamed for help. I screamed for Vanessa.

Over and over again until my voice was hoarse, until I finally saw her halo poke out from the trees. I felt a wave of relief crash over me as her eyes met mine. And her eyes were as crimson as the stain on my t-shirt.

"Kian!" She called. "Kian! Kian, wake up!"

What?

"Wake up, Kian!" Laine shook me, and saw panic melt into relief as my eyes opened and met hers. "You were totally flipping out.," she whispered. "Were you having a nightmare?"

I groaned, clicking a remote next to my bed to raise it up a bit. I rubbed the sleep from the corners of my eyes, wincing as I felt the pain meds start to wear off. My stitch-ache combined with the soreness of my arms and legs collaborated in a joyless symphony of pain. Laine pressed the call button for the doctor as she watched me shift. Finally, feeling a bit more awake and real again, I answered her.

"Yeah. I guess so," I muttered, and my voice was hoarse. Just as hoarse as it has been in my dream minutes earlier. I saw Laine frown, nodding her head knowingly.

"Yeah, I got them last night too. It was so freaky and vivid, like I was seeing you get stabbed all over again…" She trailed off, then looked up at me apologetically. "Sorry, I'm sure it's worse for you." I shake my head, straightening my legs out a bit more.

"Nah, you were there, too," I observed. "Plus, I don't even remember getting stabbed all that well, so your nightmare was probably much more vivid than mine," I lied. Laine hummed sadly.

"I dunno. It's still worse for you," she said. We sat in silence for a bit, then I spoke. "I'm glad you're alright, Laine. Physically, at least."

She looked up at me and smiled, and I noticed for the first time the dark circles under her eyes, and the slightly pale hue her skin held. "I'm glad you're alright too, Kian. Well, alive at least."

I nodded. "Alive, at least."

Laine really is a very nice girl.

There was one person I unfortunately got to meet during my hospital stay, a person the doctors and staff had managed to keep at bay until the day after the attack. When Laine had gone home after a while, and the doctors said I had another visitor, I had hoped it was Vanessa. So, when a camera crew and a woman with chunky blonde highlights throughout her perfectly curled hair and freakishly white teeth entered instead of my savior, I was understandably disappointed.

She smiled brightly at me and extended her hand for me to shake. "Hi there, Kian!" She said, as if we were already acquainted. "My name is Partly McCloudy, I'm a reporter for the Wilsonville Daily. I'm here to interview you about your attack—"

"No way is that your name," I replied without thinking, cutting her off. She blinked at me, and some air of annoyance crossed her face before she quickly fixed it. She had clearly heard such a comment before, but let her trained politeness ignore it.

"Ahem. I'm here to interview you about your attack last night. Is that alright?"

I wanted to say no, but she had already stepped in front of the camera, given a signal, and turned on her TV smile before I could answer. "Good afternoon, Wilsonville. My name is Partly McCloudy, and I'm here with Kian Wilson, the sheriff's son, who was attacked in Wilson Woods last night by who authorities are saying may have been the killer that has terrorized our town this past month. Kian, first and foremost, how are you feeling today?"

Pause.

There was something she had said that felt a little off somehow, like something about her recap that didn't quite click in my head. Well, not about the recap itself, that was all accurate, but... I guess I'll get to that later. Pay attention, though. Names are pretty important.

Play.

Her voice had immediately shifted to one of a stereotypical newscaster, so quickly that I almost laughed. She pushed a microphone in my face, and the cameraman stepped closer to me. I blinked a bit, and leaned forward into the microphone.

"Um, not great," I said, pretty awkwardly. She gave me an expectant look, and I cleared my throat before continuing. "Not great, uh, pretty shaken up, I guess. But, alive."

She nodded, a look of feigned concern crossing her face.

"I'm sure this all must be very hard for you and your family, Kian. We spoke to the other victim, Laine Meeks, earlier today, and she explained the events and just how frightening the situation was. Do you believe you were attacked by the alleged serial killer at large?"

"Uh, I'm not sure," I answered honestly. Partly looked dissatisfied with my answer, so I continued. "I think there is, um, a good chance that it was. I'm lucky to be alive."

"And do you have any suspicions as to who the killer is, and why they may have targeted you?"

The question made my stomach churn. Of course I didn't. I was a pretty popular guy, usually, and I couldn't think of anyone who might hate me enough to try and kill me. I knew it was most likely just circumstance, being at the wrong place at the wrong time. But something about it...

"I don't have any idea why or how someone could do this," I started, gulping as I tried to come up with an answer that would end the interview quickly so I didn't turn into a crybaby on the news channel everyone in town watched. "But I'm confident that my father and the rest of the police department will catch this guy and take him off the streets, so he can't hurt anyone anymore."

Partly nearly let a grin slip, apparently I'd given a satisfactory answer. She gave a curt nod and addressed the camera.

"I think that's what we're all hoping for," she said solemnly. "Thank you again for speaking with me, Kian, and to our viewers for tuning in. Remember, stay safe, make sure you know where your children are, and report any strange people or occurrences to the authorities immediately. Back to you, James." She stood smiling at the camera for another second, before the burly-looking cameraman gave her a thumbs up and she relaxed. "Good enough?" she asked. The cameraman gave a little nod and started to pack up.

Partly turned back to me, the amicable smile returning, but not as intensely as when the camera was on. "Thanks again for the interview, you can expect to see yourself on TV very soon." She gave a little wink, as if I was supposed to feel proud for having my fatigued face plastered on the screens of everyone I knew for nearly dying. I gave her as much of a smile as I could manage, and watched as she left, the burly cameraman waving at me as he followed her. The ordeal had been draining, and I unfortunately, found myself falling asleep again. You can probably guess how well that went for me.

By the time I was discharged, I was ready to go to school. My dad tried to convince me to take it easy for a week or so, but I firmly declined. I had things I needed to do, I couldn't just sit around. Besides, with the nightmares, it's not as if I was really getting any sleep anyway. The most important thing was finding Vanessa. I had my plan all laid out. Ask around and search every nook and cranny for her at school, then thank her profusely and vow my life to her. From then on, we'd become best friends and carry that valuable bond for the rest of our lives.

Unfortunately, life had other plans. As soon as I arrived at school, I was swarmed by a mass of people. Now, I was a pretty popular guy, what small town football player isn't, but this was unlike anything that'd happened to me before. You would think I still had Killers knife hanging out of my side with the way people ogled me. I couldn't hear myself think over the questions. Oh, the questions! Did it hurt, was it really the serial killer, how'd I escape, did I kill the guy, was there a lot of blood, was the killer cute? A cacophony of inquiries swirled around me as I tried desperately to wade through the crowd. I threw out a few halfhearted answers as I tried to escape, yes it hurt, I don't know, someone saved me, no I didn't, I don't remember, how should I know? No matter how many answers I gave, the questions kept coming.

Luckily, my best friend, Marco Vienna, pushed through the crowd.

"Alright, alright, people. The survivor will take your questions later. He's got English," Marco yelled over the noise, putting his arm around my shoulders and leading me away. People tried to follow us, but rolled their eyes and moved on when Marco delivered them a very rude hand gesture.

"You're a lifesaver," I exhaled, leaning against my locker as Marco grinned.

"You're welcome." I winced as he slugged me in the arm. "And you suck. I texted you for days, you couldn't bother to let me know that you were still alive?" He shut his locker and I trailed behind him as we weaved through the crowded hallway.

"Sorry, I just wasn't really up to talking to anyone."

"I was worried, man. You shoulda heard the rumors that

were flying around when the news broke." He shook his head with a low whistle as we slid into our seats. I chuckled darkly.

"Yeah, I've heard a few." It was all pretty expected, I probably would have been just as curious if someone I knew got attacked like I did, but seriously. Some people had too much time on their hands.

Marco leaned over his desk and locked eyes with me. "So. Tell me what really happened." His eyes gleamed with curiosity and I rolled my own.

"You're so annoying. But, fine." I leaned closer to him, looking around before lowering my voice so only he could hear.

"You know Vanessa?"

"Nah."

I rolled my eyes. "The school hermit?"

"Oh, the one with the eyebrows?"

"No, bro, the girl with the locs. She's in math with us? Always takes a nap in the library during fourth period?"

Nothing behind those big ole' eyes of his. I groaned. "Alright, whatever. Well, she's the one who saved me and Laine."

Marco raises his eyebrows. "Saved you?"

I nodded frantically.

"Dude, she came out of the trees out of nowhere, throwing rocks and stuff. Knocked the guy out cold. Then she drove me and Laine to the hospital. She's not the best driver, almost wrecked my car, but she got us there, right? Then she just disappeared. Left the hospital while me and Laine were getting checked out and just dipped." I searched his expression to see if he was as awestricken as I was, but all that remained on his face was a frown.

"That's low key kinda weird though. What if she was in on it? Why would she just be in the trees right at that moment?" Marco pondered aloud. I mirrored his frown.

"What do you mean? How could she have been in on it if she saved me?"

Marco shrugged. "You know, like those stories about those EMTs who almost kill people, just to be the ones to save them and get praise for it?"

"Right… but those are psychopath EMTs. Vanessa is just a student. How could she pull that off?" I shook my head. "Besides, no one other than you, me, and Laine seem to know that Vanessa saved us. She left the hospital as soon as we got there, and didn't even stay to get checked out by doctors. Why would she do that if she wanted the praise?"

Marco shrugged again. Thinking wasn't really his thing, evidently. I shook my head again, before I leaned back in my seat, zoning out as class began. I thought about what Marco suggested for a second, before pushing that thought away. No way. Vanessa was a hero. My hero. And I was wasting time talking with that cornball when I could be thanking her right now. But I'd have to wait until after class.

Finally, the bell rang, and I was the first out the door. I spent the whole five minute passing period searching for Vanessa, asking around about her, and finding her nowhere. All I got out of it was a scolding from my Bio teacher for being eight minutes late to class. My luck changed however, when lunch rolled around. I remembered seeing her once when I spent the lunch period in the nurse's office, eating her lunch on a flight of stairs while watching some gruesome horror movie on her phone. I went over there immediately, hoping against hope that I would finally spot her.

And there she was. Sitting in the same spot I remembered her in, munching on some carrots and a mes looking PB and J as her nose was just inches from her screen. I exhaled in relief, walking over to her quickly.

"Vanessa?" I spoke. She didn't react, and I assumed she was wearing earbuds or something. I clear my throat and speak louder. "Vanessa!"

She flicked her eyes up at me, and I grinned widely. I expected her to speak, or stand, or do something, but she just looked right back down at her phone.

My generation is doomed!

I blinked a bit, confused. Did she think I was some random or something? Did she not recognize me? "Vanessa, it's me. Kian, from the woods, remember?" I waved my hands around, trying to get her attention. "The guy you saved?" I made a stabbing motion to my abdomen, hoping to jog her memory. She didn't even bother to look at me this time. I dropped my arms incredulously, not believing I was really being ignored like this. I didn't know what she was watching, but whatever it was couldn't have been more important than the guy she had saved two days earlier standing in front of her, waving his arms like a madman. I approached her, bending down so we were eye level. She still doesn't look up, even moving her phone up to block my face from view. It took everything in me not to toss myself down the stairs then and there. Instead, I placed a finger on the edge of her phone, lowering it from her view so she'd look at me.

"What is it?" she asked flatly, finally meeting my gaze.

I frowned. "I want to talk to you."

Her expression turned genuinely puzzled. "Why?"

"Why?" I repeated incredulously. "Because—! I need to thank you!" Her face didn't change. I sighed. "Vanessa, I'm thanking you. For saving me. You remember that, right?" She nodded a bit, and I continued. "Well, anyway. You saved my life, which means I owe you it." I smiled brightly. "From the bottom of my heart, Vanessa. Thank you. I would be a goner without you." I don't know exactly what I expected, a smile, a hug, tears, who knows. But I expected a reaction at least. Vanessa wasn't in the business of providing those, it seems.

"Okay." Was all she said before raising her phone into her view again and pressing play on her video.

Okay? Okay? Was she joking?

"Uh…" I blinked, beyond lost.

She didn't bother to look up as she spoke again. "Is that it, or did you need something else?"

"Uh, that's it, I guess…"

"Cool, can you go away, then?"

I mumbled something that sounded like an apology awkwardly and started to shuffle away from the stairs. Something turned in my stomach. What was wrong with that girl? Did she even remember saving me? I couldn't let it be, for some reason. Maybe my own guilty conscience, or something. Either way, I turned back around, facing her again.

"Wait. Is that seriously it?" I asked. She still doesn't look up still.

"What?"

"I mean… no other reaction? Are you even human?"

She shrugged as if she truly didn't know, and I found that funny. "What do you want me to say?"

Her voice held no trace of sarcasm or annoyance, no real curiosity either. It was just flat.

"I dunno… Maybe something like 'no problem, Kian! Let's be friends!' or something like that?" I muttered.

She scoffed, and it's the most expressive I'd heard her react this whole time.

"I'm not saying that."

"Okay, fine, just… Geez, what are you watching?"

The sound of someone screaming, and the distinct noise of flesh being slashed open coming from her phone was starting to get to me. She finally looked up at me.

"A scary movie."

I grimaced as I caught a peak of the massacre on her screen. I looked away quickly, feeling my heartbeat quicken. "How can you watch that stuff with no reaction?"

"It's fun," she replied, and she didn't think I noticed at the time, but she turned the volume down. "Is there something else you needed, or what?"

I looked back at her, examining her mostly blank expression. As the hum of the air conditioner floated around the stairwell, I suddenly had a very disturbing feeling fall over me. I felt like the room was alive, breathing, pumping, moving. The light bulb above us flickered just barely, the sound was like a hiccup. I could feel the floor buzz under my feet, and the air was thicker than I remembered it being. I thought I was going crazy, when Vanessa stood suddenly.

"Let's leave," she said.

I followed her, relieved to be out of the suddenly alive stairwell.

A million thoughts swarmed through my head. What was that? Did I imagine it all? Why did Vanessa leave so quickly? Did she feel it too? None of these questions were answered as we heard the bell ring again. I blinked and Vanessa was gone, dipping through the hall to get to wherever her next class was.

I sighed.

Obviously, she wasn't very interested in the become-best-friends-forever plan I'd concocted. I considered giving up, but I couldn't see myself carrying on with the rest of my life that *she* had secured pretending like nothing happened. So, like any other sane and extremely grateful person would, I waited for her outside at the end of the school day. After standing up against the wall for a good twenty minutes, I contemplated whether or not she'd even walk out the door. I contemplated a lot of things, actually. Whether she'd left early, whether she was avoiding me, whether she existed.

Whether she existed?

It was a stupid thought, but it swirled in my head for a solid five minutes. Am I making her up? No, Laine saw her, too. But what if it was some shared psychosis? It's amazing the ridiculous things your mind comes up with when you're waiting.

Luckily, she walked out the door before my brain had the chance to collapse in on itself. She shivered in the cold a bit, pulling her jacket closed and zipping it up before heading toward the sidewalk. I jogged to catch up to her, tapping her on the shoulder before she could carry on.

"Vanessa, hey!"

I jogged in front of her, blocking her path. She looked annoyed but looked up at me. I wasn't too much taller than her, six inches or so? But the way she stared at me, it was almost as if she were taller. I don't know how to explain it, but that's how she looked.

"What now?" she asked.

I blinked a bit, not expecting her to sound quite so disdainful.

"I just think we should talk a bit," I started. She pulled a face, but I continued. "I just feel like I really owe you, you know? I mean, if you hadn't been there when you were, I would've--"

"I didn't do it for you," she said flatly. "So, stop thanking me."

…What?

"You didn't do it for me…? What do you mean? Who else could you have saved my life for?" It didn't make any sense. She sighed, a sigh that made it seem like I'd just asked the stupidest question she'd ever heard. Could you blame me? What did it mean to have saved me, but not *for* me?

"I did it for myself, obviously." She folded her arms.

My mind went back to what Marco said. Was it possible that she really had been in on my stabbing? Did she save me for praise like those psycho-EMTs Marco had read, or rather, seen a post about? I found myself taking a small step backwards and remembered something my dad told me when I was little as he showed me around the station.

"Anyone with the potential to save a life has the potential to end one," he said.

I didn't get it then, and still didn't get it as I stood in front of Vanessa, but I wondered if she was the person with potential my father had been talking about.

"Relax," she muttered, as if she'd read my mind and heard the long inner monologue I'd just performed. "I'm not Killer, if that's what you're wondering."

My expression must have been laced in confusion, because a second later, she rolled her eyes dramatically.

"You don't get it, do you?"

I shook my head. She tapped her foot for a second, seemingly in thought. She then took me by the arm, muttering a small command to follow her, and dragged me away from the school.

We walked for a bit, before she pulled me into the alley between the convenience store and the pharmacy. I misunderstood for a second, remembering this alley as one I'd brought a few female-friends to before to... chat... out of the view of any no townspeople. However, Vanessa didn't seem to have that same goal.

"I'm gonna die. Or, be killed, rather," she said simply.

I blinked, then frowned in concern.

"Is something wrong? Did someone threaten you? We can tell my dad, he's the sheriff so--"

"No, Kian." She looked into my eyes, some sort of urgency behind them. "I *want* to be killed. That's what I've been trying to do for like, a week." She sighed, seemingly exasperated. I felt my heart sink.

"Vanessa, you're not, like, suicidal, right...? Because, you know, whatever's going on in your life, there are people you can talk to!" I said in the most therapist-esque voice I could manage. "People love you, and stuff! I assume...!" I added.

Vanessa rolls her eyes, hard. "I'm not talking about killing *myself*, Kian."

I breathed a sigh of relief. "Oh, good. I was starting to think that maybe you didn't have people who loved you at home." I laughed a bit awkwardly, but she didn't seem amused.

"I'm talking about becoming a victim. Killer's victim. I've been trying for a little bit now, since I found Rosette. Stuff keeps going wrong, though. The first time I assumed it was my own error, but I thought I did everything right. Now it seems Killer is actively avoiding me... I mean, I know I'm not the usual profile for a target, but seriously, I've been trying all the tropes and I keep coming close..."

I stared at Vanessa as she kept talking. It was the most I'd ever heard her speak, and yet I could not understand a single word that was coming out of her mouth.

"You're joking, right?" I asked, my tone coming out a bit colder than I meant it to. She blinked in confusion.

"No? Have you been listening?"

"Yeah, I've been listening, but nothing you're saying makes any sense. Are you saying that you *want* to be one of the serial killer's victims? That you want to die?" I searched her eyes for some semblance of humor, some trace that maybe I had misunderstood her. But as I stared at her, I knew she was completely, utterly, and horrifically serious.

"Yes, Kian. That's what I'm saying."

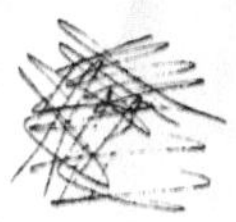

TIP FOR AN IDIOT #2: LOCK YOUR DOORS, FRONT, BACK AND BALCONY

A LONG SILENCE.

"... So, like I was saying, there are people you can talk to–"

"Kian–ugh!" I brought my hand up to my forehead in annoyance. He was looking at me with that idiotic look on his face, the stupid look people give you when they're *worried about you*. The same look adults used to give me when I wouldn't play with the other kids, the same look teachers give me when they talk to me about my "antisocial behavior." I didn't like that look, clearly, and I wanted Kian to stop.

"I'm bored, alright? Bored. This whole town, my whole life — all of it is boring." I sighed, catching my breath for a second. "I want to enjoy myself for once. I want to enjoy *something* for once. I'm pretty sure this is the only chance I'll get to be a part of something interesting."

I looked into his eyes, hoping for some semblance of under-standing to show on his face. I knew it wouldn't appear, though. Kian Wilson has never experienced boredom in his life. He's never not been at the center of something he enjoys, and he's never been... Well, anyway. I could tell he didn't get it.

"Have you tried, I dunno, sports or something?" he asked

quietly. "I feel like there are a lot of activities that would be a little bit better to try than having someone kill you. Like, knitting, or something."

"Kian, do you really think I haven't tried everything?" I sighed, rubbing my temples. "This is the first time I've had something I wanted to do in like, ever. And I'm not changing my mind, so don't try to convince me."

We stood there in silence for a while until Kian spoke again.

"Why did you save me?"

I looked up at him, a question on my brow.

"You said you didn't do it for me," Kian elaborated. "But I don't see how you saving me and your big goal of being murdered align."

"I did it for me," I said, dead serious. "I was worried that if Killer got you and Laine, or anybody else for that matter, he'd get burnt out or caught before he got to me. I don't want to miss my chance."

Kian didn't reply for the longest time. He just stared at me, and I wondered if he thought I was some sort of psychopath. When he finally reacted, he just laughed. I didn't get it back then. But he laughed, and for a second, I wanted to laugh with him. It sounded ridiculous to him, I'm sure, but I was painfully serious.

"I don't believe you," Kian hummed. I didn't respond, and he sat on the ground against the brick wall. "Can I call you Ness?" he asked.

"No."

"Why not?"

"That's not my name."

"Well, obviously. It's a nickname."

Silence.

"What, do people not give you nicknames?"

I don't reply. People don't say my real name, let alone a nickname.

"You should call me Ki."

"Why?"

"Because we're friends now."

His voice was cheery, as if I hadn't just confessed the plans I had for my own murder. I think he was trying to save me back then. I think he thought he could do it by simply being around. Maybe he did. I don't know.

"You're weird," I said as I scooped my bag off the ground. I walked out of the alley, leaving him on the ground. It didn't take him more than a few steps to catch up to me, though, and we walked in silence back toward the school. We passed the courtyard, and I paused before heading on my usual route home. "Are you going to follow me home?"

He shrugged.

"Do I need to? If I let you walk by yourself, are you gonna try to hitchhike so you can get picked up by some freak?"

I rolled my eyes. "Go away, Kian. We aren't friends."

"Too late, I've already decided. Stay here for a sec." He jogged into the school parking lot, and I kept on my path home. A minute or so later, Kian's jet-black Volvo pulled up next to me.

"Get in!" he said, a childish grin on his face.

I wanted to ignore him and keep walking, but I could see exactly how the rest of the interaction would go if I did. Plus, it was cold out. So, I opened the passenger door and slid in.

Kian has a habit of humming while he drives. It doesn't matter if there's already a song on the radio playing, he's gonna hum whatever he wants to. It's like he's always happy to be driving. It's such a mundane and trivial task, yet he hums. Maybe it's the teenage sentiment of finally being able to have control over that part of your life, or maybe he just loves his car that much. Or maybe he's just happy. I don't hum.

He turned up the radio and made a noise when he heard what song was playing.

"This one's so good." He grinned. "Right?"

I shrugged. "It's okay, I guess."

"*Okay?* Are you even listening? This is a masterpiece."

"How would I know? I don't listen to music."

If he cared for his car any less, he would have slammed on the brakes. He whipped his head in my direction.

"*You don't listen to music?* How is that even possible?" he asked incredulously.

I shrugged again.

"Not too fond of music."

"*Not too fond of music?*"

"Are you just going to keep repeating everything I say?"

"I just don't understand how you could possibly be 'not too fond of music.' I mean, that's literally unheard of."

He made it sound like I'd just confessed to killing a puppy. I sighed. "I just find most music kind of boring. I don't hate it or anything. More indifferent, I guess."

Kian shook his head, frowning as he pulled into my driveway. I didn't remember telling him my address, but that's a topic for later.

"Indifference is worse than hatred," he said, almost sadly.

I scoffed a bit and got out of the car. "Thanks for the ride," I muttered before heading to my door.

"Thanks for saving my life! See you tomorrow, Ness!" he called from his window.

This boy was going to be a pain. Not as much of a pain as the situation that waited for me inside my own home, however. I thought I'd be able to avoid my aunt and slide up the stairs to my room, but as I entered, the town sheriff was sitting next to my aunt on the couch, which suddenly lacked its plastic cover. I knew things would not be ideal.

"Vanessa, come over here," my aunt said, giving me that 'behave-or-else' look. I resisted the urge to turn around and walk back out of the room, reluctantly making my way over to the couch.

The sheriff stood, and for a second I was worried. I don't

know why; I had done nothing wrong. Maybe it's the energy the sheriff brings. It made you feel like you're guilty, despite the lack of a crime. The only thing I can attribute to his being here is Rosette.

Maybe they were considering me as a suspect again?

I couldn't see why. They made it pretty clear the last time how little help I really was. I considered a few other explanations. Maybe I killed Killer in the woods that day, and they found his body and my fingerprints. It wasn't too likely, but Killer did seem out cold a bit long...

The only possibility for the sheriff's presence that I hadn't considered explained why he hugged me. It was sudden, and beyond uncomfortable. I wondered if he'd ever hugged anyone before, because while I had little experience, I was certain this was not how it was supposed to go. My arms were pressed to my side, digging into my ribs.

Maybe I was the one doing it wrong?

Whatever.

I didn't get the chance to adjust before he let go. I stared blankly, waiting for some sort of explanation as my aunt grinned goofily in the back.

The sheriff squeezed my shoulders. "Vanessa, thank you for saving my son. I can't tell you how grateful I am."

Oh. That thing. I remembered Kian mentioning who his father was, and it made much more sense seeing Kian's dad. They look pretty similar, but Kian's hair is lighter, and so are his eyes. There was also a hardness in the sheriff's eyes Kian didn't have. I wondered if he would gain it someday and, for some reason, I hoped he wouldn't.

"Uh, yeah, no problem," I muttered. My aunt's eyes shot daggers at me, but what was I meant to say?

"If you ever need anything, really, anything, you've got the Wilson family and the entire station in your corner," the sheriff said earnestly.

"And Killer?" I asked. The sheriff blinked in confusion. Another thing he and Kian had in common.

"I'm sorry?"

"Killer. I mean, the killer. The serial killer who attacked Kian and Laine. Have you guys found him yet?"

The sheriff shook his head, shifting a bit. "Unfortunately, not. We got Laine's description and have been searching the woods for a while, but if I could get you down to the station, it could prove very helpful in catching him." The sheriff put a hand on my shoulder, peering down at me with sincerity. "Rest assured Vanessa. You're in no danger, especially with the town curfew we're implementing. We're gonna catch this guy."

"I'm sure you believe that," I responded honestly.

My aunt stood with a speed I didn't think her bionic hip would allow. "Vanessa! Show some respect to the sheriff!" she fussed.

"Oh, no worries, miss. I understand." The sheriff smiled at me, maybe to comfort me. "Don't you worry, Vanessa. If you ever feel unsafe or want to be in proximity to the authorities, you and your lovely aunt are always welcome at my house. My wife just came home from her trip yesterday, and she'd just love to meet you."

"Would Kian be there?" I clarified.

The sheriff blinked. "Of course! Provided he isn't out messing around with his buddies again. You know teenagers," he added with a laugh to my aunt, who laughed much too hard in response.

"Then I'll pass," I said finally, turning and heading up the stairs.

My aunt fussed after me, and the sheriff called out more words of gratitude. I silently prayed that one day my walls would grow thicker as I shut my bedroom door. I sat on my bed and I grabbed my phone from my pocket, aiming to pull up another movie to study. As the screen lit up, I saw a text from an unknown number. It read:

heyy it's ki! my dad got your number from your aunt, save my contact :)

My aunt's sudden friendliness was becoming a large pain. I rolled my eyes, moved to delete the conversation, then paused. After thinking about it for a second, I saved his number, just so I knew to ignore him when he called. His contact was the only one outside of my aunt's and two... other numbers... that I had saved. None of which I ever planned on using. I tossed my phone to the side and laid back on my bed. I didn't see the point in searching for a new tactic to secure my murder if I wasn't even sure if Killer was still alive. I had hit him, like, three times? Maybe my strength was greater than I thought it was.

After a few minutes of silent stewing, I heard the front door shut and lock, and my aunt came clunking up the stairs. She moved fast for an old lady and without so much as a knock; she pushed the door open with her head cocked, arms folded, and that nasty look she wore.

"You got no manners, Vanessa!" I didn't reply, letting her go on a tangent. "That sheriff is kind enough to offer you support, and his nice little son is giving you some company. How hard is it for you to have a little decorum?"

"I don't see why I have to." I didn't want to give her the chance to tell me not to talk back, so I steamed ahead. "The sheriff is annoying, his son is annoying, I'm annoyed. I'm not allowed to be annoyed anymore?"

"Girl, don't nobody care about you being annoyed! You need to be *respectful*. You're lucky I didn't have that sheriff put you in a cell for the night with the way you're speaking to me!"

"That's not how anything works."

"You always got something to say. *Mm*-mn-mn." She shook her head and finger like a cartoon. "Ever since you were a baby, you caused all kinds of trouble, made your parents crazy."

My fists clenched suddenly. She was wrong.

"No, I wasn't."

"Yes, you were, little girl! Always in mess—"

"That wasn't me."

"Just throwing your whole house out of sorts—"

"I said that *wasn't me!*" I shouted, standing up. My aunt wasn't a short woman, but she looked a little smaller now that we were eye to eye. She just stared at me for a second as I huffed with frustration. I didn't like when she brought them up. I didn't like when she brought *him* up. I *hated* when she confused us, like we were anything alike. Like I wasn't the one who'd been stuck with her for the past ten years. Like there was a life out there where I was the fortunate one. Or, whatever. I hated it.

"Whatever. Y'all both just like your daddy, anyways." My aunt fussed under her breath, shuffling out of my room. "Acting like I don't know which one of y'all is in my house. Like I'm blind. I'm not that old!"

I sighed, closing my eyes. Well, if my plan couldn't come to fruition that night, I might as well get some rest. I wanted sleep normally, but I couldn't resist grabbing the cloth again. Taking a breath before I put it on, I braced myself for whatever nauseating nonsense would slip into my dreams. After drifting for a bit, I plunged into a sea of darkness and sleep overtook me.

That night, I dreamed I was sitting in my aunt's house. I sat in the living room, and my aunt was in her chair next to me. She was drawing in a little notepad and watching the TV, but the TV wasn't moving. It was the news. That woman with the chunky blonde highlights and uncanny white teeth stood in front of the camera, staring straight ahead.

I got up, stepped to the window, and saw the mailman at the neighbor's mailbox.

Just standing.

So very still.

The sky above him was as red as ever.

I turned to my aunt and asked her what was going on. She glanced up at me; her hands a blur as she sketched, and something was very different about her. My aunt, who has been old for as long as I could remember, looked twenty years younger. The wrinkles on her skin were faded, the cloudiness her eyes normally held was nowhere to be seen. She opened her mouth to speak, but closed it again. I urged her to say something, anything, because I could tell she knew what was going on. She didn't, though. She just shook her head and looked down, almost sadly, at her notepad where only incoherent scribbles resided. I looked out the window again and saw Killer. He was moving, but not like my aunt. It was almost like he was gliding, stiff as a board down the street. I watched him for several seconds, or maybe minutes, or hours...

The dream was very vivid, like the ones before it, which probably was a direct contributor to the amount of time it took me to wake up when it happened.

The buzzing.

It was loud, louder than it had been back in the stairwell, but not as loud as in the forest. My skin twitched from the sound, and I sat upright in bed. I couldn't say exactly how I knew where it was happening, and to who, but I knew. Someone was about to die. No, not someone. *Kian.*

As I pulled my clothes and shoes on, the buzzing grew louder with every step. I bolted down the stairs, grabbing my house keys just before rushing out the door. It was the middle of the night, no earlier than one or so. The street lights flickered above me as my feet thudded on the pavement, pushing my legs as fast as they could carry me. I didn't know where Kian lived, but the way the buzzing grew louder with each step, I was going in the right direction. The houses grew bigger, and farther apart as I ran, before finally, the buzzing was as loud as it could possibly be.

I skidded to a halt in front of a large, white mini mansion with Kian's car parked out front, next to the sheriff's. I looked around, not seeing Killer anywhere near, but I knew he was close. I didn't want to ring the doorbell, lest the sheriff or Kian's mother answer instead of him. Luckily, I swiped my phone from my dresser before I left, so I called him. He didn't pick up. For one quick, horrifying second, I thought I was too late.

That my plan had gone awry, I mean.

Then I saw him. Not Kian, but Killer, climbing up the metal trellis against the house to a balcony. I relaxed a bit, knowing I still had a little time to save the idiot.

I rushed to the bottom of the trellis, shaking it, hoping I could knock it loose. The structure of the thing was a bit too sturdy for it to work, but I got Killer's attention. He turned to look at me, and I got a glimpse of his now cracked (my fault) white mask before he turned back and climbed faster.

I stared for a second in disbelief.

He couldn't even bother to come down and kill me now that I was actively trying to thwart his plan? Did I smell bad or something?

I remembered how quickly time was slipping away, so I straightened up and climbed the trellis after Killer.

One time, back in third grade, I went rock climbing for some kid's birthday party. That was the age when if you were going to invite anyone from your class to your birthday, you had to invite everyone, so that's why I made the list. I remember being encouraged by the birthday kid's mom to join the other kids climbing on the rock wall, rather than watch *The Shining* on the little tablet I brought along with me everywhere at that age. I remember reluctantly setting my tablet down, getting on the wall, and promptly falling off mere seconds later. The other kids had laughed at me, assuming I was truly so unathletic I couldn't do something that came easily to everyone else.

In reality, I just wanted to get back to my movie. It was at a really good part - the maze scene - my favorite. I assumed that if I made a spectacle about falling and shed a few crocodile tears, the adults would feel bad and let me go back to my tablet in peace. It worked, obviously, because what monster makes someone else's kid get back on the rock wall after they cry?

I spent the rest of the day sitting in the corner by myself until eventually even the parents forgot about me when it was time for cake. Someone's mom was supposed to give me a ride home, but after watching them pull away without a second thought, I ended up walking. I don't think my aunt ever even realized I walked for two hours back home, by myself, at eight years old. I don't think anyone ever realized. Before that day, I probably enjoyed climbing, at least a little bit. But after, I didn't really want to do it ever again. Which was probably why I fell.

Falling off was enough to stir the trellis a bit, and Killer lost his footing. He tripped and fell halfway down before catching himself, and I took the bonus time to run to the front door and try to find a way in. It was unlocked. *Unlocked.*

Time and time again!

I didn't waste time dwelling on how perfectly idiotic Kian had once again proven himself to be, I just busted open the door and rushed inside. It seems even bigger on the inside as I ran through the foyer and up the stairs. It didn't take long to figure out which room was Kian's, his door had a jersey with his name and the school mascot hanging off the back of it. I took a chance and assumed it'd be unlocked, and I threw it open just in time to see Killer sliding open the door to the balcony.

"Kian! Up!" I shouted, and he jolted awake. He looked as if he had been barely sleeping, anyway. His eyes widened when he saw Killer approach him, but something in them relaxed when he saw me. I grabbed him from his bed by his arm and bolted from the room. He trailed after me, then sped up and

dragged me with him. He made for the hall, but I yanked him toward the stairs.

"No, my parents!" he yelled, pulling me to a stop.

I wanted to keep going, to get him out of the house entirely, but he looked at me with this desperate, pleading look, one that normally wouldn't get a rise out of me. I don't think I've ever shared that look, not over a person. At least, not in a while, but I yielded. Besides, what if Killer *did* go after his parents? After the sheriff? The sheriff would surely shoot Killer and injure, if not kill him. That would throw a major wrench in my plan.

So, I allowed Kian to drag me into a room down the hall, which turned out to be the bathroom. I locked the door quickly, slapped his hand away when he tried to turn on the light, and placed my hand over his mouth to stop him from speaking. He held his breath, and his eyes were wide with fear. We heard Killer's feet thud down the carpeted hall, and finally come to a stop in front of the door.

"Stay here," I whispered to Kian. "Now's my chance. Once he kills me, you'll have some time to get your parents up and get out, so just wait 'til you hear me scream."

I cleared my throat a few times to prepare my perfect, bloody murder scream, and I started toward the door. Suddenly, Kian grabbed my arm, yanking me back before I could take another step.

"What are you—Let go!" I whispered furiously.

"Are you insane? I'm not letting you out there!" he whisper-yelled back.

"Not your decision!"

I tried to rip myself from his clutches, but I couldn't overpower him. I kicked at him, hoping to hurt him and get away, but his grip didn't relent. He shifted, however, and used one arm to hold both of mine firmly pressed into my sides (Maybe this method of hugging is hereditary), as the other hand covered my mouth. No matter how many times I tried to bite at his hand, he didn't let up.

I listened in dismay as Killer walked away, his footsteps going further down the hall.

Crap! I was missing my chance! I readied myself to attempt another escape from Kian's vise-like grip when he went rigid. Looking up at him, I watched as the color drained from his face.

"He's going toward my parents' room," he whispered.

I took his moment of distraction to finally break free, bolting to the door before he could grab me and flinging it open. Killer was almost at the end of the hall, but he turned around to see me. I pulled the bathroom door closed, and with Kian tugging at it on the other side. I stood wide open, just short of spreading my arms as I waited for Killer to come at me.

It took about ten seconds for me to realize he wasn't. He just stared at me, or I assumed he was, considering I couldn't see his eyes. It wasn't until Kian yanked the door open and stepped out did Killer step toward us again.

I was getting beyond frustrated. Kian stood next to me, and I could tell Killer was going toward him, so I stepped in front. It was as if I'd drawn a pen line in front of an ant the way Killer stepped back.

Like I was diseased, and he didn't want to catch it.

We must have looked comical for a minute there, because every time Killer made a move, I'd mirror it to put myself perfectly in his path. It went on for a solid thirty seconds, and after a while we all just stood there, feeling silly. At least *I* felt silly. I doubt Killer felt anything at the time.

Twenty-seven seconds.

That's how long we stood there for, unmoving.

The next person to move was Killer. He seemed to charge directly at me, and I tensed, knowing this was my chance. I watched him raise his blade, and I opened my mouth, ready to scream. I felt the air being sliced around me, and felt the cool tip of the knife graze my skin just barely, before I felt my shoulder hit the ground. Kian's shoulder pillowed my head, and I realized he'd tackled me.

Saving me.

Thwarting me.

I hate this kid.

The loud thump combined with the small cry I'd got out was enough to stir Kian's father, and moments later he stormed out of his room. Killer stood over Kian and I, knife raised, poised to strike, but the crack of the sheriff's shotgun was enough to motivate Killer to leap over the banister and out the still wide-open front door. Kian covered me when we heard the shot, and I noticed how different he smelled now from when I carried him in the woods. The overpowering, oaky cologne scent gave way to a softer linen scent, as if his clothes had just come out of the dryer. I could also smell the sweat he'd broken into from all the action, combined with the warmth his arms provided. It wasn't unwelcome; I had been cold. But... I was glad when he got off of me. The kid is heavy.

"You kids alright? What on Earth is going on?" the sheriff yelled, shotgun still in hand, just in case. Kian stood and offered me his hand, which I declined, standing on my own. Kian didn't answer his father, instead turning to me.

"Are you okay, Ness? Are you hurt?" He checked me over with his eyes rather than waiting for an answer. He saw the minor cut I received from Killer across my arm and put his hand over it to stop the barely there bleeding.

"I'm fine," I responded begrudgingly.

The sheriff rushed over to us to confirm he hadn't shot us, and a woman, who I can only guess is Kian's mother, emerged looking terrified from their room. Kian looks more like his father than his mother, but they share a hair color. She was short but sturdily built. I'd only ever seen her maybe once or twice around the town. Probably at the grocery store or something. Which is why it felt a little inappropriate for me to see her in pajamas.

The sheriff ran down the stairs to catch Killer, and I sensed I wouldn't be able to simply slip away to find Killer again, as this situation is probably difficult to explain.

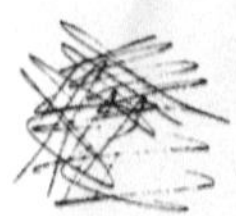

KIAN'S NOTE #2: RE: LOCK YOUR DOORS, FRONT, BACK, AND BALCONY

IF YOU'VE NEVER HAD to explain having a girl in your room at one in the morning, you have never known true discomfort.

I know my parents weren't upset with me as we sat stiffly in the living room, Vanessa on my left and my parents sitting in front of us. They were most likely relieved; their son just escaped death for the second time in a week, but I still had to explain why Vanessa was there. This was around the time I realized I truly had no idea why Vanessa was there, or how she'd even gotten in. The buzzing that'd been in the air since I woke was gone now, and I was a bit more awake than I had been, even while running from Killer. I glanced over at Vanessa. She looked as neutral as ever, if not a little impatient.

I won't lie. She made me mad. Very mad, actually.

I was forever grateful to her for saving me once again, but she was constantly, *intentionally*, putting her life in danger, and it *really* irked me. I just didn't understand how she could not value her life like that. I mean, I had already been targeted by Killer *twice*. If I had Killer actively avoiding me, best believe I would have been using that to my advantage. But here she was, sulking next to me because I didn't let her die.

My father cleared his throat. He had been running around

the town for an hour searching with the entire station for Killer. It seems right after he left our house, Killer just disappeared. The rest of the station was still out looking, and my father still had his shotgun next to him. For some reason, it made me want to laugh. The shotgun, loaded and ready, laid menacingly across my mother's precious white suede couch, which was perched atop a fuzzy white rug, and it was funny.

"So. Do you two want to tell us what happened here tonight?" my father said slowly, eyeing me with that 'you did something wrong,' look.

But I hadn't done anything wrong. Had I?

"I dunno, Dad. The guy came in from my balcony, I guess. I didn't lock it last night," I explained.

"Idiot." Vanessa muttered.

She had just thrown herself at a murderer, but sure, I'm the idiot.

"Ness saved me. Again." I turned to look at her. "Thanks, Ness."

She folded her arms and rolled her eyes as she slouched further on the couch.

"Vanessa, you're a hero," my mother whispered. She had tears in her eyes, as she'd had since she came out of her and my father's room an hour ago. She stood, approached and took Ness' hands in hers. Ness looked beyond uncomfortable, but didn't squirm as my mother continued to thank and praise her. I resisted the urge to roll my eyes and thought back to those psycho-EMTs. I wished *that* was Ness' motive for saving me instead.

My father narrowed his eyes in thought. "Vanessa, how did you get in?"

"Front door. It was unlocked. Much like every door in your house," Vanessa responded flatly. My father still had a question on his brow, so Vanessa continued. "I saw Killer--- ahem, *the killer* climbing up to Kian's balcony, so I, uh, ran in, or whatever."

My mother threw her arms around Vanessa, thanking her profusely. My father nodded his head solemnly, and he looked like he was going to cry as well. I stood, pulling Vanessa out of my mother's grip.

"I'll walk her home," I said.

"Absolutely not." My father stood. "I'm calling her aunt to come pick her up. It's dangerous out there. We still haven't found the man who attacked you yet. No way am I allowing the two of you to walk around this late."

"Please don't call my aunt," Vanessa said quickly. "She's sleeping, and if she wakes up, it'll be a whole thing."

My father opened his mouth to protest, but my mother spoke before he could.

"Stay here tonight, Vanessa. We'll wait until the morning to call your aunt. Come with me. I'll show you to the guest room."

Before Vanessa could refuse, my mother was practically dragging her up the stairs, arm hooked in hers. I watched them go down the hall -with Vanessa looking back at me miserably and disappear around the corner. I rose, sighing as I started towards my room.

"Not so fast, Kian." My father stopped me. "I need to get your statement."

I groaned.

"Can't I do that in the morning?"

"No, I need to get it now while the suspect's description is fresh in your mind."

"Dad, I'm tired —"

"We need to catch this guy —"

"I didn't even see his face; can I just go to sleep —"

"Anything you can remember is a help—"

"*I'm tired, alright?!*"

My father froze, and I didn't wait to see any more of his reaction, or whether he was going to yell back at me. I didn't care. I turned on my heel and stormed up to my room. I shut the door, locked it, then rushed to the balcony to lock that door too. As I sank onto my bed, I exhaled, realizing I'd been holding my breath this whole time.

I didn't mean to yell at my dad. I know he was just doing his job, or trying to, at least. I know he was overwhelmed and was just trying to protect me, but I was tired. Vanessa got to go to sleep, and I wanted to go, too.

At the same time, I knew I wouldn't get any rest. If the nightmares were bad since my stabbing, I knew they'd only get worse now. Not to mention how my eyes flicked over to my locks every ten seconds, checking them constantly. But the thing I knew would keep me up the most was Vanessa.

Something was off about her. A lot of somethings, actually. This was the second time in a row she just happened to be at the same place at the same time as Killer, right in the nick of time to save me.

Psycho-EMT style.

I knew the motive she told me, but that didn't explain how she knew I was in danger. There she was, just down the hall from me, and it was the perfect opportunity to get answers.

I waited until my father retreated to my parents' room before unlocking my door and slowly pulled it open, wincing at each creak the hinges produced. I made sure the coast was clear and stepped out, tiptoeing toward the guest room as quietly as possible. I didn't technically need to sneak around like this, but I thought it'd be better than my parents seeing me and having another awkward thing to explain. Arriving at the guest room, I knocked softly on the door and whispered through the crack.

"Ness, it's me. Open the door."

There was silence for a bit, and I wondered if she was genuinely asleep. That seemed like a foreign idea after all that'd transpired just an hour earlier, but most things she did seemed foreign. Soon enough, however, the lock clicked, and she pulled open the door ever so slightly. Ness eyed me as she peeked out.

"What?" she hissed.

"Are you decent?"

"Gross, don't ask me that. But yeah."

"Let me in."

"Why?"

I swear, she can be so stubborn for absolutely no reason. "Just let me in, Ness. I need to talk to you," I whispered urgently.

She eyed me for a second, the same way my father did sometimes. It made me squirm a bit, and I considered turning away, but finally, she opened the door. I slid in, shut and lock the door behind me and flipped on the lamp on the desk while Vanessa sat on the bed.

"Go ahead, talk," she said, stifling a yawn.

I racked my brain, trying to think of what to say first.

"How did you know?" I settled on folding my arms. She quirked a brow.

"Know what?"

"That I was in trouble."

Vanessa frowned, seemingly in thought, as if she too didn't know. She opened her mouth and closed it before opening it again.

"You don't hear it, do you?" she asked quietly.

Somehow, I knew what she was talking about. I had heard it, and I had just realized I didn't hear it anymore. The buzzing noise, whatever it was. The same noise I heard in the stairwell. I heard when Vanessa woke me up.

"Not right now." I answered, studying her carefully. "Do you?"

She gave me a look. A look of understanding, of relief from my understanding, maybe, and shook her head.

"Not right now," she repeated.

We sat in silence for a bit.

"Do you know what it is?" I asked after a while. She shook her head again, looking at her hands.

"Anyways, that's how I knew. I heard it, and just... knew."
Another long silence.

"I think something's wrong with the town, Kian," Vanessa muttered. "The whole town. It's all wrong."

I slid into the desk chair, resting my elbow on the desk as I waited patiently for Vanessa to elaborate.

"The buzzing, Killer, the victims — all of it is weird." She sat up a bit as she spoke, her eyes boring into mine with a sudden intensity. "Not just weird, perfect. In regard to the victims, I mean. The perfectly placed stab wounds, the presentation of the bodies? Like, come on. A red cloth over their faces? It's straight out of a movie, Kian. Especially when you look at the choice of victims. Mack and Rosette had nothing in common except for being the perfect stereotypes. A Black kid being the first victim, and a pretty blonde being the second victim that made the town really jump. That's the same pattern half of the most popular horror movies out there follow and have followed since the seventies."

She stood and paced as she talked, ramping up. But something she had said caught me.

"Wait, wait, slow down," I urged. She stopped speaking, giving me an annoyed look.

"What?"

"There was no red cloth on Rosette," I noted. "I read the case file when my dad wasn't looking. There was one on Mack, but not on Rosette. So, it isn't all that perfect, is it?"

Vanessa looked puzzled.

"What do you mean? Yes, there was —" She paused suddenly, eyes widening. "Oh, right?" She brought her hand up to her mouth, letting out a short, dry laugh. "It must really have mattered, then, huh," she muttered to herself.

"What are you talking about?"

She turned to me, examining the obvious confusion laced on my face. "I was the one who found Rosette."

...Huh??

My eyes widened, and I opened my mouth to speak, but she held up a hand to silence me. "I found her in the girls' bathroom. She had the exact same wound as Mack and had a red cloth over her face. I took it." She winced as she said the last part, and my brain nearly exploded.

"*You took it?!*"

She shushed me, eyes flicking toward the door cautiously. "Yeah, I took it, alright? Don't ask me why, I just did."

"*You just did.* "

"Don't start that repeating me thing again."

"I'm just... *Why?* Genuinely, what would possess you to not only tamper with evidence of a murder, but *steal it?*" My eyes must have been bulging out of my head, but she just shrugged, only the smallest ounce of regret present on her face. "Vanessa. Do you realize that's a serious offense? You could go to jail for that! Not to mention you could have thrown off the entire investigation. What if the killer's fingerprints were on that and the police could have used it to track the guy down?"

Vanessa shook her head. "No, that wouldn't have been the case. Killer's got half a brain. He wouldn't have left any fingerprints. Duh. And I just felt like I needed to take it, okay?" She sat at the desk, drumming her fingers on it in thought. "Listen up for a second. Anytime there's that buzzing sound, Killer is around. That, or something to do with one of his murders, is taking place. But I heard the noise after I grabbed the cloth." She had a slight frown on her face when she grabbed a sheet of paper and a pen from the desk, and jotted the time and incident when she heard the buzzing.

"In the stairwell," I offered quietly, still very much overwhelmed by the troubling information she present.

"Right." She noted that too. "And in the woods before that, when I saved you and Laine. And, of course, tonight, when Killer was breaking into your house. Or, rather, when he popped in for a visit, considering every door in your house was unlocked," she added with a roll of her eyes.

"How was I supposed to know someone was gonna try to kill me in my sleep?" I muttered.

"Maybe by the fact that there's a killer on the loose and, I dunno, the fact you've already been targeted once?"

She flashed me a look, daring me to say something else. I decided it was in my best interest to stay silent. Her attention returned to the paper.

"We just need to know what this buzzing means. It's all too perfect for it to not be connected to Killer. If we figure Killer out, I can figure out how to get my perfect death, and you can figure out how to stop ruining it." She had a morbid grin on her face, and I wondered once again whether or not she was a genuine psychopath.

"Right... or..." I offered, "We can use this information to save our town." She pulled a face, but I continued. "Think about it. If this buzzing really has something to do with this guy, it may be some sort of pattern he's following. We figure it out, we can give it to the police, and they can use it to catch the guy!"

Vanessa looked positively uninterested.

"Yeah, whatever. You can do that after I get my perfect death. Who knows, maybe my murder will help you out on your little high school detective quest."

She went back to writing, and I couldn't help but frown.

"I still don't get why you're so set on being murdered," I whispered. "Ness, there's so much to life that —"

"Not your decision," she snapped. "I already told you not to try and convince me." She sighed, and I noticed something in her face changed. "Now, let's just focus, alright?"

I fell silent, and she set her pen down.

"The buzzing. It's familiar, somehow. Don't you think?"

I shrugged. "Maybe? I dunno." I thought for a second. "Doesn't it sound a bit less like buzzing and more like... clicking? Like, rapid clicking?"

Vanessa thought for a second, then looked up at me. "You

might be right, now that I think about it. But what makes a clicking sound like that?"

We fell quiet again as we tried to think of something. There were plenty of things that could have replicated a sound like that, but nothing either of us thought of seemed to make any sense. Finally, Vanessa groaned. "Alright, whatever, I can't think of anything right now. Let's sleep on it." She folded up the piece of paper she'd been writing on and slipped it into the pocket of her sweatpants. She started toward the bed, but I spoke up.

"Wait. Can I ask you something?"

She turned, frowning. "Isn't that what you've been doing this whole time?"

"One last thing, I swear."

She sighed, plopping down on the bed. "Alright, shoot. Then leave, so I can go to sleep."

I nodded, studying her carefully before asking my question. "Why do you call the guy Killer?"

She raised an eyebrow. "Why?"

"Mhm."

"He's a killer, isn't he?"

"Yeah, but... iI's just odd. Most people would say 'The Killer', but you just say 'Killer', like it's his name or something."

Vanessa hummed a bit, shrugging her shoulders lightly. "I dunno, actually. I guess it has to do with how the whole situation feels. Like... a movie. And he's just another character. He's so much like every other movie murderer I've ever seen, so it just feels right to refer to him like that."

I nodded slowly. "I guess I get it. But, Ness... This isn't a movie. It's, you know, real life. I don't think you should forget that."

TIP FOR AN IDIOT #3: DO YOUR RESEARCH

When Kian said that, he looked at me more seriously than anyone really ever had. More seriously than I thought he was capable of.

I didn't like it.

"I'm not so sure of that, Kian," I responded honestly. There was a part of me that already knew, even then. He looked at me in this strange, almost pained way, and I was tired of looking at him. "Go away, I'm tired," I muttered as I slid under the blankets and made a shooing motion at him.

"Okay, okay." His chair scraped against the floor as he stood. "Night, Ness," he whispered.

"Turn the lamp off on your way out."

The dream was different this time.

I was back in my aunt's house, standing in the foyer and staring through the living room. It felt weird standing there, not like I was standing in the home, well, house I'd grown up in, but like I was standing in a place I'd never seen before. My aunt was there, old again, but not old like I knew her to be now. Her wrinkles were present, but not the cloudiness in her eyes, not yet.

I realized I was holding bags in my hands. This wasn't a dream, it was a memory. A memory that I didn't like to think about. A memory with Person lurking just behind me. Person, and two other people, who I could see much clearer than Person, who were taller than me, quickly left me standing there in front of my aunt, without saying goodbye. Even Person disappeared from my peripheral, and I was alone. Alone with my aunt, I guess. But alone.

Pause.

I've thought a lot about that dream for a very long time. Even after everything. I'd deduced a few theories about the other dreams I was having, but I never shared those theories with anyone else. Not for a long time, at least. Not until, you know, this. I thought perhaps the dream was different because I didn't have the cloth with me. That seemed just as reasonable an explanation as the situation itself was reasonable.

I resolved after that to carry the cloth around with me as often as I could. Now, this decision would prove to bring some of its own issues, including how often I would see Person in my peripheral. I couldn't necessarily attribute those facts to the same thing, but I did anyway.

You have to understand something about me, about this world I'd found myself in. I was in a place I wasn't supposed to be in. I had filled a role I wasn't supposed to fill. Someone would tell me something later that made everything about this time make much more sense, and it was the concept of something being an abomination and the disorder that the universe tends to lean toward and its greatest achievements. In any case, things were weird. Normal decisions, normal judgements, normal truths. None of those things fit in a world like this.

Play.

The next morning, Kian's mother gave me one last grateful squeeze before letting me go and allowing me to get into my aunt's car. The sheriff leaned against it, chatting with my aunt. He gave me a nod and a bright smile, thanking me once again. I was tiring of all the gratitude from the Wilsons, but I simply nodded back, knowing if I did anything less than that, I'd get an earful from my aunt.

My reaction didn't end up mattering, as I got an earful from my old-again aunt, anyway. Sneaking out in the middle of the night, going to Kian's house, and being a burden on the Wilsons for the night were all criminal offenses in my aunt's eyes, and she didn't relent until we were back in the house, and she was in front of her outdated soap operas again. I didn't even bother mentioning the fact that I had, once again, *saved someone*, as I doubted it would have made a difference, anyway. I retreated to my room and reluctantly got ready for school. I was just in time to miss my bus and started on my walk in the cold. As I was walking, I thought more about my underdeveloped theories about Killer. The clicking, and the cloth in particular.

The cloth could have been written off as Killer's signature, but something about it was so familiar. Beyond what I'd watched in the movies. And the clicking simply had no explanation. It too was familiar, but not like the cloth. The clicking seemed like it would be easier to find an explanation for it.

Say Kian and I were right. The clicking sounds happened whenever Killer is around, or when we're around a product of Killer. In that case, why could I hear it last night from my house, when Kian and Killer were near a mile away? And how come I didn't hear it with Rosette until I'd taken the cloth? How come Kian didn't hear it until he saw me in the woods?

There was a sizable piece of the puzzle we were missing,

and I knew it was essential in order for me to gain my perfect murder.

"Ness!"

A familiar idiot's voice called from a familiar Volvo, knocking me out of my thoughts. Kian slowed down next to me, waving. From this angle, I could see the dent I'd made in Kian's car with the rock I'd thrown in the woods. It was worse than I'd remembered.

"Get in!" he said cheerily.

It was cold, and I'm not too fond of the cold, so I got in.

He hummed, per usual, as he drove to our school, tapping his fingers carelessly on the steering wheel. At first glance, he looked positively cheerful, but as I really studied his face, I couldn't help but notice the dark circles under his eyes. Personally, I'd slept excellently, especially without the buzzing or *clicking* in my head. But Kian looked like he hadn't gotten a wink.

It made sense. After narrowly escaping death twice in one week, most people would have nightmares. I wondered how he convinced his parents to even let him out of the house after last night's incident.

"My parents tried to keep me home, but I convinced them I'd be safer at school than home alone," Kian said suddenly, as if he'd read my mind. "My dad's sending officers to the school just in case, though."

I frowned. "Wouldn't it make more sense for them to just cancel school? I mean, the town isn't that big. It doesn't seem wise to have people out of their homes with Killer still out there."

Kian scoffed. "Guess they know there's no use in canceling school, while freaks like you run around anyway."

He flashed a grin, and I rolled my eyes. Of course, they wouldn't close the school. That made too much sense. I resolved to better suspend my disbelief. My mind went to what

Kian said the night before, though. He was right, this wasn't a movie, so movie-logic didn't apply.

Then what was with all the stupid decisions the people around me kept making?

We arrived at school, and Kian dropped me at the front while he went to park. As I stepped from his car, I experienced something I hadn't experienced before.

People looking at me.

Not just looking, *staring*. I wondered if I had something on my face before hearing people whisper about me getting out of Kian's car. One thing I hadn't realized was how much of an attention Kian attracted, so much so that people were actually whispering my name.

My name.

I didn't realize anyone actually knew it.

I slid past people as best as I could, catching small snippets of gossip - some of it featuring me - as I made my way to my first period class. It was less than comfortable being the topic of people's conversation, so I avoided high-traffic areas anytime I had a free moment. I drifted through the art center, where few people spent any time. It was a product of our defunded art program. It wasn't like the people at my school were Picassos anyway; I guess. I was halfway down the hall, towards the dark room, when I heard it.

The clicking.

I tensed up, feeling the noise creep up my spine, ticking rhythmically on my shoulder blades. *Kian. Where was Kian?*

I was certain he was the source of this. Killer had to be on his tail, and I knew very well he was not equipped to keep himself alive without me there. I spun around, trying to figure out where the sound was coming from. I followed it back down the hall, but it was the loudest in front of a room I'd never entered before. Outside, the sign next to the door read FILM CLUB. *Why was Kian in there?* Not wasting time thinking about it, I threw the door open.

The room was almost completely dark, save for a small square of light on the wall in front of me.

"Kian? Where are you?" I called out.

"Hey—shut that door!" someone's voice replied.

I didn't recognize their voice, so I focused on locating the sound. The lights in the room flipped on, and a girl who I recognized vaguely from elementary school stepped toward me.

"Yo, are you alright?" she asked, concern etched on her face.

I didn't respond, searching the room hastily. Where was Kian? I knew he wasn't here. I didn't see Killer anywhere, either. The clicking was echoing in my bones, but it was different than it normally was. Less in my head, and more *around*. I turned to the girl.

"What's that noise? That clicking?" I asked urgently. She blinked, then a look of realization came across her face.

"Oh, that? Sorry, I've gotten so used to the noise that I don't really notice it anymore," she said with a small laugh as she made her way to the center of the room. For a minute, I wonder if she is in the same predicament as Kian and me, if she had had a run in with Killer too. Then, she approached a weird, old looking machine with a big circular gear on top of it. At the press of a button, the clicking stopped.

"Sorry about that. It's pretty annoying for people who aren't around it all the time."

The circular gear stopped moving and the white box on the wall disappeared.

"What is that thing?" I asked after a minute of silence, my shoulders relaxing some in the quiet.

"A projector," she replied, grinning broadly. "A 1959 Argus eight-millimeter projector, to be exact. Isn't it great?"

"A... projector? Like, for old movies and stuff?"

"Mmm hmm! C'mere, I can show you how it works!" she said excitedly. It looked as if no one had ever asked her about the projector before, and like a kid, she was excited to show it off.

"So, Kian Wilson isn't here?" I clarified.

She deflated a bit. "Uh, no. If you're one of his girlfriends he asked to meet somewhere, you've got the wrong room."

I nearly gagged hearing that. "Yeah, no way. I was just... nevermind, it doesn't matter." I rubbed my temple, trying to ground myself again. This projector-thing made the exact same noise as when Killer was around. I had a hunch as to why, but I needed a bit more proof. "Tell me about this projector thing."

The girl lit up and nodded enthusiastically. I walked over to where she was standing, and she eagerly started explaining all the parts and pieces of it. I only half-listened. Most of what the girl was saying sounded like gibberish.

"And this part moves the film—"

"When does it make the noise?" I asked, cutting her off.

"The noise is the sound of the film moving through the reel, and the little shutter inside opening and closing. That's why you hear it while the movie plays." She looked at the projector fondly, resting an arm on the table where it sat. She said something else, but I couldn't hear her. All I could hear was the clicking in my head, even though the projector was off, and Killer was nowhere near us. I didn't just hear it anymore, I *felt* it.

When the movie plays, huh?

It all started to make sense. The clicking, the town, the victims, the red cloth, Killer, the stupid mistakes—it was all exactly how I had described it since the very beginning. Everything around me seemed perfect all of a sudden, and my face stretched into a grin. I had been right all along, and the words Kian whispered to me so seriously the night before became obsolete.

It was all a movie. A horror movie.

We're stuck in a horror movie.

This was... The. Best. Day. Of. My. Life.

Now, you would think I made quite a big jump there, but it only seemed appropriate. There's a level of disbelief you must suspend to truly enjoy any horror movie, so if our town was stuck in one, it would only make sense to make a few reach-y judgements. Besides, I didn't have time to really develop my theory. I'd already accepted it as fact, so now I needed a strategy on how to use it to my advantage.

I'd tried a variety of careless actions before to become a victim, yet none had worked. Only around Kian did I find myself in any Killer-related situations. As frustrating as this was, I could work around it. Killer struck me the night before, in Kian's house. Which meant Killer had the capacity to kill me. He only needs the *motive*.

The *bait*.

The idiot!

"Are you alright?" the girl asked suddenly.

I realized I must have looked a bit insane, and I let the grin fall off my face.

"Yeah—I gotta go. Thanks for explaining this, by the way. You don't know how much you helped me today."

The girl turned red and muttered something I didn't quite catch as I rushed out of the room to go find Kian. If I was going to put my plan into motion, we needed to start as soon as possible.

It wasn't difficult to find Kian; he was where he normally was during the free period, sitting in an empty classroom with a crowd of his biggest fans. He sat on a desk, tapping his feet on one of those uncomfortable plastic blue chairs, but quickly slid off the desk when he saw me.

"Ness, hey!" he greeted me cheerfully. "I was looking for you. You left your house keys in my car this morning."

Marco Vienna, who had been sitting right next to him, frowned. He leaned over, murmuring something in Kian's ear, who just brushed him off and stepped closer to me. I think I heard Marco say something mean, but I couldn't care any less about other people at that moment. I didn't say a word as I grabbed his arm, dragging him from the classroom. Oddly enough, he didn't protest nor inquire any further about where we were going. It wasn't until we slipped from the gymnasium back door, onto the street and into the alley between the pharmacy and convenience store did he say anything.

Kian leaned against the wall, folding his arms. "Alright, it must be something important, then, right?"

I nodded, looking back and forth down the alley to check if anyone was listening. Save for a stray kitten or two, we seemed to be alone.

"Kian, I'm going to say something, and you're not going to believe me. But try to suspend your disbelief until I'm completely finished, okay?" I stared deep into his eyes, hoping he'd take my words at face value, and really hoping he'd understand.

"Okay."

While I often criticized Kian for his blind trust rooted in his own general ignorance, there are times in which I really admired him for it.

"The town is stuck in a horror movie," I started. "I have reason to believe it's just our town, considering the small-town trope, and the fact that Killer only seems to be known locally. This explains Killer's targets, as well. Rosette–the beloved, pretty blonde; you–the rich, popular, football and girl player; and Laine–your girl of the week. Clearly the stupid mistakes every victim and the police keep making are credited to plot-convenience, as well as Killer's elusiveness and appearance."

I paused for a second, partially to catch my breath, and partially to build suspense.

"And you want to know how I know all this? *The clicking.*

That's the piece of the puzzle that really pulled it all together. This girl showed me this old projector that makes the exact same clicking noise. I heard it before when I went to this vintage horror movie festival-thing, which is why it sounded so similar. The clicking happens every time something pertaining to Killer happens, which would make sense if we were in a movie. Like, we hear it whenever the film is rolling, you know? Anyways, that's the theory…!"

I'd outstretched my arms in a "ta-da" fashion, a satisfied grin on my face. Throughout my monologue, I'd been pacing back and forth, I realized, so that there was a dip in the dirt following my path. I finally examined Kian's expression, which I'd neglected to notice throughout my rant.

One thing about Kian, he's not very good at hiding his thoughts. He's so expressive that every emotion, concept, or opinion he has is clearly written on every feature of his face. I don't think there's ever been a time in which I wondered if he was being honest with me or not, or anytime where I've questioned his true feelings. I guess he's never really had to hide what he was thinking, anyway. He trusts so easily, so completely. At least, he used to.

As I looked at his expression then, I could tell exactly what he was thinking.

"Ness…" he started slowly. "I think we should get you to a hospital. You're unwell."

KIAN'S NOTE #3: RE: DO YOUR RESEARCH

She rolled her eyes in the same way she always does, this time with more urgency.

"Kian—"

"Uh-un," I cut her off. "I don't believe it." I folded my arms, peering at her as firmly as I could. "I told you before. This is *real life*. Not some movie. Everything you just described is pure coincidence. I mean, a projector. Really?"

She frowned. "I told you to suspend your disbelief."

"It's not easy."

"Try harder, then."

Silence.

"Ness, this is delusional behavior, you know that?" I rubbed the back of my neck, suddenly very uncomfortable. "I mean, I get what you're saying. Really, I do. But I just can't see how all that means we're really living in a movie."

She sighed, sitting on the ground against the wall. "I know you can't. I can't say I'm surprised."

I sank to her level, folding my arms over my knees.

"There are a few things that don't line up with my theory," she admitted. "Like, for example, my own death. How it simply

won't happen, I mean. I've gone through plenty of the situations movie victims usually die in. Left my doors unlocked, walked through dark alleys by myself, answered mysterious phone calls with no caller I.D."

For a second, I wondered how she'd survived this far, not because of Killer, but because of how genuinely stupid those moves were to make even if you're *not* living in a horror-movie.

"That was why I was in the woods that night," Vanessa continued.

I glanced at her, eyes wide. "Really?"

She nodded, and there was a small pout on her lip. "But you and Laine were right where I wanted to be, and I knew that you two would get plucked off instead of me. That's why I saved you."

I looked back down at the ground, wiping a bit of dust off my shoe. I still didn't think she was telling me a hundred percent of the truth for her motive, but I let it go.

"But when I got close to Killer to hit him with the rock, he didn't even attempt to protect himself or attack me back. Even when I showed up at your house... You saw the way he evaded me. I was wide open, too. That's weird, isn't it?"

I nodded reluctantly. "Yeah, I guess. Maybe it's someone you know."

"I don't know anyone."

"Some secret admirer then?"

"Have you met anyone who really knows who *I* am, Kian? Who's had a conversation with me?"

I thought for a second, remembering the blank look Marco gave me when I mentioned Vanessa to him. "No, not really. Only Laine and my parents, to be honest."

"And they only know about me because I saved you and Laine. Besides, I'm not the type of person for anyone to 'admire', so that's out," she muttered.

I wanted to say something, but I decided against it.

"The point is, Kian, that isn't normal behavior for a real-life serial killer. So, there's got to be an explanation for it all. I know it sounds like a reach, but how else can you explain me knowing Killer was going to attack you?"

We sat in silence for a bit as I processed the information in my head. She had several points. Especially when I thought of my dad and the station. My dad wasn't dumb, and if Killer was following such a simple pattern, shouldn't the police have been able to catch him by now? And she *did* know I was going to be attacked, and it was not like the psycho-EMTs. I could tell that much. Somehow.

"I know it all sounds weird, but there are more factors I've been looking at that I can try and show you, but you won't accept any if you've already decided that I'm insane. So... can you try and believe me?"

Her voice was smaller, softer than I'd ever heard her speak before. I looked at her, and there was a sort of desperation in her eyes - faint but present - pleading with me to understand her. She'd always had that look in her eyes, but it was so faint I wondered if anyone had noticed it before me.

"Alright. I believe you."

Personally, I hate horror movies.

I don't see the appeal of being scared. The cold sweats, nerves on high, heart beating like crazy… It's pretty much my least favorite feeling. The only reason I even took Laine to the woods that night was to show her I was tough and stuff, but the whole time I was freaked out. It made no sense for me to leave the car. I don't know why I did it. But when I did and got stabbed, when I saw Vanessa poke out from the trees, the clicking got so *loud*. So… Firm. Like it was, I don't know, upset with me. Like it was upset at all of us, like we'd messed something up. Like it was telling, no, *commanding* us to follow the plot.

"Plot," I whispered. "If this is a horror movie, there's a plot."

Vanessa seemed to light up, nodding enthusiastically.

"And if the clicking happens when," I continued, "uh, the film is rolling? That would probably be the time in which we're the most susceptible to the plot, right?"

Vanessa nodded again, leaning forward a bit. "That's right. I suspect it's harder for people not to do stupid, clichè stuff when the film is rolling."

I nodded with a frown. "Yeah, it is, but that still doesn't explain you. There have only been two deaths, so we'd be closer to the beginning of a movie. Me and Laine were supposed to die in the woods, weren't we?"

"I believe so."

"So, the killer coming to my house was him trying to finish the job and set the plot right?"

She doesn't answer, perhaps not having considered that herself.

"If that is how it works, then that means you're the one throwing off the plot, Ness. By saving me."

She looked up, tilting her head slightly. "That shouldn't be possible. I hear the film rolling too, but I don't do dumb stuff. If whatever it is that's controlling the town — 'Plot' let's call it — is powerful enough to compel you to put yourself in danger, why doesn't it work on me?"

"Maybe because you know so many movie tropes?" I offered.

She shook her head. "Everyone knows not to investigate when you hear a noise, and you did anyway. Not to mention leaving your doors unlocked with a killer on the loose–"

"Alright, you don't have to point out all my shortcomings. I've got the stitches and scar to remind me, thanks," I grumbled, kicking a pebble with my foot.

"*I'm saying* those are things everyone is knowledgeable about, so I shouldn't have any special ability to resist Plot's control. Unless..." She furrowed her brows, pondering something conflicting.

"Unless?"

She looked up at me, a frown laced on her features. "Unless the one dumb thing I did really messed something up when I found Rosette."

It was my turn to frown. "What do you mean?"

She was silent for a moment, deep in thought. Then she reached down and drew a line in the dirt. "Pretend this is Plot. A timeline for how things are supposed to go."

She drew a circle at the beginning of the line.

"This represents Mack's death. And this," she drew another circle to the right of the first, "represents Rosette's."

She drug her finger from the bottom of the second circle, drawing a downward line. "Let's make these little lines represent when we hear the film rolling. I heard it when I found Rosette. Did you?"

I shook my head, drawing my knees up. "I didn't start hearing it until the woods."

"Exactly." She nodded as if she'd expected my answer. "And I didn't hear it before I found Rosette. Not when she was killed, but when I found her. Specifically, *when I picked up the cloth.*"

She emphasized the last part, but I didn't get it. "So?"

"*So*, I didn't notice it until I took the cloth. It got loud all of a sudden, aggressive. And it's been like that since."

I hummed a bit. "Yeah, I didn't notice it until I saw you in the woods. Like, I didn't hear it in the car or anything. Only when I saw you with the rock."

"Now, I hear it whenever Killer is around you," Vanessa observed.

I'd forgotten that detail.

"But the question is *why?*" Vanessa suddenly looked completely sure of herself. "Killer is following the classic horror movie plot line. Small town, high school victims, a knife as a less than convenient weapon of choice, and his signature is the red cloth. In the movies, the signature usually has some huge significance to Killer's motive, and it ends up helping the protagonist in revealing Killer's identity and eventually defeating him. Without it, without that *consistency*, there's ample room for plot holes. How can one attribute the victims to each other without that signature? That's why I started to hear the film rolling. When I removed the signature, I messed Plot up."

"Ness, slow down. You're making my head hurt."

She rolled her eyes, then leaned back over the timeline, drawing another horizontal line over it. "The original line is how things are supposed to go. How Plot wants them to go."

"So, we're just accepting 'Plot' as an entity now?"

"Shut up and let me finish." She drew a connecting line from Rosette's circle on the original timeline to the leftmost edge of the second line. "This new timeline began as the result of me messing things up. A result of Plot *recalibrating*. Killer didn't strike again for like, a week after Rosette, right?"

"Yeah, I think?"

"And when he came back, he came for you. But I was in the woods, too. I was able to save you and Laine. That wasn't supposed to happen, so when it did, you started hearing the rolling, too. You also messed up Plot, just by surviving. Which is why it would make sense for Laine to hear it, too. We'll have to ask her about it. I think messing Plot up knocked us into some sort of sentience." She drew a circle on the second line, I guessed to signify the woods, and then a third line above it, connecting to the circle. Another timeline.

"Sentience?"

"Yeah, or, some level of breaking the fourth wall, so we suddenly hear the rolling, and can figure out from when Killer is about to strike."

"That... makes some sense," I muttered. "But how, if we're in this movie controlled by this Plot thing, were we even able to mess it up?"

Ness furrowed her brows. "I'm not sure, honestly. I'm not sure about any of this. There's still something else we're missing." She paused, thinking a bit and taking a breath before flicking her eyes up at me. "Has anything changed for you? Since I saved you?"

"Uh, yeah? A random guy in a white mask has been trying to kill me?"

"No, that's not what I mean." She rolled her eyes. "I mean in terms of your very existence. Anything that would make you interesting enough to be a primary victim, something you didn't have before I saved you."

"Your words make very little sense, you know that?"

Ness glared at me, and I sighed as I shook my head. "I don't know. Besides Killer targeting me, I can't think of anything about me that's changed."

Ness frowned. "We'll have to keep thinking about that. In any case, I think I can confidently say I wasn't supposed to be any more than an extra who found a body in this, and you and Laine were just supposed to be second-rate victims. I think Killer will keep trying to kill you until the movie gets back on track with its predictable plotline."

It was starting to make some sense. "But why doesn't Killer kill you? That's still unaccounted for."

Vanessa nodded solemnly. "I haven't figured that part out yet. I mean, it would make sense for Killer to get rid of me, since I keep saving you and messing Plot up. The only reason for Killer to not kill me is if he didn't have the ability to, especially since I was only supposed to be an extra in this. But the only way he wouldn't have the ability to is if I had some insane Plot Armor." She glanced at me, noticing my confusion. "Plot Armor prevents a character's death when their survival is crucial to the story. In most horror movies, though, the only two characters with that kind of Plot Armor are Killer and the Final Girl."

"Final Girl?"

She rolled her eyes, letting out that signature sigh. "We really need to get you some movies. Yes, Kian. Final Girl. The trope of the female character who is the only one out of the victim pool to survive Killer and is usually the one to defeat Killer in the end."

"So, maybe you're Final Girl, then," I offered. She hesitated, then shook her head.

"Nah, I don't fit the profile. Besides, that wouldn't explain why Killer was avoiding me. Final Girl can be injured, she just can't be killed."

"Well, he got you a bit in my house before I tackled you."

"I still don't forgive you for that, by the way."

"I'd do it again. Aren't I a bit like your Plot Armor?"

She scoffed, and we fell silent.

"So," I spoke up after a while. "Plot hates us, you in particular, and the clicking is a good indicator of whenever Plot is trying to kill me."

"Pretty much."

"And you might be low key immortal."

She shook her head. "Doesn't make sense. If Plot was in control, and I was screwing Plot up, why give me immunity?"

More silence.

We heard the bell ring distantly, signifying the end of the school day. Vanessa stood up, dusting herself off a bit, and I followed suit.

"What do we do, Ness?" I asked quietly as we walked back to the school.

She shrugged. "I'm going to keep finding a way to become a victim."

I frowned. "Shouldn't we use this information to help the police?"

"It doesn't work like that. Plot controls the town. What can the police do? Besides, do you really think anyone would believe us?"

She had a point, of course. I was still having some trouble believing it all. No way my dad would get it.

"And if you *are* Final Girl?"

She stopped walking. She was ahead of me only slightly, so I stopped too. I couldn't see her face as she spoke. "If I am, then the next course of action is simple. If I can't die, nobody can."

TIP FOR AN IDIOT #4: DON'T BE PETTY

"WHAT DOES THAT MEAN?"

Kian asked some silly questions sometimes.

"I mean, I'm not gonna let anyone become a victim before me," I said, turning to face Kian again. "If I'm able to hear the rolling when you're in frame, maybe I can hear it when other potential victims are in frame, too. I've saved you twice before. I'll just keep saving people until I can become a victim."

Kian blinked at me, then opened his mouth to say something, closed it, and opened it again.

"That's the pettiest thing I've ever heard, Ness."

I stared at him for a second, then couldn't help but laugh. He gave me a look like he'd never heard someone laugh before, his eyebrows raised slightly. Maybe he stared at me like that because he'd never heard *me* laugh before. That would probably explain how surprised he looked.

Honestly, it was a bit of a surprise to me to hear my own laugh. I was self conscious for a second, wondering if my laugh sounded strange, wondering if he hated it.

But why should I care?

"I guess it is sort of petty. But I'm doing what you want, right? Helping the town," I pointed out. "If there's some reason

Killer won't kill me, I'm gonna thwart him and Plot until he will."

Kian frowned, shifting on his heels. "I don't think it's a good idea—"

"I'm using you as bait, by the way."

His eyes went wide. "What?"

"I think Killer is gonna keep going after you so Plot can get back on track. So, I'll just stick with you, and keep saving you for as long as I need to. You're welcome." I turned back on my path, walking back to the school building to retrieve my stuff before going home. I think he stood still for a while before he dashed to get his car.

He pulled around the front to take me home, and I was surprised he still wanted to be around me after all we'd figured out that day. I assumed he was afraid of Killer, and he was keeping me around so I'd keep saving him. Neither of us realized for a long time how little of a hero I actually was.

I'm not Killer though.

We arrived at my house, and I slid out of the passenger seat and shut the door behind me. Kian put his car back in drive before I tapped on the window. He rolled it down, a question on his brow.

"Where are you going?"

"Home?"

"Are you dumb? Did we not just talk about this? Get out of the car. You're staying here."

He looked confused, but put his car back in park and got out. He stood slightly behind me as we walked to my door and grabbed the back of my sleeve before I could open it.

"Wait. Won't your aunt be annoyed? I don't want to intrude," he muttered, looking very much like a little kid.

"Why are you touching me?" I asked flatly.

He went red and pulled his hand back. "Sorry, I get touchy when I'm nervous."

"Creepy. Anyways, don't worry about it. My aunt likes you."

Kian smiled when I said that, and he visibly loosened up. I unlocked my front door; we stepped in and he looked around the front room with a small smile on his face. I pointed to where he could take off his shoes and wondered whether he was quietly judging the place as he drifted around the room. It wasn't like I lived in a shoe box, but my house could have probably fit in his kitchen, so… I resolved not to think about it too much. I'd never been self-conscious about my house before. Well, I'd never had anyone over before, but that was beside the point.

"Let's go upstairs," I mumbled, motioning toward the steps.

Kian frowned. "Shouldn't I say hi to your aunt first?" He had a really goofy expression on his face as he wandered into the living room, not waiting for my answer.

"No, Kian, you'll just annoy her —"

"Hi, ma'am!" Kian said cheerily as he stepped toward my aunt. She was in her usual spot, the old recliner chair in front of the equally old television. I expected her to yell at him for interrupting her soaps, or yell at me for bringing him home without telling her first, or all of the above. Instead, her face lit up in a way I've never seen it do before, and she stood.

"Kian, baby! Vanessa didn't tell me you'd be paying a visit!" she said, matching his cheery tone. "C'mere to the kitchen. I got some food for you."

This was incredible. When was the last time she'd offered me any of her food after school? When was the last time she'd greeted me so happily? Never!

She turned back to look at me, and I thought for a moment I'd get some of that good-time-auntie treatment too. "Close your mouth, Vanessa, unless you want to swallow a fly. And quit that staring."

Of course.

Growing more and more impatient by the second, I leaned,

albeit moodily, against the wall as I waited for Kian to stop scarfing down whatever my aunt had whipped up. When he finally finished, he bounced out of the kitchen with that stupid grin of his.

"Your aunt's an amazing cook, Ness," he commented, mouth still full.

I made a face. "Whatever, let's go upstairs."

I took hold of his sleeve and dragged him behind me up to my room, ignoring the calls of my aunt for me to keep my door open. I closed it anyway and tossed my backpack on the floor by my bed. Kian looked around as if he's never seen someone else's room before, staring at the old posters I never got the chance to take down and the ratty stuffed animals piled up in the corner. He picked up a particularly beat-up looking bear that I appropriately named "Bear."

"He's cute." Kian grinned as he manipulated the bear's limbs to make it walk.

"I wouldn't be surprised if Killer tried to get you again tonight, so you'll just stay here so I can keep an eye on you."

"What's his name?"

"Bear. I think I've got an old hunting knife in the closet somewhere. I'll teach you how to use it, so you're not completely useless to me."

"You named him Bear? Geez, we need to work on your creativity."

"Can you focus?"

He pouted, setting Bear down before plopping on the ground next to it. "Sorry. What were you saying?"

I doubted I'd get out of this situation without rolling my eyes to oblivion by the end of it all. "I'm giving you a knife. It's small, meant for, I dunno, gutting or something."

I rummaged through my closet for a while before pulling out a bag full of weird hunting and fishing tools. I tossed the bag into Kian's lap.

He looked impressed, pulling out the knife from the bag

with a grin. "Where'd you get all of this stuff? You don't seem like the hunting type."

"Hand-me-down." I sat on my bed, tugging my phone from my pocket. "We should call Laine over here, too. It would make sense for Killer to go after her too."

"Hand-me-down from who?"

I didn't respond. Kian seemed to clock how little I wished to talk about it, and didn't press any further. "Your aunt is really nice," he said quietly. I snorted.

"To you."

"Not to you?"

"Take a wild guess." I pointed toward the knife. "Unsheathe it."

Kian obliged, tossing it up in his palm a few times to assess the weight. "Nice. I think my dad has one like it."

"So you know how to use it?"

"Kind of."

"Good." I leaned back a bit, letting my head relax against my headboard. "Use it on the bear."

He made a horrified expression, dropped the knife, and pulled Bear close. "No way. I'm no monster."

I rolled my eyes and sat up again. "I just want to make sure you're doing it right. A common mistake in all horror movies is a victim carrying a knife they don't know how to use. They always end up freaking out and dropping it. It's so annoying. What's Laine's number?"

He tossed me his phone, and I flipped through it to find Laine's number. I frowned a bit, noticing his wallpaper: a picture of him and Marco, sitting on the football field with Laine hanging off of Kian's arm.

"What's wrong?" he asked, setting Bear down.

"Nothing." I shook my head. "You're still friends with Marco?" I inspected the image of Laine and Kian with a grin that Marco didn't share.

"Uh, yeah, 'course. Why?"

I shook off the strange feeling on my shoulders. "No reason. This is annoying." I tossed Kian the phone. "I can barely work that thing. You call her."

Kian snorted. "That's 'cause your phone is from, like, centuries ago. You gotta upgrade."

Yeah, right, I rarely used my phone. Why would I need a new one?

His fingers flew fast across his screen and the little send tone played as he shot Laine a message. "She should be here in a few." He dropped his phone and picked Bear back up.

"Stab it."

"No."

"It could be the difference between your survival and your death."

"Guess I'll just have to die then." He had a smug look on his face, as if he'd just won the argument.

"Why are you so stubborn?" I asked, exasperated, scooting back against my headboard again.

He gave a small shrug, the triumphant grin still on his face as he went back to doting on Bear. Kian was interesting in the sense he wasn't too concerned about appearing hyper masculine. He wasn't feminine, but he wasn't jumping at the opportunity to fake-kill something with a hunting knife. I didn't understand him, really. Despite having Killer on his tail, he didn't look stressed or afraid. He seemed calmer than me. But I noticed the dark circles under his eyes and the stifled yawns he hid behind a hand. He hadn't slept peacefully in some time, obviously, but he wasn't moody or irritable. He was... him; I guess.

"You'd better not die," I added, before pulling out a small notebook from under my pillow.

The blue cover was slightly weathered, and the pages had started to peel from the broken spine. Kian made a noise.

"Is that your diary?" he asked in a teasing tone. I shook my head, opening the book towards him and flipping through the blank pages for him to see.

"Never used it before, but now seems like a good time." I leaned over to grab a pen from my desk, shaking it a bit before doing a quick scribble test on the corner of the first page. "Alright," I started. "First things first: the town is stuck in a horror movie."

"Naturally."

"This means typical movie logic applies. Anything that wouldn't typically appear in the real world is fair game."

"So, like, aliens and stuff?"

I thought for a moment, then shook my head. "Probably not. I doubt with how it's all gone so far that Plot will go a sci-fi horror route. I'm thinking more like multiple Killers, a traitor in the victim pool, underground organized crime conspiracy, et cetera."

Kian let out a low whistle. "That's a lot."

"I know. But we just have to identify which tropes are happening before they happen, and we should be able to find our way out of them."

"How do we do that?"

I hesitated. Considering how likely it was that Plot was adjusting things based off the typical plot points I kept messing up, it was pretty much impossible to predict what would happen. Plot didn't give me much time to think about it, however, as the film began to roll.

"You hear that?" Kian whispered. He suddenly looked how he was supposed to — scared. He clutched Bear with one hand, so hard I could see his knuckles turn white. I guess he really did get touchy when he was nervous.

"Yeah, I hear it." It was impossible not to. "We're in frame, I think." His expression made me want to calm him down. "That doesn't mean Killer is here. It just means something important to the story is happening."

He relaxed ever so slightly and put his other hand atop the hunting knife. We waited in silence for about three minutes until we heard my front doorbell ring. Kian tensed up again, and I stood. I pressed an ear to the bedroom door, listening to see if my aunt was answering the front door. After a while I knew she wouldn't, so I pulled open my door. "No splitting up, Kian. Follow me."

He hesitated, but leapt up when he realized I would not wait for him. He took hold of the back of my sleeve, his nervous tick returned, but I allowed it. As long as it meant he'd stay close and not do something stupid, I was fine with it; I guess.

We walked down the stairs, Kian bumped into me more than once, and the impatient visitor rang the doorbell again. I took hold of an umbrella placed next to the door and instructed Kian to get ready to stab someone on my signal. He was practically hiding behind my shoulder by the time I opened the door, umbrella brandished.

It was just Laine.

She gave us an odd look, and Kian breathed a sigh of relief. I let the umbrella fall to my side and stepped to the side so Laine could walk in.

"Why are you two being freaks?" she asked, eyeing the knife Kian still held tight. "Were you expecting the serial killer to ring the bell?"

"Yeah," Kian and I said in unison.

She gave us yet another strange look, took off her shoes, and glanced around the front room like Kian did. I'm forced to remember her wealth as well. She turned back to me, smiling.

"Vanessa, I meant to tell you," she started.

I wondered if there was something that changed within the last week or so that made people want to hug me out of the blue, because that's what Laine did.

"Thank you for saving me," she whispered.

Oh, right. I did do that, didn't I?

I muttered a small 'no problem,' and slowly removed myself from her embrace.

"So, why am I here?"

I quickly led the two idiots back up to my room before my aunt had the chance to act a fool about me bringing yet another guest into her house without telling her.

"Ness, we're still in frame," Kian pointed out urgently.

"I know," I replied as I shut the door and locked it.

It's a wonder my aunt still allowed me to keep a lock on my door, or a door at all, considering she'd been threatening to take both away since the moment I arrived on her doorstep. I never really understood why. It's not like I do anything that warrants that. Most kids get their door taken away for sneaking out, delinquency, or daring to exercise their right to privacy, but I never did any of that.

Well, I'd tried it for a minute, but sneaking out isn't very fun when you have nowhere to sneak out to. No one to sneak out with.

I guess that's why I still have my door...

Laine sat on my bed and crossed her arms with a look of suspicion on her face. "Why am I here? Are you guys ever going to tell me?"

"Why are we still in frame? Does that mean Killer's here?" Kian stood beside the door and stared toward the back window as he clutched the knife tighter.

"I don't know," I replied, closing the blinds. "Probably."

"What are you guys talking about?"

Laine was getting annoyed, but I couldn't really focus on her right now. I suspected Killer was around, if not already in my house. I thought about my aunt's safety for a minute, before remembering that she's genuinely too stubborn to die.

Unfortunately.

Kian paced a bit, ramping up. I ordered him to sit down, because now he was stressing *me* out. I turned to Laine, as serious as I've ever been.

"Laine, I'm going to tell you something that doesn't make sense, so you'll need to suspend your disbelief for a minute, okay?"

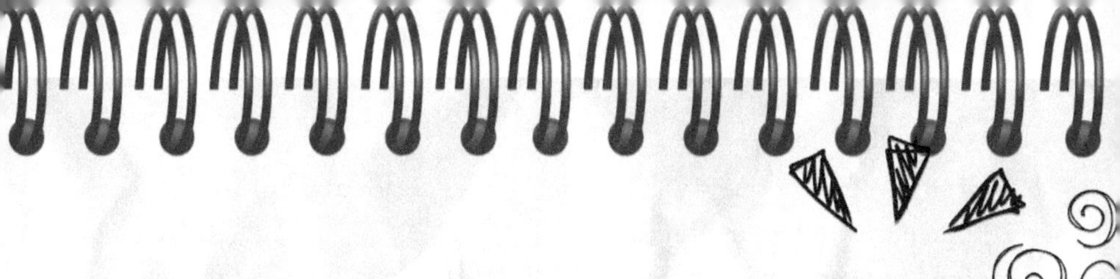

KIAN'S NOTE #4: RE: DON'T BE PETTY

LAINE DIDN'T BELIEVE VANESSA, understandably.

She started to believe her when the ax came through the door.

It took Vanessa almost a full minute to respond to the situation, long enough for Laine and I to scream and for the ax to strike the door again.

"My door," Vanessa muttered.

She was stuck in a daze almost, so I grabbed her shoulder and shook her firmly to get her mind back in the same room. It seemed to work, at least a little, and she moved less than urgently to the window. Ness slid it open and glanced out of it warily.

"Alright, we've got to — Laine be quiet for a second — We've got to jump," Vanessa said, swinging her leg over the ledge.

"*Jump?*" Laine was in absolute hysterics.

"We're only on the second floor, c'mon."

Vanessa motioned for Laine and me to follow. I hesitated before grabbing hold of Laine's arm and pulling her to the window. Laine thrashed around wildly, and it took a lot of strength out of me to keep her from accidentally throwing herself out the open window.

"Laine, relax," I shouted. "I'll go out first, and catch you two, alright?"

Laine caught her breath for a minute, pale and shaking, but listening. She nodded, and I could hear Vanessa sigh from the windowsill. I swung my leg over the edge, trying to see how to fall without hurting myself. I finally decided on a route, swinging my other leg over and standing on the edge of some exposed brick. Stepping off, I lowered myself until I hung by my fingers on the ledge. With a bit of a prayer and the sound of the ax hitting the door again — accompanied by some Laine screams — as encouragement, I let go, hitting the ground easier than I expected to. The ground was soft and damp, despite the fact that it hadn't rained in weeks. I shook myself off, then stretched out my arms toward the two girls waiting in the window.

"Jump!"

Laine shook her head wildly.

"I'll catch you, Lainey, I swear."

"Don't make promises," Vanessa scolded. "Movie mistake! Too sure of yourself and she'll miss you and snap her neck."

Obviously, this statement didn't help Laine, but Killer broke the door down. This was the first time I'd learned about the joy that is movie-timing. Had it taken Killer one less second to break down the door, Ness wouldn't have been able to loop her arm around Laine's waist and jump down in time. Laine was still screaming, grasping at her neck wildly as she pushed herself off the ground to make sure it wasn't broken. She was fine, a little bruised, but fine.

Ness, on the other hand, had taken the brunt of the fall, and she sat still on the ground, hand enclosed around a gnarly looking ankle. I rushed over to her, but she waved me away.

"I'm fine. Is Killer still up there?"

I turned to look up at the window. Killer stared down at us, or at least I think he did. We still couldn't see his face. He stayed in place for a few seconds, the surrounding curtains blowing gently in the night breeze before he turned away and walked through the now demolished door.

Gone.

Ness had gotten herself up by that point, and shifted on her feet in annoyance. I quickly made my way to her, supporting her weight despite her insistence on her not needing it. I helped her over to the bushes, dragging Laine by the hand behind us. We crouched down, shielded from view by the prickly leaves. I don't pray too often, not anymore, but I prayed then. I prayed Killer wouldn't walk out the front door and find us, especially with Ness unable to run. I would carry her, of course, but we'd only be so fast.

Ness must have sensed my increasing unease, or maybe she didn't. Maybe she placed her hand on mine by accident, but either way, it calmed me down some. It didn't last long, however, as I realized something.

"Ness, your aunt!" I whispered frantically. I made a move to stand, to leave the bushes and run back into the house, but Ness caught my arm, yanking me back down.

"She'll be fine," Ness hissed. "She's not actively being hunted, and if she were, she'd be dead already. Who is actively being hunted, Kian?"

"We are," I mumbled.

"That's right. Now stay down until we're out of frame."

It only took a few more minutes for the film to stop rolling, and I stood first, helping the still shaking Laine to her feet and going back to support Ness. We climbed out of the bushes, and Ness pulled from my grasp, hobbling to her front door.

"It's not safe, Ness—" I started, but she'd already pulled open the door.

"Unlocked," she reported. "I didn't lock it when Laine came in, did I?"

She looked positively frustrated with herself, and if I

wasn't sure it was a trick of the moonlight that barely grazed her face, I would've thought she'd teared up a bit. She hobbled back inside, and we followed her, with Laine hiding behind my shoulder. Ness bent at the waist and peered down at muddy footprints trailing from the front door and up the stairs.

"Muddy footprints? It hasn't even rained this week..." I pondered aloud.

Ness made a snorting noise, straightening up. "Movie-logic. Unfortunately, our movie looks to be the cheap cliché type. Explains your haircut, Ki."

I self consciously touched a hand to my hair, then shrugged my shoulders. "Whatever. You know I look hot."

I decided not to point out her use of a nickname for me, afraid that if I called attention to it, she wouldn't call me "Ki" ever again. Still, I couldn't hold back a smile despite the situation.

We walked up the stairs, my hand at the small of Ness' back in case she fell, since she rejected my offer to carry her. She went to her aunt's door and made us to wait in the hall while she checked, though she kept the door cracked to make sure we didn't move a muscle and get ourselves killed. I peek a bit. I wanted to know if her aunt was okay. After a few moments, Ness came, rolling her eyes.

"She's fine. Told you — too stubborn to die."

She shut the door, mumbling something I couldn't quite make out to herself as she ushered us back into her room. Laine sat on the floor, hyperventilating, but Ness just stepped over her.

"Do you believe me now?" Ness asked Laine.

I thought she sounded a kinda cold, but knew it was better to not point that out. Laine couldn't respond for the longest time and her voice shook when she finally did.

"So... that's what the clicking has been?" she whispered.

Ness blinked for a bit, then an odd grin stole over her face.

"So you've heard it too? Before today? Since the woods?" Ness leaned forward as she asked.

Laine nodded. Ness clapped her hands, flopping down on her bed.

"That's awesome. Theory update: we can hear the film rolling even when we're not in frame. Must be able to hear it anytime *anyone* is in frame. That's a new layer of cool."

"But why?" I frowned, sitting on the ground next to Laine and throwing my arm over her shoulder. She leaned into me, and I could feel her heartbeat against my chest. Ness shrugged.

"I dunno. Maybe because we're sentient. Aware of our situation. Our little version of breaking the fourth wall."

She was practically giddy. Much too high-spirited considering how she'd just jumped out of a window to avoid Killer.

"Sentient because of you," I guessed. "I didn't hear it before you showed up. Something about you broke our fourth wall."

"Maybe it's because mine was already broken. Mine broke the moment I decided to become a victim." Ness grinned up at the ceiling. "Sentience is contagious. And it's catching!"

Laine looked like she was about to pass out.

Ness called the police and went back to wake her aunt. By the time my father, other officers, and news anchor Partly McCloudy arrived with a burly cameraman behind her, Ness's aunt was full on fussing at her on the front lawn. First about having Laine and I over, then about a variety of random, irrelevant shortcomings Ness's aunt seemed to find important to mention then. I felt bad for Ness, but she hardly seemed to notice. She was too bu watching Laine, who was giving a shaky statement to an officer.

Ness would have never admitted it, I think, but I saw a flicker of protectiveness in her eyes, akin to that of a mother looking over her child. It was kind of a funny sight, considering how often Ness would claim not to be very interested in the delicacies of others' emotions. I never really believed her when she said that, anyway.

Partly was yapping to the camera, as usual, and bothering some annoyed looking officers as she tried to breach them and get to Ness. She would be smarter to approach a hungry polar bear than Ness right then, considering the dwindling patience I saw on her face as her aunt continued to throw a fit. Partly seemed to clock this as well, and she did a turnabout to approach Laine, instead.

"And here is one victim of this brutal attack now, Laine Meeps." Partly said. Her over enthusiastic voice didn't match her words.

"Meeks," Laine corrected softly.

Partly didn't seem to hear. "Miss Meeps, can you tell us what happened here tonight during this vicious, violent attack on such a *poor* neighborhood?" Partly demanded cheerily. "Was it related to the known gang activity associated with neighborhoods of a similar *demographic?*"

That last part made Ness and her aunt whip their heads around, pulling the same '*The hell did she say?*' face as Laine turned positively pale.

"Uh…" Laine looked back and forth between Partly and Ness, unsure of what she could say in relation to what information she could give that wouldn't mess with Plot and put us in deeper trouble, but also probably what answer she could give to the second part of the question that would make it sound less cancelable.

An officer shooed Partly away before she could bother anybody any further, to Laine's clear relief and my own. Ness's aunt fussed to herself as Ness made her way over to sit next to Laine.

Before the police had arrived, Ness had already told us we needed to stay over.

"No way! What if the guy, Killer, or whoever comes back?!" Laine exclaimed.

Ness shook her head, waving her off. "He won't hit up the house twice in the same night. Probably. But if he does, I'll handle it. This is smarter than letting you two go home, where I can't protect you," Ness said with confidence.

I'd never seen her like this before. She looked excited and insane. While it was interesting and kind of nice to see her grin so easily, I couldn't help but wonder why she was acting like this all of a sudden. Especially when Laine was so freaked.

She seemed sort of insensitive.

As I finished giving my statement, Ness's demeanor switched, and she casually and inconspicuously slid her little gray trauma-blanket off her shoulders and onto Laine's lap.

I managed to convince my weary looking father that Ness and Laine were so shaken; they wanted me to stay with them. My father looked on with suspicion, but he allowed it after getting permission from Laine's parents and Ness's aunt. This worked well for us for two reasons. The first: Laine's parents were pretty hands-off the majority of the time, I had noticed. For as long as I could remember, Laine governed herself. She never worried about a curfew, or getting grounded, or really any rules. I used to envy her. Not at that moment, though. At that moment, she looked like she needed parents. The second reason was the fact that Ness's aunt would agree to anything my father, or I asked, so getting her permission was as simple as not having Ness ask for it. This clearly annoyed Ness, as anyone would be, and it was funny watching her pull faces behind her aunt's back.

Once it was all settled, and the police had gotten our state-ments, the crowd on the lawn left, including Partly. My dad, however, paused for a second and pulled me to the side.

"Son, this is, what, the third time you've been caught in the middle of this? Did something happen? Did you upset someone to make them target you? Any enemies or threats I should know about?"

My father spoke like a sheriff, with parental worry seeping into his tone. It was... annoying. I wished that the worry came *first*. I know it was an odd thing to ask. My father was trying to get to the bottom of the case. That's his job. And that's what it felt like. All the time.

"I dunno," I muttered. "No threats or anything, no." I hesitated, wanting to tell my father the truth. A part of me still believed that he could fix it, like any naïve kid would think. "Maybe this guy just wants to finish the job," I said finally, hoping it was hint enough for my father to come up with some grand plan and save all of us.

I doubted it would work, though, so I hurried back into Ness's house before my father could change his mind, though I could tell he wanted to.

IT TOOK A WHILE, but Laine managed to fall asleep. Ness let her sleep on her bed while I camped on the floor in an old sleeping bag. Ness didn't lay down. Instead, she sat at the desk, doodling on the edge of the notebook.

"Ness."

She looked back at me, her eyebrows raised slightly. "Thought you were asleep."

"Nah. Can I ask you something?"

She chuckled, yes, *chuckled*, and turned back to the notebook. "Am I allowed to say no?"

"Nope."

"Then sure."

"What the hell is wrong with you?"

She stopped drawing, pausing for a second. She turned fully in the chair to look at me; her face unreadable. "Can I ask you a better question?"

"I guess."

"Why do you trust me?"

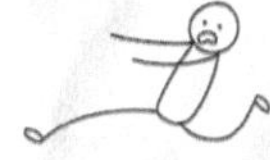

TIP FOR AN IDIOT #5: IF THE EVIDENCE POINTS TOWARD AN ANSWER, ACCEPT IT.

HE DIDN'T RESPOND at first. Then he shrugged.

"Because. I like you."

He said it so simply, as if it was an obvious answer, as if it was something I'd expect him to say. I just sort of stared at him for a while.

"You don't even know me."

He smiled. "I know you enough to know that without you, I'd have been killed, like, thirty times already." He sat criss-cross and picked at the worn edges of the sleeping bag. "It'd be kind of hard not to like you."

I frowned. "I don't do it for you."

"I know. And that's not the only reason I like you. You're funny."

I snorted. "You must not have a very good sense of humor, then."

He hummed a bit, leaning back on his hands as he peered up at me.

"You gotta give yourself more credit, Ness," he said, a soft smile on his face.

I didn't really understand. It's not like I was talking down to myself. I was just stating what I believed were facts. I'm not a funny, nor interesting, or likable person.

I'm plain.

Less than plain – insignificant. That's how I've always been, and that's how I intended to stay. The only time I've ever wanted to be more than that was when I decided to become a victim. My murder. My perfect death. It's the only way I wanted to go out.

Kian yawned loudly and laid back down. "C'mon, let's go to sleep," he muttered.

I shook my head. "Not tired."

"Well, I can't sleep with the sound of you tapping your foot, so at least pretend to sleep."

I rolled my eyes, but slid off the chair and onto the makeshift bed I'd made on the floor next to Kian's sleeping bag.

"We're so close, people might talk," Kian cooed dramatically, but he stopped playing around when I hit him with a pillow. I allowed myself to settle in, willfully accepting the blanket of darkness to drape over my eyes...

I REMEMBERED some of my dreams that night. At the time, it seemed all jumbled and meaningless, but I think it's important to mention now.

This one felt like a memory, too, but it was all distorted. I was in a house that I recognized from... a long time ago. I was in the living room, sitting crisscrossed on the floor in front of a tv, staring at some out of focused movie. There was someone sitting next to me, staring at me as I watched, but I didn't look at them.

At him.

I didn't look at him, but he was looking at me.

Person.

Per usual, I could see him out of the corner of my eye, which was enough for me to not want to look any farther. I couldn't really move, anyway. But he could, and he did, standing up and behind me. I wanted to get up and move as he placed a cloth over my eyes, a *red cloth*.

But I didn't move.

Maybe I couldn't, or maybe I didn't want to.

Either way, I didn't, and only a second later I was back at my aunt's house, and I couldn't see him from the corner of my eye anymore. But I knew he was there.

I DON'T HATE a lot of things, but I hate being woken up suddenly. Thanks to Kian's panicked shouts, I didn't really have a choice. I sat up straight and looked around the room quickly to see if Killer had come back for round two. He hadn't.

My eyes fell on Kian next, whose eyes were pressed firmly shut. He thrashed around, covered in sweat, and murmured to himself in distress. That a dream could throw someone into a vulnerable state, then paralyze them with unimaginable terror and take firm control of their mind…

It was weird, and I didn't like it.

I touched Kian's shoulder, gently shaking him. When he didn't wake and grew more distressed, I tried a firmer approach and grabbed his shoulder roughly and shook him while tapping the side of his face. He jolted awake, panicked and out of breath. He looked around the room wilder than I did, as if he was still stuck in whatever purgatory that had trapped him overnight.

"Kian–Kian, relax. You're okay, it was just a dream," I said firmly, and he finally looked at me. "You're alright. I'm right here."

Instant relief raced across his face, followed immediately by weakness and he to collapsed onto my shoulder.

"Ness," he whispered, still catching his breath. "It was so real, I thought..."

I didn't really know what to do, so I lightly patted his shoulder, offering about as much comfort as I was willing and knew how to give. "Just a dream," I muttered, hoping he'd calm down.

He did, eventually, and I monitored the rise and fall of his back as his breathing steadied. Due to the heaviness of his head, my mobility was limited, and all I could do was wait for him to get up. It must have been at least ten minutes, or maybe five or two, before he finally sat up. He wiped his face a bit, but not before I caught sight of the dampness on his cheeks. He was a bit of a crybaby, I observed, but I doubt bringing that up would have helped any.

"Sorry, I just," he started, voice barely audible. He didn't finish his sentence, but I nodded.

"Was it about tonight, or the woods? Or your house, maybe?" I asked, running through our run-ins with Killer so I'd know which was weighing on his mind the most.

"The woods. It's always the woods." He drew his knees up, curling into a ball about as little as he could manage. I nodded a bit.

"Makes sense. You were stabbed that time. Plus, that was before we knew what we know now. Your first run-in. It'll always be different because of that, and I wouldn't be surprised if it's the topic of all your nightmares from here on out."

He let out a small, pained, dry laugh, shaking his head a bit. "You're not very good at comforting people, are you?"

"I wasn't aware that was what you wanted me to do," I

answered honestly. We went silent for a bit, and I spoke again. "I'll stay awake with you."

"You don't have to–"

"You were yelling pretty loud. I doubt I'll be able to get back to sleep, anyway."

It was a lie. I could've easily gone back to sleep. In fact, I probably would have slept as soundly as Laine was, but it was already almost five, so I'd have woken up in a few hours, regardless. And I felt bad, oddly enough, sleeping when Kian couldn't. Like I'd said before, I never thought I was much of an empathetic person, so it made little sense to me back then, but I stayed up with him the whole night, mostly in silence.

When the sun finally peeked over my yard, I tried to wake Laine. She resisted, and I wondered how she could have slept so soundly through Kian's fit, and after the ordeal we'd gone through mere hours earlier. Perhaps she was more like me than I thought. Eventually, reluctantly, she woke up, and Kian sat next to her on my bed.

"Alright," I started. "We've got, like, an hour before school starts, so here's how this will go. Laine, you can use the bathroom first. I've got some clothes you can wear, I think we wear the same size. I'm not super fashionable, but I think you might like–"

"Hold on, pause," Laine interrupted, staring at me incredulously. "We're going to school? *Today?*"

I didn't really understand the question, but Kian seemed equally vexed as Laine was. "Yeah? It's a Wednesday..."

"Vanessa, we just got chased out of a window by a serial killer!" Laine shouted.

I blinked at her for a second. "Yeah, but, we've got a math test..."

"Oh my God, Ness," Kian said suddenly, mouth hanging open. "I thought you were immune to stupid movie mistakes?"

I realized the miscommunication and shook my head, sighing a bit. "No, you guys don't get it. We have a math test.

When was the last time you saw someone in a movie get cut down during a math test?"

"You know that one music video with the emo kid with a gun?" Kian started.

"Not the same. I said it is a *horror movie.*"

They went quiet, perhaps trying to think of a movie to serve as evidence for their claim. I continued before they could find one.

"School is the safest place for us right now."

I waited for them to protest, but Kian finally agreed with me. Laine was more reluctant.

"Plus," I added. "There are going to be more people added to the victim pool, most likely kids from our school. If we can scope them out now, we can explain the situation and then we have a leg up on Killer, and I can prevent him from killing you people before he gets me."

"You're still on that?" Kian sighed.

"Oh my God, she's insane…" Laine muttered to herself.

"And," I continued, slightly annoyed. "Strength in numbers. If the whole victim pool is sentient, the chances of us dying go down significantly."

Kian folded his arms, deep in thought. "I guess you're right," he said after some time. "But how are we supposed to figure out who's gonna join the victim pool?"

"Good question. All we can do is look at who Killer has already targeted, and try to find the connection."

We piled into Kian's car and Laine stewed in the backseat.

"Isn't the connection between all of us our school?" Kian asked suddenly from the front seat.

"That's one of them," I said. "But it's not enough. If Killer was the type who wanted revenge on the entire school, the horror-type would be completely different, something closer to where he could pull a *Carrie.*"

Kian peeled his eyes from the road to toss me a questioning

look, but I waved it away. "His method isn't efficient enough for the school to be the problem, is all I'm saying," I clarified.

We drove in silence for a while before Kian glanced at me once more.

"How's your ankle?"

I frowned. "What do you mean?"

"Your ankle. You twisted it bad last night, right?"

I did. Peering down at my unbruised, untouched ankle, I nodded. Kian looked down, too, and we briefly made eye contact.

"Yeah. I did. Looks like Plot is messier than we thought."

WHEN WE ARRIVED AT SCHOOL, Laine jumped anytime anyone brushed past her. Kian put a reassuring arm around her shoulder and kept her close, letting the brunt of the hallway traffic hit him rather than her. I thought Kian was interesting for that, how simply and seamlessly he moved around to protect her. I realized Kian was actually a very good person, if self-sacrifice made someone good. I wasn't too sure.

"If it's not just the school, then what other connections are there? What do me and Laine have in common with Mack and Rosette?" Kian asked as we shuffled into our math class.

I shrugged. "A lot of things. For one, Rosette was blonde, like Laine," I observed.

Laine let out a curt, dry laugh. "Right, like someone's gonna try to kill us because we're blonde," she exclaimed.

"I'm just making connections. And keep it down," I scolded. I shivered after saying that. I felt annoyingly like my aunt. "That's clearly not the only reason, but it could be one. Another could be reputation. Mack, Rosette, you, Kian, are all pretty popular, right?"

Laine rolled her eyes. "C'mon, how cliché is someone going around killing people just because they're popular?"

"That's the point."

Throughout the test, I could hear Laine's foot constantly tapping… Unrelenting. I felt bad, I think, but it was to be expected. As soon as we got out of class, she ran to the bathroom. Rosette's bathroom, to be specific.

Rosette's bathroom was turned into a memorial for her, one that I had visited a few times since I found her. I harbored some guilt from drawing inspiration from her and thought about how much better it would have been for both of us if we'd switched places. I sat in there when no one else was around a few times during my free periods, just sort of staring at the place I found her. Although the floor had been cleaned, and she obviously wasn't there anymore, I could still see her there, my dream version of her on the ground. I gave her pen back, at least, setting it next to a teddy bear someone else left for her.

Knowing what I know, I followed Laine inside swiftly.

"Laine, you shouldn't go into the bathroom by yourself. This is where Rosette was found, remember?"

Laine splashed her face with water. "Though, I seriously doubt Killer would kill here for a second time. He's repetitive, but not lazy."

Laine slammed her hands down on the counter, and I couldn't help but jump a bit.

"WILL YOU SHUT UP?!"

I blinked, confused. "Uh.."

"Like seriously! Shut up!" Laine clutched her forehead and groaned. She took a few deep breaths. "I'm sorry, Vanessa, I just… I don't want to hear about Killer right now. I don't want to hear about how close I am to dying every time I do, like, anything!"

I stayed silent, which was probably for the best, and I

watched her cry. She dropped her arms and head onto the counter, her shoulders shaking.

I'd only ever witnessed people cry from afar. I'd never had someone burst into tears over something *I said*. It was weird. I felt really… guilty? I don't think I had ever felt truly guilty for anything before. Before all of this, I guess I hadn't done much to feel guilty over before all of this.

I didn't know what to do, so I thought of what Kian would do. I approached her slowly and tentatively placed a hand on her shoulder. I opened my mouth to say something Kian would say, but Laine spun around and hugged me before I could. She sobbed into my shoulder.

"I'm scared, Ness. I'm so scared," she whispered.

My nickname was catching. I put my arm around her, trying very hard to be empathetic, and patted her back gently.

"I know, I'm sorry. I didn't mean to scare you," I replied softly. It only felt right, as I was the one who made her cry.

We stood like that for a while and I constantly checked over her shoulder until she had calmed down some. Finally, she straightened up, wiping her eyes and laughing awkwardly.

"That was so embarrassing." She looked at herself in the mirror and groaned. "I look awful."

"No, you don't," I noted honestly. "You're pretty. Just a little streaky."

Laine stared at me for a second and laughed again. She reached into her bag and wiped her face with a makeup wipe, and tossed it away. Then Laine threw her arm over my shoulder.

"You're sweet," she said as she led me out of the bathroom.

I didn't really agree, but I was worried if I said it, she'd cry again. I really didn't want that, because I wasn't sure I could be more comforting than the first time, and repeating the same method probably wouldn't be that effective.

Kian was waiting for us outside the bathroom, earning him a few odd looks. He gave me a questioning glance when he noticed Laine's sniffles, but I just shook my head. Better not to talk about it, lest she cry again.

We moved through most of the day with no incident. Laine's nerves calmed, Kian relaxed as usual, and I was vigilant as ever. About halfway through the day, I relented some and focused on identifying any potential victims. I had my eyes on the more popular kids, but I couldn't exactly rule out the losers and fellow hermits, could I? The pool of potentials was way too big. Luckily, one of them ran right into me.

"Woah — sorry!" the person said. They crouched down to pick up the laptop they'd just knocked out of my hand and nearly dropped it again.

"Sorry about tha— Oh!" The person straightened up, and I recognized them as the girl who'd shown me the projector. She must have recognized me as well, because she smiled awkwardly.

"Hey, it's you again," she said. I nodded and opened my mouth to speak, but Kian got the jump on me.

"Jo? You still go here?" he asked stupidly.

She just gave him a weird look, then looked away. "Yeah, Kian. I do," she muttered.

Kian had a silly grin on his face, and he playfully slugged her in the shoulder, which I doubt she enjoyed.

"Awesome! Been a while. How come we never hang out anymore?" Kian wondered aloud.

I saw the faintest eye roll from the girl named 'Jo', and she shrugged. "You tell me, Kian."

She turned away from him and back to me. "Anyway, you're Vanessa, right?"

I blinked, not expecting her to know my name. "Yeah. And you're Jo."

She grinned and nodded. "Hey, I know you were interested in the projector and if you ever want to come to Film Club and check it out, you'd be the, uh, second member!"

She spoke fast, with a stutter now and then. "I'll even make you vice president!" She laughed a little, then stopped laughing abruptly.

In any other circumstance, I would have said no immediately and walked off, but something about this girl caught my eye. Particularly the venom I saw flicker behind her eyes whenever Kian opened his big mouth.

"Actually… Can we all join?"

Laine, who had been ignoring most of the conversation, leaned up against the lockers and whipped her head over to look at me. "Uh, Film Club? Not for me." She shook her head in emphasis, but Kian piped up.

"C'mon, it sounds like fun! Plus, then we can hang out with Jo again!"

"Who?" Laine narrowed her eyes as I rolled mine.

"Quick sidebar, one second," I said to Jo. I spun around, taking hold of both Laine and Kian's arms and pulling them into a huddle a few paces away from Jo. "We're joining this club."

"No way—"

"Shh. We're joining. I think Jo might be a potential victim. Or worse, a potential Killer," I said.

Kian's eyes widened. "Killer? How do you know?"

I frowned. "She matches the profile a little. Especially considering she used to be friends with you, Kian. And now you're popular, and she's the president of a one-member film club. See what I'm getting at?"

Kian thought for a second, then nodded slowly. "Yeah, I guess. But if there's a chance she's Killer already, shouldn't we steer clear?"

"I'm not sure she is Killer yet. It's too soon in the story for Killer to be unmasked, so right now, Killer could be anybody. I suspect Killer's identity has already changed at least once." I folded my arms, peering at the ground. "I suspect there may even be more than one Killer."

"That makes this infinitely harder," Laine groaned.

I nodded.

"Which is why we need to weed out any potential Killers as well. Which means befriending Jo," I concluded.

Laine frowned, but I shrugged.

"That's our best course of action. And she seems less idiotic than you two, having knowledge of movies."

I ignored their offended scoffs and continued. "Plus, she got this close to us, so who knows whether she'll end up on Killer's list, too?"

They finally agreed with me, and our little huddle broke. I walked back over to the still awkwardly waiting Jo, putting on as much of a friendly look as I could manage. "Sorry about all that."

"That's okay." Jo shifted on her feet, clearly expecting a rejection.

"So…" I'd never joined a club before, and something about it was weirdly exciting. I was probably just a product of the weirdly exciting movie world we'd found ourselves in, but I wasn't sure that was really the case. "Got room for three?"

I DON'T THINK I'd ever seen someone as enthusiastic about movies as me before Jo. The second we showed up in the film room after school that day, she'd whipped out a bunch of older films and started showing us how the projector worked.

Laine and Kian jumped when they heard the noise, and the three of us exchanged looks. Jo didn't notice, still caught up in her explanation of all the bits and pieces of the old projector.

She showed us a silent movie on the projector, commenting on the history of the film and all the nuances that went into building it. It would have been interesting if it was Dracula or Frankenstein or something, but it was some slapstick comedy that Jo found hilarious.

Laine was visibly bored, but Kian nodded along to what Jo was saying, engaged. I doubt he was super receptive to all of her words, as flashes of confusion would flicker over his face, which he quickly fixed to look engaged again. If there was one thing Kian could do, it was pretend to understand stuff.

I was on edge the entire time. I was certain Killer would make a move during the meeting. It would only make sense. We were some of the only people left in the school building, watching old movies as the sun set. It always set so early.

No one else was on high alert like I was, so I had to stay vigilant for everyone else. Especially for Jo, considering she didn't know anything about what was going on.

Before arriving, Kian, Laine, and I discussed telling Jo, but we decided it was best to wait to see if she'd actually join the victim pool. Like with Laine, it would be easier to explain after Jo had seen some of the strange occurrences that transpired when Killer was around.

So we sat waiting for something bad to happen and we didn't have to wait long. Since it was late, the first 'meeting' ended and the four of us gathered our stuff to leave. Laine was ready to go first, while Kian stretched with a loud yawn as he stood.

"Hey," Jo whispered to me, distracting me briefly from my vigil. "Thanks for coming. It means a lot, really."

She gave me a soft smile, and for a minute I wasn't sure how to respond.

"Yeah. No problem. You're um, helping us, to be honest."

She gave me a questioning look and opened her mouth to say something, probably about my odd statement, before she stopped. Staring just past my shoulder, she murmured a small "Who..?"

I frowned before turning to see what she was looking at. It took me a second to recognize a figure sat in the back of the classroom, shrouded in the shadows. They were almost perfectly still; only the slow rise and fall of their shoulders with each quiet breath, proof that they were a real person.

"I thought you only had us as members, Jo," Kian said suddenly, having spotted the figure as well.

"I do."

Slowly, the figure stood, and I suddenly realized of the presence of a sound that should have stopped when the film ended several minutes ago.

Someone grabbed my arm, yanking me the rest of the way out of the room. It was Kian, of course, my arm in one hand and Laine's in his other. I had just enough time to grab hold of Jo, creating a counterproductive human chain for a few steps before we all collectively fell in line, sprinting from the art hall. Killer was behind us, walking eerily calm, in true villain fashion.

Kian lead the group, but Jo was slowing down. She was out of breath, clearly not the athletic type. I couldn't blame her, neither was I, but we were so close to the exit of the school. Then we could pile into Kian's car and get out of there. For a second, I had forgotten my curse, one that quickly turned into an asset in that moment. I slowed to Jo's pace, grabbing her arm.

"Kian!" I shouted.

He had stamina. I knew he could run back, scoop Jo up, and get the three of them out of the school and into the car. I'd stay back and keep Killer at bay, and maybe, just maybe, achieve my perfect murder!

Kian must have guessed my thinking. He turned, let go of Laine's hand, rushed back to Jo, picked Jo up and threw her over his shoulder (impressively enough), and caught back up to Laine (disappointingly enough).

There was a split second where he looked at me, and I recognized it as him asking me what the plan was. I mouthed a small "go" and slowed to a stop, taking a breath as I turned around to face the still very slowly approaching Killer.

I wondered if the blade he held was the same one he'd stabbed Kian with. I'm sure it was. It's odd how my mind wandered in that second, so much so that I don't even remember running again. This time, however, I ran toward Killer. I don't remember if he kept walking, or if he'd stopped moving for a second. I don't even remember winding my arm back.

But I do remember the weird, fleshy and hard feeling of my fist colliding with Killer's stomach.

KIAN'S NOTE #5: RE: IF THE EVIDENCE POINTS TOWARD AN ANSWER, ACCEPT IT

WHERE COULD she possibly have learned how to throw a punch like that?

I mean, damn. I felt it, and I was all the way down the hall. Killer absolutely *folded*. I would have laughed if I wasn't so scared at the time.

It reminded me of a video Marco showed me back in fifth grade about how a punch to the gut killed that old magician, Whobini, or whatever the guy's name was, and I hoped in that moment that Ness had that strength. Killer doubled over, and my eyes flicked back to Ness. She was clutching her fist with a grimace on her face.

She turned back to me, rolled her eyes and muttered: "I said go, idiot."

Jo was still over my shoulder. It may have been the adrenaline, but she felt so light I thought she might fly away if I ran too fast. But I had a plan. I took hold of Laine again and sprinted to the front door, attempting to push it open. It didn't budge.

No, no, no!

I recalibrated, pulling the door frantically in case I'd made the all too common mistake of pushing a pull door. Still, noth-

ing. I resorted to as much violence as I could manage, alternating from kicking the door and slamming into it with my shoulder. The door shuddered, but didn't open.

"Open it, Kian!" Laine screeched.

"What do you think I'm trying to do?!"

I spun around to see how Ness was doing. Killer was still doubled over, and Ness watched him with her arms folded. I yelled to get her attention, and she gave me an annoyed look.

"What now?!" she shouted.

I motioned toward the door. "Locked."

She rolled her eyes — hard — and sighed. "Did you try pulling?"

I frowned. "I'm not an idiot."

She muttered something that sounded mean and gave Killer a last look before jogging over to us. She tried the door herself, and frowned. "Alright, so we're stuck."

Laine made a strangled noise, and Jo patted my back to put her down.

Ness continued, "He's getting up again. He's gonna come over here, and probably going to go straight for one of you."

Laine clutched my arm tight. "What do we do?" I asked, eyes fixed on the now standing Killer. He started walking, with more urgency this time.

"Just stand behind me," Ness said.

I gave her a look, and she returned one of her own, one that compelled me to trust her.

Killer picked up speed, and I quickly stepped behind Ness. Laine didn't look that certain, but followed my lead. Ness had to physically shove Jo behind her as she turned to face Killer. Then, like some sort of vigilante, Ness pulled a knife that looked a lot like the one she'd given me from her sweatshirt pocket.

Had she been walking around with that all day?

I wouldn't put it past her, especially as she brandished it so brazenly. I was reminded of the first time she'd saved me, as again moonlight peeked in through the window and danced atop her head. Her halo returned, twice as bright, twice as strong. Jo gasped behind me, and Laine muttered a small *huh*, and I knew they saw it too.

We watched, awestruck, as Ness held the blade in front of her. Killer slowed for a second, almost timid, but returned to his pace a second later. He approached heavily, mere meters from us, his own knife drawn and poised to strike Ness. As his arm reached out, Ness ducked just in time, leaving Killer's knife inches from my chest.

I held my breath, preparing for impact, but Ness was quicker. From the ground, she plunged her blade into Killer's stomach, driving forward and pushing Killer backward onto the ground. As he crashed to the floor, her hand was still wrapped around the knife. She stood, yanking it out. She looked almost brutal, despite the halo still gleaming over her.

Everything seemed to stand still for a moment, with Jo, Laine, and me in utter shock. Ness stood like she was fresh from battle, blood on her sleeve. Killer was on the ground, but he wasn't struggling. He wasn't even moving.

Or breathing.

"Did you kill him?" Laine asked shakily, the first to make a sound for at least five full minutes.

Ness glanced at her, and for a second I swore her eyes flashed solid white again. She bent down, reached her hand out to Killer's arm, but paused. "I'm going to be the last person to touch this body, alright?" Ness turns back to look at us. "This will definitely change up Plot in some way, so I'll make sure he's dead, but none of us will remove the mask, or try and discover who it is."

She bent down, closed her eyes, and felt for Killer's wrist. "Turn around. We can't risk seeing any indicator of who this is. Skin color or otherwise."

I frowned as the three of us complied. "Why not?"

"It's too early in the story for Killer to die. And considering

Killer's identity has probably changed, there's a chance that there's not an actual person under this mask." She went silent for a bit before she spoke again, this time her voice quieter.

"Dead."

We were all silent for a while, the reality of the situation finally dawning on us. Ness had just killed a guy. It was self-defense, sure. But still. A guy was *dead*. What did this mean? Would the movie end? Ness said that it couldn't be Killer under that mask, but I wasn't exactly convinced.

Jo's voice suddenly piped up, and her stable tone was almost as shocking as the situation. "She's right."

Laine and I both whip our heads in her direction, but she's looking straight at Ness. "Vanessa's right. It's too early for the killer to die. Whoever is under that mask isn't the killer."

The three of us stared at her blankly.

"How…" Ness started. "How did you know—"

"I found out a little while ago." Jo laughed a bit dryly to herself, shifting on her feet. "When you showed up at the film club the first time, Vanessa. Before that I had been… blacking out. I had big chunks of my memory just… gone. Then you came in, and I remembered things. Snippets of stuff that… that I had done. The woods."

Ness's eyes went wide. "So that was you?"

I took a step back, and suddenly I was very aware of my stitches again.

Jo looked at the ground, nodding a bit. "I think so. But I don't… I don't know. All of my memories are as if I'm in someone else's mind, someone's mind using my body. It's weird," she trailed off, and there was silence for a minute.

Laine moved closer to me.

"Then I started hearing things. Like, I could hear my projector when it wasn't on. And I was so… angry. All the time. Angry at everyone. Don't get me wrong, it's not particularly a happy life being an outcast, but I was never… not before.. Well, anyway. I was mostly mad at, like, people like you." She gestured toward me, and I frowned. She avoided my eyes as she spoke. "You, and Laine, and Marco, and all of those types."

"Popular types," Ness chimed in.

Jo looked ashamed, but nodded. "Yeah, popular types. Especially you two, actually. I think it's cause...'cause you guys were my friends."

Jo picked at her fingers, and I felt a weird pang of guilt in my chest. It was true, the three of us had been friends at one point. Back in elementary school, and for the first half of middle school. Something happened in eighth grade, though, that made us drift apart. More honestly, made Laine and I drift apart from Jo.

I had always been well-liked, but once I got tall and started leaning into football, well, that's pretty much royalty in our town. Laine had a bit of an awkward phase in middle school. I mean, who didn't? But she got really pretty in eighth grade. She also got sort of mean, which, for some people, made her worthy of their attention. Jo didn't change, though. Not at all.

She had always had some trouble making friends outside of Laine and me, but we had always been content as a trio. Laine was the first to drift away, suddenly very concerned about how she looked hanging out with a nerdy sort like Jo. I thought nothing of it. Friendships change, but Laine expected me to change as well. I liked Jo. She was my friend. But so was Laine, and now there were a whole bunch of people who were demanding my attention, and part of me assumed Jo would find some more friends too. I assumed she'd understand the circumstances and that she wouldn't be upset. People drift apart! But now, as I stood in the dark hallway of the school, a motionless Killer ten feet away from us, and her own confession to stabbing me, I realized that wasn't a very good judgment to make.

Jo's voice pulled me from my thoughts. "I wanted to kill you."

Laine grasped my arm, and Ness took a barely noticeable step toward Jo.

"When I saw you and Laine next to Vanessa. I was so angry just seeing your face and... I wanted to kill you. I thought I would. Until Vanessa said that you were all going to join my film club."

Something in Jo's face lightened.

"And you guys *actually showed up*. Then the feelings, the anger, the weird murder-y stuff, it just... went away. Like a light switch. Don't get me wrong, I still didn't like you guys, but it was back to the reason it was before: because you're both jerks. But that's not something I've ever wanted to, like, stab someone for."

Ness stepped forward suddenly and pushed Jo's bangs out of her face. Jo's light brown face went bright red and Ness hummed.

"I hit you with a rock," she muttered.

Jo stuttered as she tried to speak, then cleared her throat after turning back to her normal shade.

"Yeah, I remember that a little. There used to be an enormous bruise there. It was there this morning... I take it... it's gone now?" Jo said, staring at the ground as Ness stepped back.

"Yeah, it's gone. When exactly did you hear the projector?" Ness inquired.

Jo thought for a moment. "Well, I think I started hearing it after the woods. But I didn't really pay attention until you showed up at film club. After that, it got louder." She frowned, absentmindedly touching a hand to where her bruise allegedly used to be.

"Right after the woods, I remember waking up in my house. I wasn't sure how I got there, or what exactly had happened before. I remembered seeing you, Vanessa. And that's all I could remember until I saw you again."

I exhaled a bit. "So Ness really is the common thread

between sentience," I concluded. "What's that phrase for when characters, like, realize they're just characters?"

"Breaking the fourth wall," Ness answered. She turned back to Jo. "The town is stuck in a horror movie. That's the conclusion. Do you believe me?"

Jo thought for a second, then slowly nodded. "Yeah. I believe you."

I learned then that Jo was pretty good at suspending disbelief, something Laine and I never really got down.

"But... does this mean that I'm the killer?"

Ness thought for a moment, then shook her head. "You don't have any more murderous urges toward Kian and Laine, right? Well, besides the usual ones fueled by their stupidity?"

"Hey!" Laine and I said in unison, but the other two ignored us.

"Nope. Not anymore," Jo replied.

Ness nodded and folded her arms. "Looks like you've been demoted to a member of the victim pool, then."

We all went silent. Jo looked green, and Ness moved back toward the body on the ground. "If I take off his mask, it'll drag someone innocent into it," she muttered. "But if I don't, who knows how Plot will change?"

"Don't do it," Jo said.

Ness looked toward her, and Jo raised a finger to the air. "You hear that?"

I looked up too, though I didn't need to because I realized what Jo was referring to.

The film was still rolling.

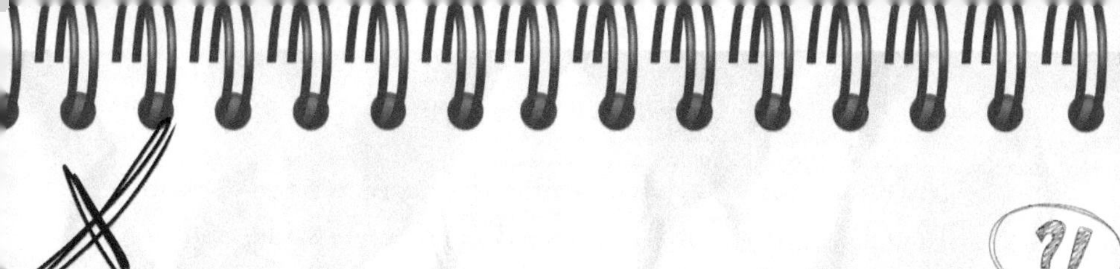

TIP FOR AN IDIOT #6: NAMES ARE PRETTY IMPORTANT

It was still rolling, though I couldn't guess why until we heard sirens and the familiar blue and red lights shined through the windows.

A little less than a minute later, the front door swung open, and in stepped three officers with their bright flashlights, Kian's father just behind them. The sheriff looked shocked, then pretty pissed, when he saw Kian, Laine, and Jo in front of him. His expression softened a bit when he noticed me, though I do not know why, but then he grew stern again.

"What are you kids doing in here? You four are breaking and entering!" the sheriff said, brows furrowed.

Kian steps forward, his voice small. "Dad, it's not what you think—"

"We were attacked," I interrupted, gesturing to the corpse behind me. I was surprised the sheriff hadn't seen it earlier, and even more surprised when he didn't look fazed.

"Attacked, hm?" the sheriff repeated, as if he didn't believe me.

"Uh, yeah? We were here for a club, stayed too late, and got locked in. Sort of. Then we were attacked by Killer — I mean, that killer. You know, the one that y'all haven't caught?"

My aunt would have had a fit if she heard the tone I used with her beloved sheriff. The sheriff's eyes grew wide, and he withdrew his gun from its holster. I wanted to tell him it wasn't necessary, and that I'd taken care of it, but he spoke before I could.

"Which direction did he go?" the sheriff asked, and the other officers had their guns out too.

I startled. "What do you mean? He didn't go anywhere, he's right there—"

"Ness," Kian said suddenly, cutting me off. I glanced at him, then at his shaking finger that pointed behind me. He was pale. Well, paler than normal, as were Laine and Jo.

"You're kidding, right?" I said aloud as I realized what had happened.

Kian shook his head, and I turned around, but I already knew what I would see. Or, rather, what I wouldn't see.

THE OTHER OFFICERS at the station laughed when we explained that the freak I killed had gotten up and walked away as soon as they'd arrived. The sheriff didn't laugh.

"You know, Kian. This is a serious matter. It's disgusting for you to lie and use this situation as an alibi for breaking into your school." The sheriff's voice was chilly, and I wondered if this was how he always sounded when he scolded Kian.

"I'm not lying, Dad, Geez!" Kian groaned. "I told you, he was there, chasing us with a knife, or ax, or something, and then Ness... Ness.."

Kian grew frustrated, and it was clear his father didn't believe him. I felt, I dunno, bad for Kian. He wasn't a liar. He was objectively much more honest than I'd ever been. Still, his father didn't listen until I asserted Kian was telling the truth.

"I thought I killed the, uh, guy," I muttered. "But he must have been... I don't know, pretending."

The sheriff raised an eyebrow as I continued, outlining the events to make it sound more believable than it actually was. The sheriff nodded along, and Kian stayed silent, arms folded and clearly annoyed.

Good, now he knows how I feel.

Still... I felt bad. I took a breath when I had finished recounting the story, and Laine, who had been interjecting with "Yeah!" and "Literally," nodded her head finally and leaned back in her seat as if she'd done the bulk of the explaining and exhausted herself. The sheriff was quiet for a second, processing the absolute information dump we had just delivered to him, then let out a deep sigh.

"And this all happened?" he clarified.

"Yes."

"If you were to testify to this in court, you wouldn't be perjuring yourself, right?"

"Odd way to ask if I'm a liar, but yes."

He nodded slowly, then clicked something on the laptop in front of him. We waited in silence for a long time as he typed away, before he eventually sighed again and shut the laptop.

"Alright," he said. "I'm having a unit search the school."

Kian, who had been sulking for several minutes, looked up as his father spoke.

"I'll let your principal know that we're shutting down the school for the time being, implementing a town curfew, and will be preemptively halting all preparations for the Harvest Festival until we catch this guy."

The Harvest Festival. I had forgotten about that.

An all too common quirk of an all too common small town. It was undoubtedly some sort of device Plot was going to use to create a bloodbath. It was lining up perfectly. This shift would start the apex of Killer's streak, and the point where we'd have to be the most vigilant. Chances were, Killer was injured, likely slower, but angrier, so we couldn't get cocky. I'd saved the pool all this time, but once we got to the apex... Well, I could only carry so many people on my back. We'd have to distance ourselves from everyone else to make sure no one else could join the pool. That meant no police, no Partly, no parents, no other students. We'd have to disappear.

Understandably, the others were skeptical of disappearing during the height of Killer's streak.

"He's going to find us, regardless. If we keep it to just the four of us, we won't risk anyone else joining the pool," I explained to Jo once we left the station and got back to my house. '

The sheriff took Kian away and called Laine's parents to come get her. He tried to call my aunt, too, but I slipped away before he could. As for Jo... I didn't know why her parents didn't come to get her. I didn't notice, actually, not until I realized she was walking beside me back to my house. The film stopped rolling once we left the station, and its sudden absence made the whole town seem so much quieter, so much emptier.

"That makes sense," Jo said.

I could feel her eyes on me, but I chose not to meet them.

"I'm sorry all this is happening to you, Ness."

I didn't understand that. Out of everyone in the pool, I was the only one who chose to put myself in this situation. Everyone else had fallen in by pure circumstance. Hell, I'd even dragged Jo into the victim pool just to avoid having her become Killer. What was the point, anyway? There would always be a Killer, it didn't really matter who it was. The roles were all set; the actor was irrelevant.

"Nothing is happening to me," I said finally. "It's happening to all of you, not me."

Jo frowned a bit, but said nothing more. We got back to my house, and my aunt was already asleep, so she couldn't cuss me out for bringing Jo back without telling her. We got to my room and called Laine and Kian, neither of whom answered.

This made me ant, but I had a good amount of confidence in using the film rolling as an alarm stem, so I resolved to stay awake until we could reunite. Jo accepted a change of clothes I gave her and settled in to go to sleep. She didn't though and ended up sitting awake with me.

"Ness?" she blurted, and I recognized my nickname as a cemented one.

"Mhm?"

"I think there is something we're missing."

I nodded. "I think so, too. What are you thinking about?"

"Well, did you see how things changed when the film stopped rolling? In the station, I mean."

I tilted my head and shook it.

"I was watching Kian's dad when he dragged Kian away. He was talking to Kian, hushed, and he looked angry. Then, the rolling stopped, and it was like... like a switch flipped. He put an arm around Kian's shoulder and rushed him out, talking about taking him to the hospital and having him checked out and stuff."

I frowned. I hadn't noticed that.

"Same with Laine's parents. When they showed up, they hugged her. I think her dad even started crying. Then the rolling stopped, and they looked like it was an inconvenience to them to be there. Like they were more frustrated with having to pick Laine up than with the fact that their daughter almost just died.." Jo shook her head. "It was so weird. I've met Laine's parents, and they were not the same before the rolling stopped as I've known them to be."

I thought back to our theories about the rolling, about Plot. "It makes sense," I concluded. "If the rolling happens when the movie is playing, then it would make sense for people's personalities to change. But not if we truly were just characters." I stood, suddenly aware of a very important fact. "We didn't start as characters, Jo. Whatever has happened in this movie hasn't always been here. We haven't always been like this."

Jo looked spooked. "The town existed before the movie. Whatever started this didn't create us, it just.."

"Repurposed us."

I thought back to my question to Kian, about whether anything about him as a person had changed since I saved him. "Either whatever is controlling this town has a serious recycling of characters problem, or we didn't begin as characters."

"So something about the rolling puts Wilsonville into some sort of trance? Making them subservient to the Plot?" Jo tapped her foot on the ground.

"Yeah, I think—Wait."

I noticed something. Something very, very pressing, so pressing that I had no idea how I hadn't noticed it before. "Wilsonville. Is that what you just said?"

Jo blinked. "Yeah? Our town?"

"That's not our town's name." I remembered.

Jo looked confused, and I couldn't blame her.

"I'm certain of it. That's not our town's name."

KIAN'S NOTE #6: RE: NAMES ARE PRETTY IMPORTANT

By the time I had snuck out, picked up Laine, and got to Ness's house, my father had already called my phone.

I knew he would check Ness's place for me first, so when we saw Ness and Jo waving us down on the lawn, I urged them to get in the car, drove to the edge of town to buy some time.

Ness and Jo were visibly shaken, and I'd never seen Ness like that. No matter how many times I asked them to explain, they shook their heads and wanted to wait until we were at the edge of town. The entire ride there, they stared out the window and pointed at every building, making odd exclamations.

"See?" Ness kept saying, jabbing her finger at the window. Jo would groan, looking queasy, and point out another building. They kept this up incessantly.

"What is wrong with you two?" Laine asked, annoyed, but Ness and Jo never responded.

They practically fell out of the car once we got to the woods. Ness insisted we drove through to get to the edge of town from there. I was reluctant, for obvious reasons, but obliged her nonetheless. I knew it was the only way to get Ness and Jo to explain just what was wrong with them. There was

another odd moment in the forest with a sign that said they were leaving Wilson Woods, which belonged to Wilsonville, and entering another, privately owned section of the woods.

Laine and I got out shortly after Jo and Ness, who were pointing at the sign frantically.

"Alright," Laine said in frustration. "You two better start talking before I genuinely go insane."

Ness and Jo started speaking at once, making for a cacophony of incomprehensible ramblings, until Laine gave a look that made them both stop. Ness took a breath and spoke.

"Kian. What's the name of the town we live in?" she asked, her voice slow and careful, loaded with information she wasn't sharing.

"What kind of question is that?"

"Just answer. Please don't tick me off right now."

"Okay, alright. Wilsonville. Obviously," I answered.

Ness and Jo exchanged unreadable looks.

"What's the name of our school?"

"Uh, Wilson High?"

"Our old school?"

"Wilson Middle, Wilson Elementary."

Ness suddenly looked giddy, a look Jo did not share. "The pharmacy?"

"Wilson Pharmacy."

"Convenience store."

"Wilson's Quick Stop."

Laine made a face, a realization that I hadn't come to yet.

"Daycare by the bank?"

I was getting annoyed. "Wee Wilson Childcare. What is this about?"

"Where are we right now, Kian?"

"Oh, my god." I rolled my eyes. "Wilson Woods. Literally, what is this about?"

"Kian." Ness looked at me seriously, but I could see the excitement in her eyes. "What is your last name?"

"Wilson."

Wait. What?

"Wilson... I'm.." I racked my brain, trying to think of how this was possible. I knew my family had money, but how could I have not noticed that literally everything in town was named after me?

"Remember what I asked you before?" she asked.

"Just how rich am I?"

"Not that rich," Ness answered. "At least you weren't, not before I saved you." She turned, pointing at the sign. "What does that say, Kian?"

I peered at it. "You are now leaving Wilson Wood- No, wait." I stared harder, realizing that was not at all what it said. "You are now leaving... leaving..."

"Watercress Woods," Laine said quietly.

Ness clapped her hands, and Jo looked positively green.

"Do you guys know what this means?" she asked, her eyes twinkling with an intensity I've never seen before. I wanted to say no, but she already knew I didn't.

"Things really did change when I saved you. Roles changed. This town was something before the movie started. We were something before the movie started. Something, or someone took control of us, of this whole town, and they turned it into their live set." She turned to Jo. "That's why the rolling changes personalities. That's why every one of us is a stereotype. Well, except for me. We weren't always like this."

Laine gripped my arm, and I tried to wrap my head around all of this.

"Where there's one change, there's many," Jo piped up. "We thought about it last night. Kian, you weren't always a quarterback, right? Now you are."

I thought about it. I couldn't remember a time where I wasn't a quarterback until I could. It was as if one day I had changed, so suddenly and seamlessly, that no one even noticed. "Yeah." I managed to get out weakly.

"And, Laine. Have you always been the head cheerleader?"

Laine looked like she was on the verge of a breakdown, and she shook her head. "No, I don't think so," she stammered.

"I don't even remember when I started Film Club," Jo admitted. "One day, it didn't exist. The next day, I was president, and never even noticed I hadn't been before."

"And," Ness continued, pointing between Laine and I. "You two are supposed to be dating, but you haven't acted like a couple since I saved you both the first time. Do you remember being a couple before Mack?"

"No," Laine answered before I could. "Not at all. Unless you count that one time in middle school."

Jo rolled her eyes, and Ness spoke up again.

"This goes for other things within the town, too." She paced. "When your dad mentioned the Harvest Festival last night, I was surprised I had forgotten about it. I hadn't. It didn't exist until that moment." Ness clapped her hands. "Can any of you remember a single Harvest Festival before this year?"

None of us could.

"If our town had been created with the sole purpose of being the setting of a movie, we'd have memories that align with current events, if any. We wouldn't have conflicting ones. That tells us two things. One, we aren't just characters, we're actual people. And two, whatever is pulling the strings in this town has us in some sort of hypnotism. A hypnotism that keeps all the townspeople acting according to the script that Plot says, while never being aware of it."

"A hypnotism that Ness broke," Jo declared. "Hence our sentience. Now, Ness thinks she became sentient because of something to do with stealing a red cloth and messing up Plot's continuity. Then, from her sentience, she woke you two by saving you and making you an anomaly."

"We also messed up Plot's continuity by surviving," I muttered, repeating the theory Ness shared with me days prior.

It made a good amount of sense now that we knew what we knew.

Jo nodded. "And so did I, by becoming friends with you guys. Well, with Ness."

"So, the common thread is Ness," Laine concluded.

Ness grimaced. "That seems to be the case, yeah."

We all went silent, each lost in thought. The whole situation was near impossible to believe, yet here we were.

"How do we end it, then?" Laine said after a while. "Can Ness just like, make the whole town sentient?"

"Not without saving the whole town from certain death first," I guessed.

"But she didn't save Jo, right? Jo joined the victim pool and stopped being Killer just because she befriended us."

"But I was sentient before that," Jo muttered. "Remember? I became sentient when Ness hit me and saved you two in the woods. I knew what I was, what I was doing, but... I couldn't stop. I was still Killer. My role didn't change until you guys came to Film Club."

"That changes things." Ness claps. "That changes the rule. Sentience doesn't pull you from Plot's control. Jo must have become sentient from not killing you two. That didn't pull her entirely from the hypnotism when the film is rolling."

"What if the rule is different for Killer?" Jo said. "Think about it. Killer is the most important character in a horror movie. You can have any number of victims, of any sorts, but without Killer, it isn't complete. Whatever is controlling Plot and everything may hold on to control of Killer much tighter than everyone else."

"So Killer is more susceptible until they aren't Killer anymore." Ness hummed.

Laine groaned. "This is making my head hurt, bro."

I nodded, and Ness waved us off. "In the end, it's all just trying to understand this place so we can end the movie. But it's mostly for my sake. You all are leaving. Now."

We turned to her, confusion spiked on all our faces.

"What are you talking about?" I asked. "Why would we leave?"

"Because. The way the movie is going, it's looking like Killer is gonna ramp up soon. If I'm Final Girl, you all being around me is a liability. And I'm not sure I'll be able to keep you all safe in the moment, so you're leaving. Just for the time being, until I get rid of Killer," she said it so simply.

"No way," I said, shaking my head. "No. We aren't leaving you."

"I'm gonna be fine, unfortunately. Final Girl can't die, remember?"

"Still, what if your role changes? It's not safe. I'm not leaving you."

"Not a choice," Ness said sharply. "No offense, Ki, but you three are kind of out of your element. You can't do anything against Killer. We've established that. Killer actively avoids me, and when he does get near, it's damn near impossible for me to lose. And if I'm focused on keeping you three alive, I can't focus on getting rid of Killer. If I can't die, nobody can, remember?"

Laine piped up before I could, which was probably for the best, because she was calmer than I felt at that moment. "Ness, we couldn't possibly leave you alone. That would make us, like, totally sucky friends."

"Friends?" Ness repeated. "This isn't about friendship, Laine. This is about survival. The fact of the matter is, none of you will survive this. If I slip up, if I take my eyes off of you for one second, you'll die."

Ness shook her head, and I could see genuine distress in her eyes. Distress she would never admit to, of course.

"You're leaving. That's final. It's just for a few days. That's why I had you grab your stuff."

Laine opened her mouth to protest again, but I gave her a hand a small squeeze and shook my head.

"Alright, Ness. We'll go," I spoke up.

Ness met my eyes, and I could swear I saw a flicker of emotion, one that dissipated just as quickly as it had appeared.

"Good. Get in the car."

We obliged, and Ness leaned into the driver's window. "Go to the next town and stay in a motel or something. Your dad will probably come to me for your whereabouts, and I'll send him your way when I think things are going to get dangerous. That way, your dad won't get caught in the middle of it trying to do his job."

"Thanks, Ness," I said softly.

"Not doing it for you," she muttered, stepping from the window. "Don't even think about coming back, not until I personally come and get you guys. Got it?"

I nodded, but I could tell by the look on her face that she knew I was going to come back anyway. I wouldn't bring Jo and Laine with me. I wouldn't allow them to come back into the line of fire. And that was the most Ness could expect from me. We both knew that.

"Don't die, Ness," Laine called as we started moving.

"Couldn't even if I tried. And I will," Ness replied, waving slightly.

I wondered as I drove toward the sign if Ness would hold off and be fine until I came back, but soon we realized we didn't need to worry about such a thing.

It was a good thing I was driving slowly to avoid hitting any of the trees that leaned onto the little dirt path in the woods, otherwise the damage to the front of my car when we hit the Veil would have been much worse.

TIP FOR AN IDIOT #7:
FORGET THE DAMN CAR.

THE FACE KIAN made when he hit it would have been comical if the fact that he hit it in the first place wasn't extremely troubling.

It was still kind of funny.

Sorry, insensitive.

Anyways…. I jogged over and Kian climbed out with a thousand-yard stare, rushing to the front of his car to assess the damage. It didn't look great, definitely not something you could buff out, but that wasn't the worrying part. As Jo and Laine stumbled out of the traumatized Volvo, all four of us focused on something formally unexplainable.

Kian hadn't hit anything.

The front of his car pressed against the air, crumpled as if they'd hit a concrete wall. We all stood in complete silence for a considerable amount of time, trying to deduce what exactly this meant.

"My car," Kian muttered, almost in a trance.

"Did something run across the path?" Laine asked shakily.

I shook my head. "Nothing was there."

"My car."

Jo crouched down, peering at the damage cautiously.

"Whatever made this dent should have been big enough for us to see."

"My car."

"Forget the car, Kian!" Laine yelled, exasperated.

Kian made a strangled sound and leaned against his precious car and its damaged hood. The rest of us stared at the car for a few seconds longer, before Jo yelped. Laine and I looked over at her as she looked around for a second.

"What is it?"

"Something was behind me," she murmured. "I swear. I leaned back, and it felt like I hit something."

"There's nothing there," Laine said, but I had already put my hands out and walked toward where Jo looked.

Sure enough, nothing was there, and I walked uninterrupted. But when Jo tried? Well, it was surreal watching her hit the air in front of her as if it were a solid wall.

She looked at her hands, then the woods, then me, several paces in front of her. We were stunned for a moment, before Laine mimicked Jo's movements. Same outcome.

"Kian, you try," I said.

They stared at me, then motioned they couldn't hear me. I stepped to their side and repeated myself over the sounds of Laine and Jo freaking out. Kian was still in a sort of daze, so when he walked forward, he didn't even put his hands out, and groaned loudly when his face hit the invisible wall.

No matter how far I walked, I ran into no obstacles. Jo and Laine hit the solid air repeatedly, as if they could break through with their fists. Finished with my experiment, I walked back to the others.

"What the hell is happening?" Kian finally muttered, the cause of the knot on his forehead having knocked him back into reality. Or whatever this was.

I took Kian's hand and tried to pull him back through this invisible barrier. It didn't work. As soon as I got through, we were ripped apart. I stepped back to their side.

"Alright," I said, standing still for a second. "Theory update: you guys can't leave. And I can't hear y'all when I leave."

"YOU THINK?" Laine screeched.

"Relax. This isn't super out there. Most movies thwart the victims' plans of escape until the end of the movie, anyway. So, this just means that Plot's got a pretty tight grip on you guys."

"Why can you leave and we can't?" Jo squeaked out.

"Good question. It probably has something to do with the fact that I'm the only one who can, you know, resist Plot's little hypnotism-thing. I guess this is another symptom."

Kian piped up. "Look."

He pointed toward the ground, where a small, white bunny was desperately trying to pass through the invisible barrier and get to a berry on the other side. "Plot hypnotized the bunny, too?"

Shrugging, I crossed the barrier, picked the berry and dropped it within the bunny's reach. "Maybe?"

I picked up a nearby stick and tried to toss it across the barrier. It bounced off, making a dull thump as it fell back to the damp ground.

"Hypnotized sticks..." Laine muttered beside me.

I resisted the urge to call her an idiot, as I wasn't sure what was happening, either. She was actively making more deductions than I was. Who was I to discourage her?

"So, it's more of a physical barrier, then. Some sort of veil keeping everything in, in, and everything out, out?" Jo whispered.

Something latch on to my sleeve. I didn't even have to look to know it was Kian.

"That sounds about right."

We, or, rather, Jo and Laine, spent the next ten minutes throwing various objects at the Veil and watching them bounce off. It would have been entertaining if it wasn't so annoyingly ambiguous. Kian and I just sort of sat there for a while, watching Jo and Laine without a word. Kian still held tight onto my sleeve, and I reckoned he'd stay like that for a while. Between the Veil and the destruction done to his car, I could tell his little brain had gone haywire.

I glanced at him for a second and decided I should probably say something. For comfort, or whatever.

"Ki?"

"Yeah?"

"Your car's insured."

Yeah, I settled on that. So comfort isn't my strong suit, sue me. It seemed to work at least a bit, because his grip relaxed ever so slightly.

"Yeah, it's insured. 'Course." He sighed some, kicking dirt at his feet. "I'm not insured against my father's wrath, though."

I nodded. As if I understood. How could I possibly? I knew nothing about any of that. I'd never even been grounded. My aunt tried it, but come on. I don't do anything or go anywhere already. Who is she grounding?

In any case, the 'wrath' of a father after one crashes their car is not something I've experienced, or will experience. Though, despite seeing the pure dread on Kian's face as he mulls over how to tell his father, it's something that I'd maybe like to experience. Once, that's all.

Anyways...

Kian's phone was off, since he knew his parents would call non stop after he snuck out. Since my plan to get him, Jo, and Laine out of town was thwarted indefinitely, he turned his phone back on. Oddly enough, he didn't have a single missed call. Not one text, either. That was weird, not only because of Kian's parents, but because Kian was a very popular guy. Even his DMs were dry — a discovery he whined about for several minutes.

I got off the hood of the car and approached Jo and Laine.

"Pull out your phones right quick. Any messages? Calls or anything?"

They stopped throwing things for a second, pulling out their phones and going through their messages.

"Nope," Jo said, and she didn't seem surprised at all. Made sense, she was the president of a one-woman film club. Her phone probably stayed dry.

Laine looked distressed as she refreshed the notification center of each social app she had over and over again. "Nothing," she said, incredulously.

Her reaction made sense, too. Need I explain why?

I tugged my phone from my pocket and checked it, even though I didn't expect anything. "Phones in, guys. I wanna check something."

Everyone piled their phones in my hands, Laine with some reluctance, and I jogged away from the barrier, back toward town. I'm not super proud of how quickly I got out of breath, but after a few breaks for air and getting a significant distance away from the barrier, notifications piled in on Laine and Kian's phones. Jo's and my phone stayed quiet, save for a scam email or two on Jo's, but that was to be expected. Laine and Kian caught up to me quickly (Jo did not), and took their phones back.

"So. What does this mean?" Laine asked first.

"Not sure," I replied honestly. "Something about the barrier must mess with the phones."

Kian shook his head as Jo finally caught up. "It must be something that cuts off communication specifically. The phones themselves were working fine. Even the Wi-Fi. Something about the barrier keeps people from contacting us."

I nod a bit. "That makes some sense. How and why it can do is the part I doubt we'll be able to figure out anytime soon."

"Crap, my dad's calling," Kian groaned.

"Ignore it. Don't worry about that right now. Trust me, this Veil is much bigger trouble than whatever your dad will do to you."

That proved to be true, as when we walked back over to

the Veil, I noticed something. At a certain angle, the Veil had a red tint to it. It was barely noticeable, but I saw it. Red like the cloth. It was like when you looked at the side of a mirror and found out the glass was green. But, you know, much scarier.

I stopped walking and pulled the cloth I'd kept on me out of my pocket. Kian looked at me, then the cloth, and realization crossed his face.

"You have it with you?" he asked incredulously.

I nodded. "Yeah. Don't yell at me. I have it for a reason."

"What reason? What could possibly be a reason for carrying around stolen evidence?"

Laine and Jo stopped walking, too, and stared at me.

"Ness, no way. Please don't tell me that's something from a crime scene?" Laine gaped.

I shrugged a little, and she groaned.

"I have reasons, I swear," I murmured.

Jo looked pretty green, and I unfolded the cloth. "Everyone, stay quiet until I finish speaking. I don't want to hear any judgment, nor criticism, nor skepticism. Just be quiet and believe me for a second."

They exchanged looks, knowing looks I didn't really like, then nodded for me to continue.

"I sometimes—now don't make a fuss over this — I sometimes sleep with this covering my face." I held up my hands in a halting motion as soon as I saw their mouths open. "Relax. I did it 'cause... Well, I don't know why I started, but I did. And every time I do, I have really weird, vivid dreams. Dreams that the town is like, frozen in time. Or the people are, more specifically. And the sky was.. was red. And my aunt was there— Anyways, it was weird. And I know it sounds like just a regular nightmare, but I don't *get* nightmares. And they only happen when I use the cloth. And when I wake up, any place I've moved in the dream, I've moved in real life."

I finally stop talking, and I observe their expressions for a minute. Disbelief, mixed with a little disgust.

Kian speaks first, stepping toward me a bit. As soon as I hear his voice, I know he doesn't believe me. "Ness-"

"No," I cut him off, my voice getting louder with every word. "Don't do that. Don't make me out to be crazy. Have I been delusional about any of this thus far? Has any observation I've made turned out to be too out there?"

They stare at me and slowly shake their heads.

"Look, just.." I rubbed my forehead in frustration. "Just see for yourself. Prove me wrong." I thrust the cloth in Kian's direction, looking away.

After a beat of silence, Kian took the cloth from me, holding it between his thumb and forefinger as if it were still dripping with Rosette's blood. He glanced back at Laine and Jo before looking at me.

"I'll test it, okay?"

Kian may not be the brightest, and he may get on my nerves most of the time, but he's... nice.

KIAN'S NOTE #7: RE: FORGET THE DAMN CAR

So, Ness looked kind of crazy.

By kind of, I mean really, really insane. And the prospect of putting the murder-cloth over my face made me want to gag. But she was right. She hadn't made any guesses that were too far out there since all this began. And she'd been right quite a few times. So I took the cloth from her and stepped toward my car. My poor, poor, lovely car, too young to be so injured.

"Kian," Ness called from behind me, snapping me out of my mourning.

She jogged over and opened the car door for me. I slid in and, with hesitation, laid back against the seat. She leaned in and folded the cloth into a makeshift blindfold.

I couldn't help but stare at her for a little while. The light caught her hair in a way that reminded me of the little halo she had had back at the school, and when I got stabbed. Her face was mostly stoic, but there was a hint of her stress in the way she moved. I couldn't tell you if it was adrenaline or maybe even fear, but her hands shook ever so slightly. Ness was so...

Anyway...

"Ki, if this works, you might beget scared," she whispered. Her voice was softer than I'd ever heard her speak. "Don't freak out, okay? And don't go walking anywhere. Just stay in the car." Her eyes searched mine for a second, and I nodded. "And Ki? I'll be right over here, okay? So don't be scared."

There was something in her voice that made it sound like she was more scared than I was. I was suddenly very worried about the possibility that she was right, and that whatever state I was about to put myself in would be akin to my nightmares. Even so, I nodded and gave her a smile.

"Got it," I said simply.

She nodded and placed the folded cloth over my eyes. I laid back, and tried not to think of how low key gross having this cloth on my face was, and also it was kinda wrong, and why does it feel like this—and I let the exhaustion I'd been battling since my stabbing wash over me. It seemed like it took a very short amount of time for me to fall asleep, though I'd find no rest in this sleep.

My eyes opened on their own, and I was in the car. I thought maybe I'd had a dreamless sleep, the kind of sleep I'd wished for since my stabbing, until I noticed everything had a red glow. I could still feel the cloth over my eyes, but it was as if it was completely transparent. Looking out the windshield, I saw that the sky was red, red as the cloth. Had to be a trick of the light, right? I was peering through the cloth after all? But the sky was so vibrantly red, I knew I was lying to myself.

I moved my arms, then legs, then turned my head a few times, just to make sure I could move. I felt sort of weird, and stiff, but I could move. Yet, I froze when I looked out the window. Jo, Laine, and Ness stood exactly as they had before I'd fallen asleep, moving, talking, and looking at me. But they weren't alone.

Standing right behind Ness, just over her left shoulder, was a boy. He was tall, looked around our age, with deep, dark skin and his gaze fixed on Ness. He looked so sinister, just standing there, with a hint of amusement on his face. I'd never seen him before, and I didn't like the way he was looking at her. I waved my arms at Ness, trying to catch her attention, and she peered at me curiously. I pointed frantically behind her and jabbed the window with my finger. The boy heard me and looked up from Ness, meeting my eyes. He looked... surprised. Bewildered even, and he walked toward the car. He bent down, peering at me through the window, before yanking the door open.

"Can you see me, Kian?" he asked.

His voice was smooth and low, laced with something that I couldn't quite place. His gaze on me was sharp, deep, and intense. It made the hairs on the back of my neck stand up, and my heart raced like it did when Killer stood over me at my house. I couldn't speak, nor move. The fear that coursed through my body from him just looking at me rendered me paralyzed. He stared at me for a moment, before a wide grin stretched across his features.

"You can, can't you?" He hummed. Then he leaned down and brought his face directly in front of mine. "Answer me."

I couldn't. I couldn't *possibly*. Somehow, I garnered enough strength to nod. The boy nodded along with me, that same smirk on his face mocking me.

"Weird!" He chuckled a bit, then leaned closer to me.

I wanted to push him back, to slug that stupid grin off his face, but I couldn't move.

"Kian," he said in a singsong voice. "Wanna tell me how you got out? Or, got here, I mean."

I stared at him, unable to speak, and he finally rolled his eyes.

"You have the cloth, don't you?" he asked, sounding annoyed. "Did Vanessa give it to you? She's so sneaky, I didn't even realize what she was doing. I was surprised she figured it out. Well, surprised and annoyed."

He stepped back, stretching with a yawn. "I shouldn't have even used those stupid cloths. Oh, well. Too late now, I suppose." He glanced at me. "Are you done here, Kian? What did she send you in for?"

"Who..." I managed to get my voice to work again. It was hoarse and weak, but audible. "Who are you?"

His smirk returned. It stretched across his face, sinister and almost distorted. I don't know if it was the red tint everything had, or my mind playing tricks on me, but I could have sworn his eyes flashed red.

"I'm not gonna tell you that," he hummed. "But some people call me — What was it she said? — Right, Person. Ask your little Ness about me."

He winked, and a chill went up my spine.

"It's time for you to go on back, Ki."

"What are you? Are you Plot? Do you have us all trapped here?" I finally found my voice and my ability to think. "Tell me! What is this? Are you the reason we're stuck in a... in a?"

"A horror movie?" This 'Person,' grinned. "Wouldn't you like to know? Bye-bye, now."

He reached his hand out toward my face, in a way that I thought he was going to kill me. Instead, his hand simply covered my eyes, and when I opened them again, the sky was blue; the air wasn't as thick, and Person was gone. Replacing him was Ness, her hands on my shoulders.

"Kian? Kian, are you alright?"

I realized how hard my heart was beating and the tremble coursing through my body. I wanted to tell Ness that no; I was not alright, I was freaking scared, but I didn't want her to worry. So I nodded, even though she could clearly tell I was lying.

"I'm okay. I'm okay," I repeated, probably more for me than for her.

Jo and Laine stood back, looking over Ness's shoulder in concern. Ness held the cloth in her hand and shoved it into her pocket.

"What happened? What did you see?"

"Not what," I muttered. "Not what. Who. He said... He said you'd know him as Person."

As soon as I said that, Ness froze. If she could have gone pale, she would've.

"Person?"

I nodded. "Yeah. Person. He... He was tall. Our age, or somewhere around it. Dark-skinned, thin. And his eyes..."

I shook my head, willing the image of Person to go away. I didn't want to think about him. I didn't want to see him so clearly in my mind.

"The sky was red, like you said. I could see you guys moving, though." I gulped, and took some time to catch my breath, and try to stop my hands from shaking so much.

I hated being scared more than anything. Not just because of the feeling, but the way I look when I'm scared. I used to get really scared really easily, when I was a little kid. People always called me a crybaby back then until the seventh or eighth grade. I'd changed around then, I realize. I used to think it was just Laine whose personality had shifted, and that the only thing that changed about me was the way other people saw me. But I think I got stronger.

No, not stronger. Better at faking it, I think. Braver, maybe. Being brave doesn't mean you aren't scared. All it means is that you push through, regardless. My dad told me that.

Ness hadn't said anything, and me, Jo, and Laine were all just sort of looking at her, waiting for her to say something. When she finally did, it was so strange the hairs on the back of my neck stood again.

"You really came face to face with him, then?"

I blinked a bit, then nodded slowly. "Yeah. Yeah, I did. Ness, do you know who—"

"How come I still can't see him in front of me? What did he say to you?"

"Uh, he asked me how I had gotten there. He asked if I had the cloth and said you were sneaky for giving it to me. But, Ness—"

"Was he surprised to see you? Did you catch him off guard?"

"Yeah, I think. He asked if I could see him and looked surprised when I could. He stood right over your left shoulder, just staring at you, and didn't even notice me until I tried to get your attention."

Ness nodded and rushed to speak before I could get my question out. "So he's been focused on me. If he was so focused on me, how could he not see when I gave you the cloth? Never mind, don't even try to answer that. It doesn't matter. What matters is that we can sneak up on him."

Laine piped up. "So we're just going to believe Kian? No offense, Kian, but how do we know it wasn't just a dream—"

"I believe him," Ness said finally. "Move really quick."

I think she had me in a trance for a second. Who knew being believed could make someone feel so—

"Kian, move."

"Right, sorry." I got up and out of the car, stumbling a bit before finding my balance, and stood by Laine. Ness climbed into the driver's seat, shut the door, and we watched as she covered her eyes with the cloth. We watched her for a good thirty seconds before she ripped the cloth off her face and climbed back out of the car.

"He's not showing himself to me. I can see him in my peripheral, but he just won't... Ugh!"

She threw the cloth onto the ground with an anger and frustration I've never seen on her before.

"Ness.." Jo stepped forward a bit, but Ness held her hand out to stop her. She stood there with her eyes closed, taking a deep breath before dropping her arm.

"Okay," she started, much calmer. "Alright. Here's the plan. I'm gonna use one of you as bait."

"Bait?" Jo, Laine and I asked in unison.

Ness nodded.

"If it's true that Ty—that Person is so focused on me that

one of y'all can sneak up on him, then that's what we'll do. One of you will go in and help me get him to a place where he can't avoid me."

"But if he's focused on you," Laine said, suddenly whispering. "Can't he hear us right now?"

We go silent, then I pipe up again. "I'm not sure. I couldn't hear you guys speaking while I was in there."

"Then how did he know what I call him?" Ness wondered aloud.

I looked at her. "Ness. How do you know that guy? How does he know you?"

She looked up at me. "I've been seeing him in my peripheral for a little while now. Since I picked up the cloth, I think. I don't see him all the time, usually when the film is rolling or when I've got the cloth in hand." The cloth was still on the ground.

I was suddenly really, really annoyed.

"Ness, how could you not tell me about all this stuff? About seeing people? Your dreams? Anything?" My tone was harsher than I'd intended, but I was upset.

She blinked at me for a second. "I didn't think it meant anything."

"You didn't? *Really*. I find that hard to believe. You should have said something instead of springing all this on us now."

Her eyes dropped and she something I don't think I've ever heard her say.

"I'm sorry."

I felt like the world's biggest jerk. I mean, I wouldn't have said anything if I thought the nightmares were just that. Who was I to reprimand her for thinking like a normal person for once? Why did I expect so much else from her?

"It's fine, that wasn't fair of me," I said softer. "Do you see him now?"

She shook her head.

"That's something," Jo said suddenly. "Maybe he's only around when you've got the cloth?"

"That would explain why he's in my peripheral anytime I use the cloth," Ness said softly. "That would also explain why he didn't expect Kian to show up. Maybe he can't hear us, didn't hear our plan, and didn't see me give the cloth to you."

"Maybe he can't see the cloth," Laine said quietly.

I thought for a second, then nodded.

"Yeah. I could still feel the cloth on my face, but he spoke as if he couldn't see it. He also spoke like there were more than one. He was annoyed with himself for using them."

Ness looks up. "More than one? So that probably means that the one on Mack does the same thing."

"He asked me how I got out." I remembered. "He asked how I got out, then changed his mind and asked how I got there. But he said out first."

"Out," Ness repeated.

"What if the cloth is like a door?" Laine suggested. "Like, you said the world looks exactly the same, except the sky is red, and no one moves except us. If the Person guy, or Plot, or whatever, has the town hypnotized or something, then maybe it keeps people from moving."

"Unless we're around," Ness mutters. "Everyone moves just fine when we're around. But when I was in that red sky place, everyone stood in the last place we'd seen them."

Laine and Jo nodded.

"So, it's a door to what? The real world unencumbered by Person's hypnosis?" I asked.

Ness sighed. "It makes sense, but it's all just speculation. We'll have to just ask him. Which brings me back to my plan. We'll need another cloth. I would say we could cut the one we have in two, but I don't want to risk ruining it."

"There was one on Mack," I offered. "But it's in evidence."

"So let's break in and get it!" Laine said, a little too cheerfully.

Jo and I stared at her, but Ness seemed to love the idea.

"Yeah, let's do that," she agreed.

"Yeah, let's not," I retorted. "Break into the evidence room? Are y'all crazy? Do you know how illegal and difficult that is?"

"Can't be that hard." Ness shrugged.

"Yeah, you can probably break in easily." Laine nudged me. "Just ask your dad to let you in."

"That's literally not how anything works."

"Then we'll break in by force," Ness piped up. "We'll swipe somebody's keys and let ourselves in."

"We could do that," Jo said. "Create a distraction in the station and stuff."

"It won't work," I urged, annoyed that Jo was no longer on my side. Though, I shouldn't expect loyalty from her.

Ness frowned. "We'll make it work. Just trust me, Ki."

Well, when she puts it like that, it's hard not to.

"Yeah, okay. Fine. But I swear to God, if we get caught.."

Ness grinned and nudged my arm. "We won't get caught, because you're going to be the perfect distraction."

I raised an eyebrow, but didn't fully grasp what she was insinuating until we were back in town.

TIP FOR AN IDIOT #8: JUST DON'T GET CAUGHT

"No way," Kian said immediately. "Un uh. Not doing it. Do you know how quickly my father will kill me?"

I rolled my eyes. "It's not that serious, Kian. Just start an argument and cause a scene in the station. Tell him about your car or something. Or say you're dropping out to become a SoundCloud rapper, I dunno."

"Are you kidding? No, my dad is already pissed at me enough. Causing a scene at the station would be the final nail in the coffin. He'd ship me off to military school in a second."

"Just do it, Kian," Laine groaned. "You're the only one of us who can. If either of us caused a scene, they'd just arrest us. Your dad will not arrest you, and it's the only way we can get that stupid freaking cloth."

"What happened to being on my side, Laine? We used to date, remember?" Kian whined.

Jo piped up. "We need more than just Kian, I think. Something bigger."

I thought for a second. "Alright, one of us needs to go commit a crime."

Dead silence.

"C'mon, guys. We need that cloth. Someone go commit a

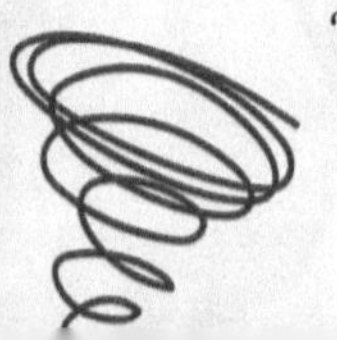

crime. Kian will distract anyone still at the station with a tantrum, and I'll get the cloth."

"Wait, why are you getting it?" Jo frowned. "Why don't you go commit a crime?"

"I'm Black."

That killed that suggestion.

Laine sighed. "Alright, I'll do it. I had a kleptomania phase, so I'm well-versed."

I decided not to pry further into that.

"Okay, Laine will go do... whatever, Kian will throw a tantrum in the station, and I will get the cloth. Jo, you be look-out." I retrieved my phone from my pocket, took Jo's and punched in her contact information, then did the same with Laine's before making a group chat of the four of us.

Actually, Kian had to take the phone from me and make the group chat for me, since I'd never done it before. I was weirdly excited, having a group with me to even make a group chat. It was exciting and odd. I didn't really know how to feel.

"Text us if anyone heads toward the evidence room. If Kian is right, that should be the door." I pointed toward a window, where a plain-looking door lay just past it.

Jo nodded and swapped seats with me. Laine hopped out first, then jogged a few shops down to one of the few big name chain grocery stores we had in town and walked in. She didn't tell us what she was going to do, but when we heard yelling and the sound of a lot of heavy things falling over, we kind of inferred. Only a few minutes later, five of the thirty officers at the station jogged out and over to the grocery.

"Not big enough," Jo murmured.

Only a second later, we heard a louder crash, as well as the unmistakable scream of Laine saying that she was being chased by Killer. *That* got some attention. A dozen more officers ran out of the station before spreading out around the store and searching for Killer.

"That's my girl," Kian murmured proudly.

"You're up," I reminded him.

He sighed, but got out of the car and trekked into the station. Jo and I exchanged looks before I got out.

"Be careful, Ness," Jo said suddenly. "Don't get caught."

I gave her a last nod before I approached the station slowly. As I got closer, I heard Kian shouting. I slipped in through the sliding doors and skulked along the wall. I didn't have to do much, as Kian was doing an amazing job. He yelled at his father, who stared in disbelief as Kian shoved stacks of papers off the sheriff's desk.

"Yeah, I screwed up the car. So what? We can afford it! We can afford everything, Dad, but you work anyway! Which brings me to my next point..."

I decided not to waste time listening, though I couldn't help but feel a little strange. Kian looked really into his performance, so much so I wasn't sure if he was really performing or not. I decided to ask him about it later and crept over to the sheriff's desk. Kian saw me and moved in the opposite direction, taking his father with him. I got to his dad's desk and searched frantically for his keys.

"And the fact of the matter is, Dad, you don't care! I mean, even if I took your keys, which are hanging off the bottom drawer to the left, and drove to Timbuktu, you wouldn't care!" Kian shouted, looking dead at me.

He was an idiot, but sometimes he came in clutch. I bent down, finally seeing the cluster of keys hanging off a blue carabiner. None of them were labeled, and I groaned. I held the keys up so Kian could see them.

"Which one?" I mouthed.

"And, Dad, even if I took your little gold key to the jail or the slightly bigger gold key with the little blue paper dot on it to the evidence room, you wouldn't notice!"

"Son, I'm not even sure what you're saying to me right now..."

I didn't wait to find out how Kian was going to explain

away that one, and bolted down the hall towards the evidence room. There was an officer in the hallway, standing at a vending machine. He turned to me, puzzled.

"What are you looking for, little lady?" he said, a bit of a southern accent piercing his tone.

Strange. Literally, where on the globe were we?

"Uh, bathroom," I muttered.

"You're going the wrong way, then." He turned, pointing down the hall in the opposite direction. "Lady's room is that way."

Crap. I didn't know what to do. He turned back to look at me, and I knew I had to come up with some way to get him to leave.

When I was younger, I used to act out scenes from my favorite horror movies when I was bored. Naturally, I learned how to scream really well, and cry on command. The second one came in handy more often than you'd expect. Something I had learned was that people, men especially, get really uncomfortable when girls cry. So that's what I did.

"Oh," was all the policeman could get out. "Uh... Are you alright?"

I shook my head, and fake-sobbed harder, while he stood there awkwardly. "Stop staring at me!" I wailed. He immediately turned around and spoke over his shoulder.

"I'll, uh, get you some tissue, little lady," he said quickly before practically jogging out of the hall. I stopped crying as soon as he was out of sight and trusted Kian to keep him bu until I finished. I hurried down to the end of the hall, where the appropriately labeled evidence room sat.

"Second, slightly bigger gold key with the blue paper dot," I murmured to myself, flipping through the keys until I found it. I jammed it in the lock, said a silent prayer, and turned the doorknob. It opened, and a wave of cool air hit me. I step inside quickly, shutting the door behind me.

Kian had given us a rundown on how things were categorized in the evidence room, but it was fairly simple. Alphabet-ized by the case name, which was just Mack's last name. Remembering poor Mack's last name was a different challenge, but I soon got to the right section.

I pulled two boxes with Mack's last name on them off the shelf and sat on the ground while I opened them up. Before I could even delve into the box, my phone buzzed.

It was a message from Jo:

somoeons cobning nesw

I frowned at the typos, trying to decipher them until the next message popped up.

someones comign ness*

commng*

cominf*

COMING*

"Yeah, I got it," I grumbled under my breath as I hurried up my inspection of the box. The first one had various pieces of clothing, but no cloth. I panicked a little, which wasn't helped when I heard keys in the door. I slid the box across the ground, ducking behind a shelf and instinctively covering my mouth with my hand.

I got caught up in the horror-movie thing. What can I say?

Someone entered the room, and I prayed silently that they weren't looking for something to do with someone with a last name starting with an V. Their footsteps went from the door around to the other side of the shelves.

Just then, I saw the red corner of a cloth poking out of the second box. I took a breath and poked my head out of the shelf to see if the door was clear. I took a breath, and stood, and in one deft movement, snatched the cloth from the box and sprinted out the door.

I didn't look back to see if the officer followed me, and raced out behind the sheriff and outside. Kian saw me, made some random excuse to leave, and raced out after me. We practically fell into the car, stood on the gas, and pulled to the grocery store where Laine was still screaming inside. We skidded to a stop in front of the store, and I leaned out the window.

"Laine! Let's go!"

She heard me, shoved past some officers, and hopped in through the window. It was dramatic and perfect and I loved her for it. Kian peeled off, going on a roundabout way to the woods. Once we arrived, we all collectively remembered to take a breath.

"Did you get it?" Laine asked breathlessly.

I nodded, holding up the plastic evidence bag that held the cloth. Laine went pale, and I looked at the cloth for the first time. I sort of wish I hadn't, as I realized it still had some of Mack's dried blood on it.

We all went quiet for a while.

Jo was the first to speak up. "We should get this over with."

I sighed and nodded. "Alright. I'll, uh, I'll use this one."

"I'll use the other," Kian said.

"Wait." Laine frowned. "Why does Kian get to go? No offense, Ki, but how reliable are you? You totally freaked out last time."

"Like you wouldn't freak out too?" Kian shot her a look, a deep frustration I'd not seen from him before. "I'm going. I already know what to expect. You'd freak out."

"No, I'm going," Jo protested. "That Person guy may already expect you now, Kian. Ness, can you see him right now?"

I shake my head. "Not right now. I guess I'm not really touching the cloth, so."

Jo nodded. "Good. Give me the other cloth."

Kian opened his mouth to protest, but Jo held up her hand to silence him, and he slumped back into his seat with a pout. It's weird how easy it is to boss Kian around, but hey, I'm not complaining.

I pulled Rosette's cloth from the glove compartment, and immediately feel Person over my shoulder.

"He's watching," I muttered.

Laine shivered, and Kian squirmed in his seat. I handed the cloth over to Jo. "Can you see him? Just out of the corner of your eye?" I asked.

Jo paused for a second, then shook her head. "No, I can't. I guess he only watches you."

"Yeah," Kian agreed. "When I went, he was just staring at you. Even when you weren't holding the cloth."

"So I can only see him when I'm holding it, but he can see me whenever?" I groaned. "Freaking creepy. How does he not know what we're planning, then?"

"He probably does," Jo muttered. "He's probably been sending curveballs this whole time. Nobody moves unless we're around. Which means he's *making* them move. He's making them act. Like puppets. So the station, any obstacle we ran into, *he* put there."

We sat for a second, letting that sink in.

"Alright," I said finally. "Let's pay him a visit."

Laine pulled two hair ties off her wrist, and we got out of the car. Laine helped us fasten the cloths to our faces like makeshift blindfolds, and a second later, we were on the ground.

I opened my eyes just enough to see the red sky. I didn't move, per our plan, and I heard Jo stand up next to me.

"Holy..." she muttered. "Y'all weren't lying."

She was quiet for a bit, but I resisted the urge to peek again and make sure something hadn't happened.

"Ness." She started again finally, her voice near a whisper. "This guy is freaking..."

She trailed off, and I heard footsteps get closer, before another voice emerged.

"Oh-ho. A new visitor, huh?" said a voice that made my blood run cold. "You snuck up on me."

"Who are you?" Jo said, and I was surprised and a little proud at the lack of shakiness in her voice.

The other voice didn't reply, but I heard more footsteps around me. I peeked just enough to see the feet of someone approaching. Shoes I recognized as Jo's and she was stepping back. I stood swiftly, withdrawing the knife I still carried in my pocket and held it toward the figure in front of me.

Even before he turned around, hell, even before we got here, I knew who he was.

Tyler.

He looked at me with a mixture of amusement and disappointment.

"Wasn't that a nice try at sneaking up on me?" He hummed and crossed his arms.

Jo stood frozen behind him, fear written plainly on her face.

"Take the cloth off, Jo. I got it from here," I muttered, eyes locked on Tyler.

Jo hesitated, but obliged.

Tyler glanced down at the knife in my hand with a frown. "Let's be real."

"Why are you here?"

"Oh!" Tyler smiled a strange, twisted smile. "You remember me, hmm? I'm glad. I was worried you wouldn't recognize me. Though we do look so similar, it isn't hard to refute."

Pause.

Let me explain something to you. At this point in time, my brother didn't exist. Neither did my parents, or anyone else I may have once considered my family. No one but my aunt existed to me anymore, and for good reason.

I had always wondered what was wrong with me. There had to have been something, right? Why else would my parents have left? Why would they have taken him with them, but left me?

I never understood how a parent could do that to their child. Pick one, and leave the other at their aunt's house, I mean.

In middle school, we briefly learned about a culture that would kill the weaker twin, or abandon it somewhere to die. I wondered if that was me, but my brother was only a few seconds older than me, and he wasn't much bigger or stronger than I was. I don't think I spoke a lot back then, but that's not entirely unheard of for a little kid, now is it? I wondered if it was because I was a girl, and our parents just assumed I'd be weaker because of it. I wondered why they hadn't just killed me.

As I got older, I stopped wondering.

I stopped caring; I guess. What's done is done, and why would I let those kinds of people take up any more space in my head? It was much easier to pretend they didn't exist. And in a way, they didn't. Even on the day I walked home from the rock-climbing birthday party in the third-grade, my parents had the decency to not answer their phones and pretend to care.

So why was Tyler standing in front of me now? Tall, and older, and real, and not that much bigger than me? And with that stupid grin on his face, like he was telling a joke I wasn't a part of? That I was the butt of? Why?

Ahem.

Play.

He folded his arms over his chest and leaned down. "Vanessa, ask me what you wanted to ask."

I stared for a second, suddenly at a loss for words. He frowned.

"Come on, don't tell me you have nothing to say! You did all this just to get a chance to speak with me, despite all the obstacles I sent your way—"

"So you are Plot then? This is all your design?" I finally found my voice.

Tyler just grinned.

"Don't come back until the movie is over, Final Girl. You'll confuse yourself and screw up my story. Just relax, I'll take care of everything. All you have to do is go along with it."

Go along with what? I didn't get the chance to ask him, because a second later, he was in my peripheral again.

"Tyler!" I shouted. "Come out and talk to me, you little— ugh!" I ripped the cloth off my face and sat up. My hands were balled at my sides, and Laine, Jo, and Kian all looked at me expectantly.

"Well?" Laine urged after several seconds of my silence. "What did he say?"

"He started all of this. I don't know why, or how, or..." I muttered. "It doesn't matter. He's not going to stop anytime soon."

I sighed and shoved the cloth into my bag, just so I would feel Tyler leaving my shoulder. I rubbed my temples in frustration, as the others just sort of stared, a little disappointed with such little information.

"I'm Final Girl," I murmured, and they perked up. "He confirmed it. Which doesn't help much of anything. All it means is he's going to keep trying to kill you guys."

They were quiet for a second, and then Kian spoke up. "Well, that's something. He's basically confirmed most of our theories, right? We're in a horror movie, Ness is Final Girl, and we're the victim pool. Killer is, well, Killer, and the movie won't end until we're all dead and Ness kills Killer."

"None of you are gonna die," I said firmly. "As long as I can keep saving you, it's not gonna happen. Don't look at me like that, Kian. You know my motive."

I stalked over to the car, yanked open the passenger side, and sat, before honking the horn for the others to join me.

"Where to?" Kian asked gently, and I responded with much less softness.

"To find Killer. We're gonna knock him sentient, no matter how hard I have to hit him."

KIAN'S NOTE #8: RE: JUST DON'T GET CAUGHT

Ness didn't explain her plan any further.

I really wished she would stop just saying things and telling me to drive.

"Drive, Kian."

"But-"

"Ki."

"Yes, ma'am."

We're not gonna talk about that.

Anyway, we drove back to Ness's house in complete silence. Ness was deeply, intensely in thought, and I think the rest of us were too intimidated to interrupt that.

I glanced in the rearview mirror to see Laine and Jo staring out of their respective windows, Jo looking paler than before. I meant to check on her after she got back from the red sky place, but Nesa rushed us off so fast I didn't get the chance to. I doubt she would have appreciated my check-in, anyway. We weren't friends, not anymore. And looking back, it really was sort of my fault.

I tried not to think about it, and my mind instead turned to Person, or whatever. How odd he looked. How familiar. I

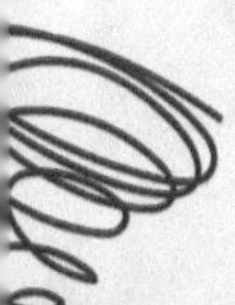

couldn't place it, and I thought there was something Ness must know about him. I wondered why she wasn't telling us.

Honestly, it was frustrating. It felt like I'd put so much trust in her, and there were things she still wouldn't share.

After all of this.

And then I wondered if I really cared about the information, or if I just wanted her to talk to me. To trust me. To—

Well, I was doing a lot of thinking, that's all.

I turned down Ness's street and pulled into her driveway.

"Something's wrong," Ness said immediately.

I glanced at her, and she seemed to have broken free from her trance.

"What is it?"

"The porch light," Ness murmured. "It's on."

"Probably 'cause your aunt is waiting for you to come home?" Laine offered, draping her arms onto Ness's seat. But Ness shook her head.

"She never waits for me."

Laine and I watched as Ness climbed out, made a motion indicating we should stay where we were, and went up to her front door. She did this little jumpy-thing trying to look in the small window on the door, and then her demeanor shifted entirely. She turned away and booked it back into the car. Before she could even shout at me to drive, the rolling started.

Jo sat up immediately as I pulled out of the driveway swiftly. "What's happening?"

"Kian's reliable father and the whole damn squad are in there. They saw me." Ness rolled down her window and stuck her head out to look behind us.

I groaned.

"He must have figured out that we stole the cloth."

Laine groaned, too. "Ness, I thought you were being careful!"

"I can only steal things so carefully from a literal police station, Laine. Do I look like the Pink Panther to you?"

"The what?"

"Uh, guys?" Jo piped up, worry filtering through her voice. "Who's in that truck behind us?"

They all looked back, and I looked in the rearview. Behind us was a large, beat-up black truck. It looked ominous as hell on its own, but the person in it was much scarier. Sitting in the driver's seat was none other than Killer, clad in his mask and hoodie, and only getting faster.

"He's gonna try and kill us. Well, y'all," Ness observed.

"YOU THINK?" Laine shrieked. "What do we do? Kian, drive faster!"

I obliged, but we were rapidly approaching a roadblock I'm nearly a hundred percent sure wasn't there before. *Curse Person's diligence.*

Ness thought for a second, before reaching over me and grabbing the steering wheel.

"You're gonna hate me for this, Ki," she warned, flashing a small, almost apologetic look.

"Then don't do it?"

But it was too late. She turned the steering wheel roughly, turning the car around until it faced Killer's truck. Everyone in the car screamed, save for Ness, of course, as she pushed down my leg and sent the car flying toward the truck. I said a silent prayer for my car to survive this, but also started a eulogy in my head.

"Sorry in advance!" Ness shouted just before we slammed into Killer's truck.

Now, I don't know if you've ever been in a head-on collision with a pickup truck in a Volvo, but let me tell you. Not fun.

And my car was already injured before, so you can imagine how it looked when we climbed out of the car. The collision was enough to knock Killer into his steering wheel and definitely stop him from driving any further.

We staggered out of my car on pure adrenaline, despite the

injuries I could see across all our bodies. Jo clutched her neck, Laine was bleeding from her head, and Ness and my legs were severely scraped up from the twisted metal poking into the front seats. But despite this, Ness still ripped the truck door open and dragged Killer out by the hoodie.

I know you may not believe me when I say this, but you've believed most of the strange things we've told you that happened throughout all of this. I swear I saw Ness's halo again. I was almost certain at this point that it had something to do with Person. Or, rather, whatever Ness wasn't telling me about her and Person, but more on that later.

This next part exhibits some behavior of mine that I'm really not proud of, so I'll let Ness tell you.

TIP FOR AN IDIOT #9: YOU HAVE ONE JOB.

FIRST THINGS FIRST, Kian doesn't *let* me do *anything*.

If anything, *I'm* allowing *him* to not tell you this part. But anyways.

I had Killer pinned down, thrashing underneath me, but I wasn't about to let up. Laine and Jo each held one of Killer's arms down, and Kian had his legs. I held my knife tight in one hand and used the other to peel up Killer's mask. Everyone held their breath as I tugged off the white mask, the elastic band of it snapping as I removed it. When I finally tossed the mask aside, I nearly cheered.

I loved being right.

Right under me, squirming and looking thoroughly concerned, was none other than Marco Vienna.

"Wha-what the hell?" he squeaked out.

"Marco?" Laine and Jo said simultaneously.

Ki, who was behind me and couldn't quite see, let go of Marco's legs immediately and stood. I'd forgotten for a moment just how close Marco and Kian were, and seeing the shock and utter betrayal on Kian's face, I really regretted not sharing my theory with him sooner. Even if I had, I doubted that it would have changed what Kian did next.

He swiftly pushed me off of Marco, sending me crashing painfully onto the concrete as he replaced my spot. He wound his arm back and delivering a punch so fast and sickening that neither Jo, Laine, nor I could have stopped him. Marco cried out, and Laine and Jo rushed to get Kian off of Marco.

Honestly, my feelings were hurt just a bit. Nobody had ever manhandled me like that before. Especially not Kian, a whole entire crybaby-softie who's just happened to be built like a wrestler.

I know it's really not the point, but damn.

As Laine and Jo struggled to restrain Ki, I stood, dusted my hands off, and grabbed onto the back of Kian's jacket.

"Ki, chill!" I yelled over the general chaotic noise of the situation.

"He's been trying to kill us, Ness!" Kian shouted back, winding up again before delivering another brutal blow.

"Kian, does he really look like someone who knew what he was doing? Plot control, remember?"

I tugged on his jacket again, yanking him back as he finally ceded some. We all sat panting for a moment, save for Marco, who writhed in pain under Kian's weight. Kian finally moved, and we thought he was going to punch Marco again. Instead, he reached down and gripped Marco's chin tight, turning him so he had no choice but to meet Kian's icy gaze.

"What do you remember?" he asked.

Marco made small, pained, whimpering noises, and it took Kian's threat of winding up again for Marco to speak.

"Nothing, nothing! I don't remember anything! I was at school one moment, and the next I'm lying here and you're freaking jumping me!" Marco's tone was panicked, and unless he was a theater kid in disguise, pretty damn genuine. Kian didn't look convinced, though.

"Do you remember the woods?"

Marco hesitated. "The woods? Like, where you were..."

"Yeah."

"Um.." Marco shifted in discomfort before nodding a bit. "A little. I don't know. It feels like a dream, but... I don't know. I remember seeing you and Laine, and then some other chick in the trees or something, and.."

Kian reached down again, grabbing and pulling Marco's hair out of his face, revealing a big, angry bruise. Kian's brows furrowed.

"This wasn't there when I spoke to you after my stabbing, was it?"

Marco shook his head as much as Kian's grip allowed him to.

"Let him go, Ki." I tugged on his shirt again, and Kian finally let go of Marco. He stood before reaching down and grabbing Marco again, this time by the shirt. He lifted him to his feet.

"Ki, I'm sorry, man," Marco whispered. "I'm sorry for stabbing you. I remember it now. I'm sorry, I don't know why I..."

Kian didn't look at Marco as he spoke. "It's not your fault."

"We'll explain later," Laine piped up.

"Guys?" Jo said suddenly.

We turned to look in the direction she was pointing, to see Kian's father rolling down the street in a squad car.

"Shit," Kian muttered.

Marco was bloody and wearing his Killer-attire. Mask and everything.

(I'm not entirely sure how he got the mask back on, but whatever).

"We gotta go." Kian bent down, tossed Marco over his shoulders, and started running back to the traumatized Volvo.

I got there first, slid into the near-mangled driver's seat, and Laine got in on the passenger side. Jo, Kian, and the still confused Marco were tangled in the back, but we had no time to get comfortable. Kian's dad approached rapidly, so I called back to the mini-driving lessons Kian gave me and pulled off with a screech.

It's lucky Marco's truck was so old and beat up - unusual considering his wealth - otherwise, the Volvo might not have worked anymore. The windshield was shattered, and the crumple zone, well, crumpled, but somehow, by the grace of my glorious Plot Armor, it still ran.

"Easy on her, Geez!" Kian shouted at me.

Laine leaned back and hit Kian over the seat, while I frantically steered us down a narrow alley. Apparently, the driving lessons weren't super helpful, and Kian yelled at me as I hit countless trash cans, and maybe one street lamp, but that's not important. The sheriff was still on our trail and his sirens were on.

"My dad is going to arrest me," Kian groaned, leaning back in his seat, and closing his eyes. "I'm dead. So dead."

"We're going to die if Ness doesn't steer!" Jo shouted over the chaos.

"I'm trying, Geez!"

In truth, I was having quite a bit of fun. I remembered this racing movie I'd watched a while ago that I hated and found myself changing my opinion. Being a little racer myself in that moment really gave me an appreciation for it. I would never admit something like that to Kian, though, because I think he'd kill me just for thinking that it was fun.

He wouldn't kill me. I shouldn't have said that. Anyways.

I made a sharp swerve down another alley, then pulled into a dark cove behind the gas station. Kian's father drove right past us, and I pulled from the cove and dashed down a steepish hill, driving along the bottom until we hid right by the river behind our school. I shut the car off, making sure there were no lights to give us away, and turned back to the others.

"Down, now, and nobody make a sound," I hissed. We all sunk into our seats, and were dead silent. We could hear the sirens somewhere above us, going up and down the streets. We sat like that for at least twenty minutes before the sirens seemed to stop.

"They're going to find us," Laine whispered beside me, and I could hear the unmistakable quiver of fear in her voice. "They're probably searching. They know Marco is Killer. I'm sure there's hella evidence in his car. They're gonna get the dogs out, and sniff for us, and find us, and take us to jail, and make me wear orange for the rest of my life. I hate orange. It's the worst color. Ness, I hate orange!"

"Okay, relax," I compelled her. "They aren't going to find us. Well, maybe they will." I thought for a second and then nodded. "No, yeah, they definitely are."

She made a whimpering sound and Jo popped up. "Let's go to my house."

I turned back in my seat to look at her.

"My parents aren't home. They're never home. I doubt the police know where I live."

"Are you sure?" Kian whispered. I could just barely make out Jo nodding in the dark.

"It's not the house I grew up in. It's the house from when... You know, Kian."

I watched as a look of realization crossed Kian's face. "Yeah, yeah, okay. Ness, let's switch."

I knew better than to pry into this strange understanding that Kian and Jo shared, and got out of the car as quietly as possible. Once we were all settled into our new positions, Kian slow rolled with the lights all off as quietly as possible to Jo's house.

It took a while, and a good amount of time hiding in alleys, but we made it to the edge of town, to a small, almost unnotice-able house standing by itself. We parked the car behind the house and got out. Jo and I supported Marco and brought him into the house, while Laine and Kian carried some of the stuff we had in the car.

Kian stayed outside for a while as the others got settled, sitting by his car and resting his head on its ruined crumple zone. I glanced at Laine, who was talking in hushed tones to Jo in the corner. Marco laid on the couch.

I slipped out of the house and sat next to Kian.

"Let's hear it, then." I nudged. "What's up? Besides finding out that your best friend stabbed you and has been trying to kill you for, like, a month?"

Kian let out a short, dry laugh. "Besides that? Nothing." His knee rested against mine. "I'm kinda cold, though."

I nodded in understanding. "It's warm inside."

He looked at me, one of those oddly deep, searching looks he always gave, before nodding and allowing me to give him a hand up.

We walked into the house together, and I called everyone to Jo's living room.

"Okay," I started. "So. Marco, I'm going to tell you something, and you're going to believe me. We're--"

"Stuck in a horror-movie," Marco mumbled. I blinked, and he nodded toward Jo.

"Jo, I could kiss you." I let out a sigh of relief at not having to explain the thing again.

Jo turned really, really red, and I wondered if she wasn't used to getting praise like this. Kian would laugh at me when I brought it up later, but that's a different story.

"Alright, well, Marco, I'm sure you have some Killer-motive in your head, right? Can you tell us?"

Marco hesitated, but nodded slowly. "Yeah. Yeah, I can. Uh, so, I killed Mack-" His voice caught in his throat, and he gulped before continuing. "Cause, you know, I was dating Rosette a while back. And she, um, she cheated on me. With Mack. Then her. And I was going to kill Kian, 'cause.." He turned red. "Well, he was moving in on Laine, even though he knows I've always had a crush on her. I guess a lot of people know. Maybe that's why Rosette cheated."

Now, I'm not well-versed on the gossip of their popular

little friend group, so I looked to Kian and Laine for confirmation. They looked puzzled, and Marco spoke up again.

"She cheated on the day my mom died," he murmurs. "The day of the Harvest Festival—"

"There it is!" I clapped my hands, and didn't bother to conceal the grin that permeated my face. "The grand motive, loss of one's mother. And on the day of the Harvest Festival! So it must be your mother's one-year anniversary. Isn't that freaking perfect?"

Judging by the mortified looks on everyone else's faces, I gathered I was the only one who knew what that meant.

"Ness. Insensitive," Kian whispered.

"Oh. Sorry. I just mean, it's the perfect motive. Well, perfect movie-motive. In real life, it would be kinda weak—"

Kian cleared his throat aggressively.

"Sorry."

Kian turned back to Marco. "Marc, none of that stuff is true. You know that, right?"

Marco frowned. "What do you mean? Of course it's true. I remember."

"Do you really? Think, Marco. Can you really remember ever dating Rosette? Ever liking Laine? Mack ever getting with Rosette? Or can you only remember the information that it all happened?"

Marco thought long. His brows furrowed as he grew distressed. "No... No, I swear I remembered it... I coulda sworn... My mother...?"

Kian softened his voice, putting a hand on Marco's shoulder. "Marc, your mom died six years ago. In the spring. Not during the Harvest Festival, and certainly not last year."

Marco's eyes filled with tears, and he stood abruptly. "No, this isn't right. It can't be. That would mean... That would mean I've been doing all of this for nothing...! I killed Mack, I killed Rosette, I stabbed you-!" Marco ran out of the room, into the bathroom, and shut the door.

Kian wiped his hand over his face and sighed. "He doesn't get that it wasn't his fault."

I nod, thinking for a second. I turned to Jo, who reclined on the couch with her knees drawn up. "Jo, do you think you could talk to him? I think you'd be able to sympathize with him better than the rest of us."

Jo looked up at me, then toward the bathroom, and got up. "Yeah, I'll talk to him. I'm not super good at comforting people, but I can probably understand what he's feeling."

"Thanks," I said, and she gave me a small smile before going to talk to Marco.

"That was really sweet of you," Laine said from behind me. I turned to look at her, a question on my face.

"What do you mean? I was being logical. Jo used to be Killer, so she could empathize with him the best."

Laine laughed a bit. "Yeah, Ness. You did that because you want to cheer Marco up. That's called *being nice*."

I frowned a bit. "I'm not nice."

"Most people would take that as a compliment."

I guessed she was right, so I conceded and sat down next to her. Kian came and joined us, and we sat waiting for a while. Jo and Marco came out after a long time, and Marco looked a little better, but still upset. He sat next to Jo on the couch, and couldn't even look at Kian.

I nudged Kian and whispered in his ear. "Go talk to him."

Kian frowned. "Didn't Jo just do that?"

"You're his best friend, and he stabbed you. How would you feel if you knew you'd stabbed me in some weird hypnosis?"

Honestly, I didn't know how he would feel. He'd called us best friends before, even though I never really believed him. But the analogy seemed to work, because he got up and went to sit next to Jo.

Kian elbowed Marco, who winced, but didn't look at Kian. Kian sighed a bit, then draped his arm over Marco's shoulders.

"Mad at me?"

Marco looked up with a frown.

"No? Why would I be mad at you? You should be mad at me!"

"But, I'm not," Kian said. "You're the one who isn't talking to me." He poked Marco's arm. "Oh, honey. Don't tell me you want a divorce!"

Marco stared at the goofy grin hanging on Kian's face.

"You're a dumbass," Marco murmured with a small smile. "I'm taking the kids."

Kian made a kis face, and Marco elbowed him. I really didn't understand male friendship. So odd.

We spoke to Marco about Tyler, well, what I let the others know about Tyler, the red cloth and such, and got him as caught up as we could. He looked confused through most of it, and distressed through all of it. It was understandable. That's pretty much how everyone had been feeling this whole time.

When we finished explaining, Jo pointed us toward the kitchen to fend for ourselves, and I found some instant coffee in her pantry. Kian leaned his chin on my shoulder.

"Nes."

"Oh, no. It's evolved."

"Isn't it cute? Nes. Not as good as Loch Ness, though."

"How about you just don't refer to me?"

He pouted and sat on the counter next to me. "Hey. Do you think this will work out? We knocked Marco sentient, but he's still under Person's control, right?"

I nodded. "Unless he's like me, and I doubt that. But it's fine." I looked back down at my coffee, stirring it confidently. "As long as we keep him in our sight, away from any weapons, and preferably restrained somehow, we should be fine." As I finished my sentence, the unmistakable sound of the rolling started.

"Uh, Ness?" His tone told me all I needed to know. I

slammed down my mug and spun around to where Marco used to be standing.

"Damn it, Kian! One job!"

KIAN'S NOTE #9: RE: YOU HAVE ONE JOB.

ABSOLUTELY NOT MY FAULT.

I turned around briefly and Marco had slipped off some-where. Not my fault, I still stand by that. Now, the fact that I had left the bag that held both Ness and my knife just sitting on the ground?

Yeah, that was my fault.

Whoopsies.

Now that we were in immediate danger, though, Ness directed her wrath from me to finding Marco. She armed herself and the rest of us with little rusty kitchen knives, and we all stood in a circle, facing out.

"The second one of us sees him, we rotate and put me in front," Ness ordered. "Chances are, he's not gonna run at us. He'll try and maintain that creepy slow walk thing, so we'll have time."

"Unless he adapts to the situation," Jo murmured. "Some Killers change their patterns depending on the situation."

"Marco's not that smart," Laine chimed in, her voice quiv-ering. "He's an idiot, actually. I don't think he can even spell adapt."

"I gotta agree," I muttered.

But Ness shook her head. "It's not Marco we're against. It's Killer. *Tyler's Killer.*"

Pause.

"Tyler?" I asked, and Ness would've gone pale if she could have.

"Person. Focus."

How could I focus after she let something slip like that?

How much was she not telling me?

Thoughts swirled through my head, so much so that I started thinking about psycho EMTs again, so I decided to chill out, focus, and put it on the back burner.

Play.

We stood like that for a few minutes, just waiting. The rolling was so loud I wanted to drop the knife and cover my ears, but I knew I couldn't. Then we heard him.

Creeping around the house, out of view, but certainly there.

Step.

Step.

Step.

And on and on. He really had his Killer thing down pat. Laine trembled against me, and Jo let out a little squeak.

Ness was steady, though.

Steady, prepared, and unafraid. At least, that's how she looked. That's how she *allowed* herself to show, but I knew she had to be a little scared. Or excited. She acts the same in both cases, so...

"He's close," Ness whispered. "Everyone, take a breath and get ready to rotate, but don't let your knife drop, or *I swear to God,* I'll kill y'all myself."

"Got it," I replied, trying to sound as unbothered as her, but my voice cracked, and I wanted to die.

The steps got closer, but I couldn't tell from which direction. Then we saw him. Shrouded in the corner's darkness, only the white of his mask visible, he looked absolutely horrifying. He just stood there, the glint of Ness's knife in his hand. I felt myself falter.

Was this my best friend?

Marco, sweet, dumb Marco?

The most loyal kid you'd ever meet, coming here to kill us? To kill me?

"Wake up, Kian! Rotate!" Ness's voice broke me from my trance, and we rotated swiftly so Ness faced Marco. She stepped forward, breaking the circle, brandishing her knife in front of her. Jo, Laine, and I fell back behind her, and Marco charged forward.

He swung Ness's knife high above his head, and brought it down swiftly, aiming directly for Ness's neck. She raised her own knife to try and block the blow, but missed and the knife connected with her arm.

Ness cried out, stumbling back as blood poured from her. Laine screamed beside me, and I instinctively moved forward to help Ness. She used her good arm to push me back, shaking her head.

"I'm fine! Stay back!"

Not even a second later, Marco attacked again. The brief moment Ness took to push me back gave Marco an advantage, and he sliced at her back. The sick sound of flesh connecting with metal filled the air. Ness fell into me, and I'd never felt like a greater piece of trash. She regained her footing on pure adrenaline, but I wasn't going to let her take this alone.

I charged forward with my little knife and stabbed at Marco's knife-wielding arm. Ness screamed for me to get back, but I'd caught the knife on Marco's sleeve and grabbed hold of his arm. He, in turn, with a strength I knew he'd literally never possessed before, used the arm I held to put me in a chokehold, and squeezed. My eyes felt like they were bulging out of my head, and every blood vessel in my face felt like it was on the verge of exploding.

If you've never been choked out before, let me tell you — not fun. Very embarrassing. And there is literally nothing you can do about it, unless you're trained or can somehow keep your mind clear and throw 'em over your shoulder when you're literally fighting to breathe. Luckily for me, Ness's mind was clear enough for the both of us, and she sliced Marco's wrist open in one swift movement.

Marco shouted, dropped his knife, and released his grip on me, and I fell to the ground, fighting to catch my breath. Ness charged forward as Marco clutched his wrist, and straight up *body slammed* him.

Where did she learn to do that? I mean, she got low, rushed him, and threw her entire shoulder into his stomach, sending him flying backward onto the hardwood floor. If I weren't still doubled over on the ground, I would have clapped.

Laine and Jo ran over to where Ness had Marco pinned under her weight, and took hold of his arms and legs.

"Jo, got any rope?" Ness shouted over the sound of Marco groaning over his wounds.

"Y-y-yeah," Jo stammered. "In the shed out back."

"Kian, are you gonna keep crying or can you get that for me?" Ness shot at me.

I wasn't crying, for the record. My eyes were watering, as is normal when you nearly get the life choked out of you.

"Yeah, yeah." I struggled to my feet, voice hoarse as hell, and still very embarrassed. I jogged out of the back door while the other three wrestled with Marco. The film was still rolling, frustratingly enough, but I couldn't hear it too loudly over the sound of my blood pumping in my ears. I jostled the old shed door open and stepped in. It was dark and dusty, which didn't help with my already labored breathing.

Then I heard Jo shout behind me.

"Kian! Duck!" she screamed.

I'd learned over the past few weeks of living in a horror movie that when someone shouts vague directions at you, just follow them. Good thing I did, 'cause if I hadn't, I'd probably have gotten more than a little trim from the giant knife Marco swung at my head.

I stumbled back, falling on my behind. Marco approached again, but Ness and Jo had managed to grab him by the back of his clothes and restrain him. I got up quickly, embarrassed again, and retrieved the rope from the back of the shed.

With Laine's help and Ness and Jo's kinda mean shouting, we got the still-struggling Marco tied up and on the ground. He writhed, trying to break free for several seconds until the rolling stopped. He went still suddenly, as if he'd fallen asleep, then he started trying to move again.

"Marco?" I called out of breath. "That you, or Killer?"

"Me." He coughed. "Geez, what happened? Did someone body slam me?"

"Nah," Ness lied. Jo and Laine helped get Marco seated on the ground.

"You attacked us," Ness said. "No, don't start looking all sad and guilty. It isn't your fault. We'll keep you restrained for the night, and I'll keep watch until the morning."

I frowned. "Let's just take shifts," I croaked.

"No," Ness said firmly. "If something goes wrong, none of you will be able to handle him. And if you can't get me up before Killer cuts you down..." Ness shook her head. "Not worth the risk."

I shared a knowing look with Laine. Ness liked to pretend she didn't care about us, but it was pretty clear she did.

"Okay." I nodded. "I'll just stay up with you, then."

"Me too," Jo and Laine said simultaneously.

Ness rolled her eyes.

"There's no point in every one of us being exhausted in the morning, then none of us will be able to handle it if the rolling starts. You guys go to sleep and stop arguing with me."

We all nodded, but even Ness knew how this would end up. We hauled Marco back inside, made makeshift beds on the floor in the living room - we decided that would be better than the slightly moldy sleeping bags Jo pulled from her basement - and huddled up for the night. Ness tried to convince us to sleep three more times before giving up.

We didn't really chat, Marco fell asleep, and Laine and Jo played with a little water-ring toss toy Jo found. I sat next to Ness, who sat with her knife resting over her drawn-up knees, staring at Marco. She shivered a little. Evidently Jo didn't have any heat. I grabbed a blanket from the ground.

"Cold?" I asked quietly.

Ness let out a dry laugh and nodded. "Very."

I draped the blanket over her shoulders, and then my arm. She started to shrug out of it, but gave up or changed her mind.

"Ness, can I ask you something?" I began after several moments of silence.

She sighed.

"Can I say no?"

"Nope."

"Then go ahead."

I hesitated before asking, glancing at her face so I didn't miss her expression. "Who's Tyler?"

She went rigid, her face became unreadable, and she didn't answer.

"C'mon, Ness." I sighed. "Just tell me, alright? Look, whatever it is, whatever you haven't been telling me this whole time, I'm not gonna judge, or be upset, or anything. You know that."

I squeezed her shoulder a bit, hoping she'd open up.

"Please?"

She was silent for several more moments before finally speaking. "Nobody. Go to sleep."

Convo over.

TIP FOR AN IDIOT #10: HE FINDS A WAY

I WANTED TO TELL HIM.

No, seriously, I did. I wanted to tell all of them, but especially him. But I just... couldn't.

No way.

I could barely even admit it to myself. This part of me, of my life and past, that I'd effectively cut out of my mind years ago, was now the thing that'd killed two people and continued to ruin the lives of everyone around me.

Now, you'd think I'd recognize that this wasn't my fault. You'd think I'd say, "Hey, so my brother is crazy, and has some weird superpowers that lets him control the minds of an entire town. What's that got to do with me?"

But I *couldn't* say that. I knew I couldn't. There was no way all of this connected to Tyler and had nothing to do with me. Especially with the role he'd placed me in? I mean, the very concept of living in a horror movie? It *had* to have something to do with me. I didn't know how, but somehow, this was my fault.

At some point, Jo and Laine fell asleep and Kian stayed awake for a few more hours. He too fell asleep after that, on my shoulder, actually. His head was heavy, but I didn't push him off.

Don't ask me why, I don't know. Maybe I just felt bad. He'd been through a lot that day. All of them had, and they wouldn't have if I had just been a little stronger, a little faster, a little better.

It started to really weigh on me how much went wrong because of me. If I'd kept my own eyes on Marco, he wouldn't have been able to get away. If I'd been a little faster than Kian, Kian wouldn't have had the chance to get between me and Marco and end up bursting a blood vessel in his eye. If I'd been stronger, Marco wouldn't have been able to break from my grip and get to Kian in the shed. If, if, if.

I hate that word.

I didn't sleep. How could I? If I fell asleep, a whole other series of incidents would stem from my neglect. I had to stay up, stay vigilant, protect the others, and Marco, too.

Protect them, protect them, protect them.

My motive had changed so much since I'd saved Kian the first time. Maybe it's because I had some guilt about all of this.

Either way, I wished I was better than I was. Stronger, I mean. Maybe then I would have been able to stop Marco.

I doubt it now, knowing what I know. Tyler always found a way to make things go the way he wants them to go.

So Marco escaped.

He was quiet when the rolling started, and I thought he was still asleep. I didn't know why the rolling started suddenly, so I woke Kian, Jo, and Laine. I only looked away for a minute.

One minute.

And that was all he needed. He did away with the rope

using one of the little kitchen knives, something that absolutely wouldn't have been possible if not by the grace of Tyler's movie logic. And then he was gone. He took the battered Volvo, too.

"*HE TOOK IT?*" Kian shouted.

Some part of me was glad he was mad at me. I deserved it. I should have been more attentive, and now Killer was loose again.

Laine ran a hand through her hair in frustration, and I couldn't help but notice her lack of bedhead despite spending the night on a hard, dusty floor. With no bonnet, either.

"I can't believe this. So he's just loose again?"

"I'm sorry-" I started, but Laine cut me off.

"We're sorry, Ness. We shouldn't have fallen asleep."

...What?

"Yeah," Jo chimed in, looking like a much more realistic version of "I woke up like this" than Laine. "We totally dropped the ball."

"What are you saying?" I asked, my voice a little rougher than I'd intended. "*I* was the one who dropped the ball. This was *my* responsibility."

Kian shook his head. "No, it was all our responsibility. We said we'd stay up with you, and then we left you to your own devices. We screwed up—"

"Stop that," I spat. "Stop pretending like we're a team. I'm Final Girl. I'm the only one who can end all of this, and it's my fault he's gone."

They all stared at me for a second before sharing knowing looks. Suddenly it felt like I was on the outside again, looking in on some joke I didn't understand, and I didn't like it. I turned away, going outside to see if I could see Marco down the road, but he was long gone.

The others joined me outside, Jo with keys in her hand. None of them spoke. Instead, they followed Jo to her garage, and she opened it revealing an old, dusty looking Honda. She climbed in, and the others followed suit. I stared after them for a moment, before Jo tossed me the keys through the window.

"C'mon, let's go find him," Kian said from the passenger's seat.

I didn't understand these kids, really. At all. But I got in anyway, and drove toward town.

All our phones had been off since we left my house the night before. Partially because we were worried if the police could track our phones. And for Lanie and Kian, to resist the temptation to call their parents.

At the end of the day, we were kids. And regular kids needed their parents when, you know, they were being hunted by Killers. Except for me, of course. Except for me...

It was another oversight I faulted myself for. Another misstep that almost ruined everything.

With our phones off, we had no way of learning that there was a warrant out for our arrest. We drove aimlessly around the town for almost an hour, leaning out of the windows, searching for Marco.

"He could be anywhere," Laine groaned. "We're never gonna find him."

"Town isn't that big," Jo offered, a rare ray of optimism. "We'll find him. We just gotta keep looking."

"We won't find him," I confirmed. "Not unless Ty- unless Person wants us to."

Kian shifted beside me, and I clenched the steering wheel harder.

We got about as far as the pharmacy when the sirens appeared behind us. I glanced in the rearview mirror, and groaned when I saw we were being followed by not one, not two, but *three* squad cars, with more approaching. At the forefront was none other than Kian's father.

"Pull over now. There is a warrant for your arrest." The sheriff's voice boomed over the little speakerphone in his car.

"Arrest?" Laine repeated hysterically. "For stealing evidence, right?"

"That must be it," Jo groaned.

Kian didn't say anything. I glanced at him, and he was pale, staring at his father behind us.

"I'm not pulling over." I clarified for the others. "We're going to have to lose them."

Once the rolling started and the sheriff got back on the megaphone thing, things got clearer.

"You're under arrest for the murder of Mack and Rosette. Pull over now."

Now, I don't know that much about police procedure, but I'm pretty sure they're not supposed to say that part until you're actually being arrested. Tyler clearly didn't know much about procedure either and didn't care.

That just goes to show how important research is before you write. Shameful.

Anyways, the whole car was in hysterics.

"Marco must have lied on us," Kian said.

"Ugh, that little idiot!" Laine shrieked. She and Jo were sobbing and shouting in the backseat, which wasn't helpful when police cars started coming at us from the front, too.

"We're dead. We're so dead," Kian kept muttering.

I rolled my eyes. "Have a little faith."

"Faith in what?" Laine cried. "We're so going to—"

Laine's thought was cut short when I slammed the car into the pharmacy.

Don't judge, alright? I had to make a quick decision, so I slammed the car into the pharmacy, blowing straight through the front window and parking in the center of the thing. I heard a screech and crash from outside, hopefully the sound of the police cars running into each other.

"Everyone alive?" I checked.

"WHAT THE HELL, NESS?" Laine screamed.

"ARE YOU CRAZY?" Jo yelled just as loudly.

"Kian? Reply immediately," I called when he was quiet for a second too long.

"I'm alive. My ankle's busted, but.." he whispered feebly.

I let out a sigh of relief and practically fell out of the car. I'd thrown the police off for just a second, and I had to act quickly before they regained their footing and came for us. I dragged Jo and Laine out, who then helped me get Kian out. Kian had probably a broken ankle and leaned heavily on Jo and Laine as they hurried to the back door.

"Ness, come on!" Jo called back.

I shook my head. "Gotta do something first. Get to the school, don't look back, and don't get caught!"

I ran around to the trunk of the Honda and retrieved the spare gas can in the back. It was full, thank goodness. I poured the gas all over the pharmacy, saying a quiet apology in my mind to the owner, Mr. Brown. I had to hurry, as I could hear the officers outside shouting.

I searched frantically for a lighter and found a whole jar of them on the front counter.

"Alright. Just light it and go." I quietly hyped myself up as I flicked the lighter open.

Wait. Not yet. I closed the lighter again and climbed back into the car. I couldn't leave the clothes. We needed them; I was certain of it. I felt around on the ground for the bag of our stuff and—

"Freeze!"

Crap.

"You're surrounded! Come out of the car with your hands up!"

It was Kian's dad. I knew it was. I slipped the bag onto my shoulder and reached for the glove compartment to grab our phones.

Mistake. I forgot I was Black.

Bang! A shot rang out, and a bullet flew through the back-seat window.

"I said get out of the car!"

"Okay, okay!" I called back, dusting the glass from my hair as I climbed back out of the car. Only my raised hands were visible from over the car, and I had the lighter between my fingers.

"Step around the car with your hands up! Don't make any sudden movements!"

I slowly stepped around the car, wondering if I was really thwarted this time. More importantly, I wondered if the others had gotten caught or not. There wasn't much time if they hadn't been as more squad cars pulled up. I had one second to do this and get it right.

Before I had the chance, my fears were confirmed.

"Dad, don't shoot!" Kian yelled.

I whipped my head toward the back door. Jo, Laine, and Kian were standing there, doing exactly the opposite of what I'd told them to do.

"I told you guys to go!"

"We weren't gonna leave you!" Jo called back.

"Son, I don't know what these girls have put into your mind," the sheriff said, his gun still pointed at me. "But Marco told me what they did. What she did."

He motioned to me with the gun.

"Marco told us she convinced all four of you kids to help her kill Rosette. Oh, and Mack."

I mean, they could at least make it a little more believable when pretending to care about Mack. Gosh.

"That's not true, Dad!"

"Marco said that Vanessa concocted this entire scheme so she could live out her dreams of some horror movie."

"That's not... entirely true?"

"You all need to turn yourselves in. Son, I know you were manipulated, and I promise you and I will figure this out together." He held his hand out to Kian, and I fight to not roll my eyes. "Come here, son. Slowly."

"No. I'm not going with you. Ever."

Something in the sheriff's eyes shifted, or shattered, maybe, and I knew I had one quick moment to act.

In one swift movement, I flipped the lighter open and lit it. The flame slid across my hand as I dropped it into the pool of gasoline in front of me. It only took five seconds for the sheriff to realize what happened, and by that time, the flame had already grown beyond what he could quickly blow out.

The sheriff panicked and looked around, presumably, for an extinguisher. His attention was no longer on me, and even if was, there was now a considerable wall of fire between us.

"Now run, Vanessa," Tyler whispered beside me. *"Here's your chance."*

Yeah, Tyler. That was the plan, thanks.

I got a better grip on my bag and headed for the back door. But the fire had spread, and flames had consumed a solid half of the store. I still had an easy path to escape, but the sheriff did not. Kian stood by the door, horrified, as Laine tugged on his sleeve, trying to get him to move. But he just stood there, staring at the wall of fire that separated him and his father.

I had a quick decision. If I stopped to help the sheriff, chances were he'd catch me, or just shoot me. But if I made a break for it, who knew what'd happen to him? I weighed my options, and one thought permeated my mind. This was Kian's *father.* He had the rare gift of having one, and who was I to take that away? After everything Kian has been through because of me?

So, with my Plot Armor and sheer gall, I climbed across the top of the car and leapt over the literal wall of fire between the sheriff and I. The smoke dominated us, and my eyes burned almost as bad as my lungs as I tried to locate him.

"Make a sound, Mr. Wilson!" I called.

He coughed.

I watched this super boring documentary once about the echolocation whales and bats have, and—

Got sidetracked, sorry.

I moved toward the sound until I could finally make out the sheriff, and I grabbed onto his arm.

"Get your hands off me!"

"Sir, I know I'm wanted for murder, but you're going to have to trust me for a second, or we'll both die. Well, you'll die. I'll be fine, to be honest."

The sheriff fought for a second more, before the instinct to survive took over and he allowed me to tug him toward the back of the store. We couldn't get to the door, but there was a small drive-thru window that I bet we could fit through. The sheriff leaned on me heavily, another trait Kian must have inherited. I glanced toward the back door again, but it wasn't visible through the fire.

"Sir, you're gonna have to go out the window. Are you listening?"

The sheriff bent at the hips and hacked violently. The smoke got to me, too, but we didn't have time for that. I slide open the drive-thru window and help the sheriff climb up onto the counter in front of it. With great effort, the sheriff tucked and rolled out of the window, hitting the ground with a thump.

"So boring." Tyler muttered beside me.

I really wish I could hit him. It was my turn to go out the window, but I saw the sheriff had stood again. He reached for his holster, and I silently curse him out. Seriously, I just saved your life, and you're gonna shoot me anyways?

Rude, rude, rude.

I'd survive, but I think being shot would be much more of a hassle than being burnt up, so I went for the second option. Trying to gauge the best and least painful way to get through the fire, I moved back toward the car.

I'd stuck it out thus far, but the smoke was really getting to me. More than I expected it to, actually. I was lightheaded, and coughing was futile to keep it out of my lungs. I tried to climb on top of the car, but the higher I got, the worse the smoke got.

For a second, I was ready to give up. I knew I'd live. I would sustain some injuries, but I'd live. And even if I didn't, who really cared? I mean, wasn't that what I wanted in the first place? Of course in this case it wouldn't have been by Killer's hand, but in my haze, I could tell the difference.

I really almost gave up. I think I was even on the ground at one point. Then I heard the others. Shouting my name, calling me, coughing. These idiots had run back into the building to find me.

Load-bearing beams fell from the ceiling, indicating that the building was near collapse.

I summoned all the strength I had left in me to pull myself off the floor. Completely numb and near delusional, I approached the car and shielded my face before jumping through an area with the least amount of flames, through the car and to the other side. I could tell my clothes caught fire, but I could barely feel the burning.

Oddly enough, I was more cold than anything. My vision clouded over, and I staggered around until the light of day pierced through the smoke.

"Kian?" I called out, coughing. "Jo? Laine?"

"We're here!" someone called back.

I couldn't see them, but I could hear someone approach and hit me with something, before grabbing me roughly and pulling me into the daylight.

"Where... Where?" I murmured.

"We're right here," Laine said. "You're okay, we're okay, it's all okay."

Then the world went black.

KIAN'S NOTE #10 HE FINDS
A WAY

I DIDN'T GET to see whether my father was okay.

I didn't see him get out of the building.

I didn't know anything, and the one person who could tell me was on my back, unconscious. We crouched down by the river, creeping slowly toward the school. Every few feet, we'd stop to make sure Ness was still alive. Despite her Plot Armor, we were still freaked out.

Jo was out in front of us, carrying the bag with our weapons and clothes, and Laine brought up the rear. Every once in a while she'd look at me, or maybe say something, but I couldn't hear her over the blood pumping in my ears. The way my father looked at me, the way he'd shifted his aim toward me, the way he coughed behind those flames...

I couldn't get any of it out of my mind. If he hadn't gotten out, if he was—

I couldn't stop thinking about it.

After some time, we arrived at the back of the school and waited behind the bleachers of the football field, listening for the officers and dogs after us. I placed my jacket on the ground and put Ness down on top of it gently, while Jo and Laine sat next to me.

"Do you think she'll wake up anytime soon?" Laine whispered after a long bout of silence.

Or maybe she had been talking, and this was just the first time I had heard her.

"She should," I murmured back. I hated how weak my voice sounded.

"She better," Jo croaked.

We were quiet again, and I stared at the angry burns that covered Ness's arms and legs and creeped up her chest.

"She literally ran through fire," Laine whispered.

"For us," Jo added. "That's why she did it. She heard us and thought we were in danger. *She ran through fire for us*."

"She'll never admit it," I said quietly.

"Yeah."

We laughed as much as the situation would allow us to. Jo rummaged through the bag for a second before sighing.

"Those burns are brutal. We need to get into the building and to the nurse's office. There should be something that we can do to, I dunno, keep them from getting infected, right?"

Laine frowned. "Won't there be alarms if we break in?" She leaned against my shoulder a bit, and I could feel her heart beating rapidly.

"That's a risk we're gonna have to take," Jo responded. Laine and I exchanged looks and get up.

After some searching for an open door, we realized we really had to bust our way in. And like any movie, there was a perfectly good, loose brick on the ground beside a window. I let Laine carry Ness on her back while I busted through the window, my hand wrapped with my jacket to avoid any cuts. Once I climbed through, I helped Jo in before we both pulled Ness from Laine's grasp. Laine hopped down from the ledge and dusted the glass from her hair.

It was lucky I kept the brick with me. I used it to smash the nurse's office window and unlock the door. We stepped inside, gently laying Ness on one of the cots before rummaging through the many cabinets and drawers for something to treat her wounds.

"Look for aloe," Laine said. "That's what you use on burns, right?"

"We need a lot of aloe," Jo grimaced. "Look at her." Laine looked like she didn't really want to.

We'd found some aloe-burn-stuff and bandages, and got to work on treating and covering Ness's burns. We had to cut her clothes off of her, since pieces had literally melted into her skin. Well, Laine and Jo cut them off. I stepped out to open some lockers until I found gym clothes that would fit her. Once Laine and Jo got her dressed again, I came back in to help dress her wounds.

"You're doing it wrong," Jo pointed at the arm Laine wrapped. "You're gonna cut off her circulation."

Laine rolled her eyes. "Sorry, didn't realize you went to medical school."

"I'd do better in medical school than you'd do in kindergarten."

"Guys," I tried, but they couldn't hear me.

"Why are you so miserable?" Laine shot. "Like seriously, what did I ever do to you?"

Jo laughed out a loud, sharp, humorless laugh. "Are you kidding me right now? What did you ever do to me?"

"Yeah. Tell me."

"I dunno, Laine, maybe be the world's biggest pick me since eighth grade?"

"*Excuse me?*"

"Guys, can we focus-" I tried interrupting again.

"Yeah, Laine. You're a pick me. You're fake, too," Jo spat.

Laine stood, throwing the bandages down. "You're just bitter because no one likes you, Jo. You've always been so jealous that people actually wanted to be friends with me and Kian—"

"Please don't bring me into it—"

"—all because you are a loser no one wants to be around, 'cause they don't want to catch your freak-disease."

"People don't want to be around you either, Laine!" Jo shouted. "They only kiss up to you because they know you'll make their lives miserable if they don't. Because you're mean, Laine. You're mean, and judgmental, and fake, all to make up for the fact that you hate yourself almost as much as your parents do."

Too far. Laine went completely silent.

"You know what, Jo?" Laine started again, her voice quiet and low. "You might be right, but you're meaner than I am. You always have been."

And with that, Laine walked out of the room, slamming it behind her as she disappeared down the hall. Jo scoffed, looking back at the bandaging in her hands.

"How am I meaner than her?" she muttered angrily to herself.

I frowned. "You're both mean," I mumbled. "All of us are. Especially to each other."

Jo looked at me, but I looked away. "We're all mean to each other," I continued. "Even though we used to be best friends. We're supposed to be friends. I mean, you were gonna kill us, Jo. And the worst part is, your motive wasn't even something Person or whoever made up. We actually abandoned you back then, and for what?"

I could feel my eyes welling up, and I willed myself not to get emotional. "To be cool? Cool to some insignificant middle schoolers? Who cares? I mean, seriously. Who cares about that stuff?"

"That's easy to say," Jo mumbled. "When you have that stuff."

I shook my head and stared down at Ness. "None of it matters, though. I'd give it all up in a heartbeat. Though, considering half the town thinks we're serial killers..." I can't help it, the corners of my mouth turn up. "Guess we already kind of did."

Jo and I were quiet for a long time before she spoke again.

"I didn't mean to say that." Her voice was quiet and fragile, and I nodded.

"I know. But you did say it."

"I know."

Silence.

"Do you think she's okay?"

"No, I don't think she is."

"I want to apologize."

"You should. But so should she." I leaned back, closing my eyes. "So should I." I turned and looked at her, and she looked so similar to how she used to be.

"I'm sorry, Jo. For what happened back then."

She looked away quickly. "You don't have to do that."

"I do. I'm sorry about how we treated you. I'm sorry I pretended like everything was fine between us after, too."

"Look, Kian." Her voice was suddenly sharp, almost defensive. "I don't need your apologies, okay? We're in a... really odd situation right now. And it was middle school. Like you said, who cares?" She stood up. "Laine's been gone a long time. We should make sure she's not dead. Do you know where she might have gone?"

"Same place she used to," I answered. Jo hesitated, then nodded. Of course we knew where she was.

Back in middle school, before we fell out with Jo, anytime Laine would get mad or upset, she'd skip class in the handicap stall of one of the girls' bathrooms. Now, that same bathroom was Rosette's, so when we found her, she wasn't in the stall. She was sitting by the little memorial people had set up at the far end of the sink.

"Go away," she murmured, not even looking up at us. Of course, we ignored this request and sat next to her.

"Remember when Kian would get in trouble for coming in here to find you in middle school?" Jo said after a long bout of silence.

Laine laughed, though it was short.

"Yeah, I remember."

"And he never understood why he got in trouble!"

"Literally! Just kept repeating that he was trying to find me, as if that would get him off the chopping block." Laine and Jo were now openly laughing at younger me's expense, which I really didn't mind. It was a moment of peace amongst days, weeks, maybe even years of chaos.

Laine and Jo kept talking about the stupid things that we went through together in middle school, and it felt like we were back there for a moment. I couldn't even remember what we'd been fighting about. Or what we'd come here to do.

After a while, though, we stood, not knowing how long we'd left Ness in the nurse's office. We walked back, but breaking into a run when we heard Ness shout.

We dashed into the office to see Ness awake, and positively freaking out. The supplies we used to treat her were scattered all over the floor, and she had her hands pressed to her ears, her eyes squeezed shut, sobbing.

"No, no..no!" she repeated through sobs. "No, *please!*"

I quickly grabbed hold of her, sliding one arm around her back and with the other I tried to pull her hands from her ears.

"Ness? Ness, you're okay. You're alright, we're right here!"

I tried to calm her down, but it took a while for her to open her eyes. She completely melted against me when she saw me, and let her hands fall away from her ears.

"I thought you... Laine? Jo?"

"Right here," Jo said quickly. She and Laine stepped forward, and I helped Ness to sit back down on the cot.

"We're sorry," I murmured as I kept my arm firmly around

her back. "We stepped away for a second. You were out for so long..."

But she didn't answer. She just sat there, catching her breath, and staring out in front of her. It was as if she couldn't hear us at all. Then she stood.

"I'll be back. Don't move."

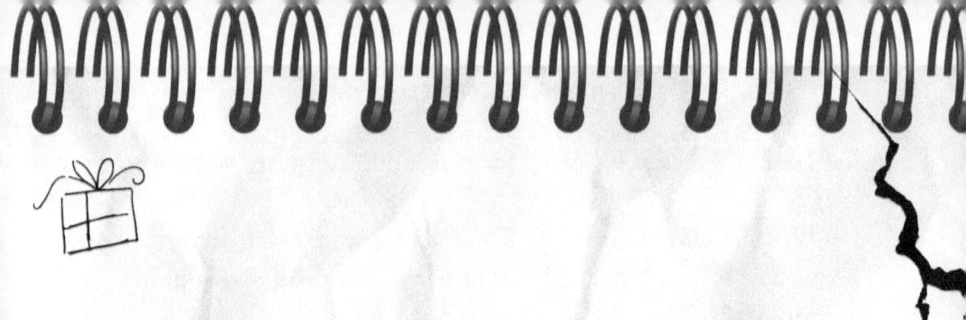

TIP FOR AN IDIOT #11: A GIFT IS ONLY A GIFT WHEN WANTED

I WAS DREAMING AGAIN.

I didn't have the cloth, so I wasn't in the red-sky place, but maybe this place was a little worse - my house.

Not my aunt's house, but *my* house. The house I left a very long time ago. The same house that had been in my first memory-dream when this whole thing started. My parents' house.

Now, I remember little from around that time. You know those stories about women whose brains force them to forget the trauma of childbirth, so they'll do it again? That was kind of like this, minus the childbirth, and Tyler was the one who wanted me back there.

I sat in front of the TV, like before, staring at some unintelligible slasher film, completely entranced. Tyler was next to me, in my peripheral, per usual.

"Isn't it great?" Tyler asked. "Isn't it fantastic?"

"Yeah." I heard myself responding. "It's really cool."

"Are you scared?"

"No."

"Do you want to be?"

Then I was in our room. We had bunk beds across the

room from each other, but we were only allowed to use the bottom bunk. The top bunk bore no mattress and stored mostly stuffed animals. We weren't allowed to use the top bunk until we got older. I sat on my bunk, looking across the room at Tyler, who sat on his bunk. He looked like him today, not like him ten years ago.

"Vanessa, do you want to be scared?" he asked.

I shook my head no.

"It'll be fun," he promised. "It'll be like you're in the movie."

That did sound fun. I nodded.

"Lay back."

I laid flat on my back, staring up at the bunk above me. Tyler approached, holding a red cloth. Mom's red cloth.

"She'll be mad if she sees you took that," I warned, and Tyler shrugged.

"We need it. For immersion. Close your eyes."

I obliged. I felt the cloth lay over my eyes, and Tyler spoke.

"Let yourself fall asleep, Vanessa, and you'll wake up in the movie. It'll be fun."

I slowly felt myself drift away, and when I woke up, I was in the living room again. Tyler and I were staring at the TV when a woman scooped me off the ground and pulled me away.

"Look at her, Aaron," the woman said, her voice high and frantic as she held me out toward a man who refused to look at me. "She's covered in bruises, scratches! I mean, *covered*."

It was true. My skin burned all over from the lacerations, especially on the bottoms of my feet. It was like I'd been running through the woods barefoot all night. That's what it felt like.

"How did she even get out there?" the man asked quietly.

"Ask your son," the woman shot back. "He's dangerous, Aaron. He's only getting stronger, and soon we won't be able to keep him still anymore. *He'll hurt her.*"

"That's our son, Marie!" the man rubbed his temple. "What do you propose we do?"

I WAS at my aunt's house. The woman and man—my parents, I think—were hugging me and apologizing. Tyler wasn't there. My parents were crying. They said they loved me. And then they were gone. And I was alone.

When I woke up, and I mean actually woke up, I was alone. I was laying down, looking up at the tiled ceiling of the nurse's office in complete quiet. My whole body stung, bad, and the pain was almost too great for me to bring myself to sit up. But I did, with great effort, and then I panicked.

I was completely alone.

Jo, Laine, and Kian were all nowhere to be found. If I was here, and they were somewhere else, I wasn't there to protect them. To save them. And I freaked.

As expected, Tyler was no help.

"They're dead, Vanessa," he whispered from behind me. I didn't even realize I was holding the cloth. *"They're dead, and it's all your fault. You passed out from the smoke and they died after bringing you here."*

"No..." I murmured. "No, you're lying. They aren't dead."

"C'mon, Vanessa," Tyler drawled. *"It's my story. What kind of horror movie would it be if I didn't kill off the rest of the victim pool? It's the day of the Harvest Festival, you know. Now you get to kill Marco."*

"You're lying!" I shout. I slam my hands over my ears to block out Tyler, but his voice rang louder and louder.

"They're dead, Vanessa!" Tyler taunted, his sing songy voice echoing in my skull. *"Dead, dead, they're all dead!"*

I couldn't hear my screaming over his voice, and it wasn't until Kian grabbed a hold of me that Tyler stopped.

"Ness? Ness, you're alright. We're right here."

I opened my eyes. I had squeezed them shut so hard my head hurt.

Kian was in front of me. Alive. Behind him stood Laine and Jo. Alive and alive.

"Just kidding." Tyler laughed this cruel, sinister laugh in my ear, and it took everything in me to not slam a nearby EpiPen through my eardrums right there.

I couldn't even breathe. It took me several minutes just to remember how. I babbled as Kian tried to calm me down, and I couldn't even say what I was talking about when Tyler spoke again.

"Come see me, Vanessa. I want to give you some spoilers."

I don't know what excuse I gave the others, but I prayed they'd stay put. I ran out of the office in a daze, clutching the red cloth so tightly blood from my palm seeped into it.

Not that you'd be able to tell either way.

I don't know how long I ran, but it must have been awhile judging by the sunset peeking through the forest when I arrived.

I found my way to the spot where everything started, where Mack died, where I saved Ki and Laine for the first time. If I looked hard enough, I could see the sign some hundred feet away that contradicts the whole of "Wilsonville." Ripping one of Laine's hair ties off my wrist and fastening the cloth to my face, I let the world change.

"Took you long enough." Tyler mocked when I finally came to. I opened my eyes and stared directly up at the red sky from the ground. Peeling myself off the forest floor, I came face to face with him again.

Sure enough, it really was Tyler. We looked similar, in a fraternal-but-still-clearly siblings sort of way. He was tall, which wasn't surprising. He was always slightly bigger than me, but he was also thin. I was definitely more sturdily built than him, so I was pretty sure I could body slam him if need be. He also didn't look like the type to run, so I bet I could outrun him, too.

I was going through so many possible escape routes and defense plans in my mind that I almost missed when he started talking.

"Cool burns. I made sure they didn't creep up to your face or your hair. You're welcome." Tyler grinned.

When I didn't answer, he sighed and spoke again. "You've got questions, right?" he asked. His voice felt just as slimy as it did when he was speaking in my ear.

"You've got answers." My voice was smaller, weaker than I'd intended, and I hated myself for it.

Tyler nodded and leaned against a tree with his arms folded. "'Course I do. This is my story, after all."

"How?" I asked. "How did you do this?"

"Well, I-"

"No, wait. Don't answer that yet. First, tell me exactly what this even is."

He grinned. "You want me to tell you? You seemed so confident you had it all figured out, though? You were always good at that, Vanny. Figuring out the ending of the movie when it had only just begun." He pushed off of the tree. "So, you were right. You're stuck in a horror movie."

"Surprise, surprise."

"I was disappointed you'd figured it out, honestly." Tyler pouted. "It was a sort of surprise. You wouldn't have figured it out at all if you hadn't taken that cloth."

His expression turned dark, and he regarded me as if he were scolding me. "Vanny, did you forget you aren't supposed to take things that aren't yours?"

"What's the significance of this cloth? And why is it so —"

"Familiar?" Tyler sighed. "Yeah, it was my mistake to use something like that. Pulling inspiration from real life has its consequences."

"They're our mother's old cloth napkins, aren't they?" The dream-memory thing came to mind as Tyler nodded.

"She always hated when I would take those, but I needed them. That's how I put you in the story. Or, at least, how I used to, before I became as well-versed in my craft as I am now. Do you remember it, Van? I gave you those memories, hoping you'd remember. When we were kids, you loved horror movies, even then. And I enjoyed making them real for you. Our parents used to tell me to look out for you since you were smaller than I was. They stopped saying that, though. They thought I was hurting you with my stories."

"Stop being cryptic." I glared. "And get to the point."

"So impatient. Well, I found out from a very young age I had an affinity for creativity. If I concentrated hard enough, I could bring a story to life. You loved movies, so you were my audience of one most of the time. I would cover your eyes when you went to sleep, and I'd tell you the story. You'd sleep walk, following my every command. Whatever character I made you, you were. Our parents didn't find out for a while. At first, they thought it was something they didn't need to worry too much about."

"'He's a good kid', they tried to convince themselves. 'He just wants to entertain her.' They were right, of course. You adored my stories, and I just wanted to entertain you. You bored easily and were so quiet and reclusive, but not with my stories. I was looking after you, like they'd said."

"Well, when they started finding you in odd places in the mornings, they got worried. The last straw was when they found you in the woods behind our house, yelling about some monster chasing you. They didn't like my stories, Vanny. They thought I was hurting you with them. They didn't understand."

Tyler shook his head, visibly annoyed, maybe even angry. "They decided I was dangerous, but I was getting stronger. I could put them into stories, too. I'd even tried it on some of the neighborhood kids. Our parents knew soon they wouldn't be able to control me. So, they separated us. They couldn't just abandon me. No, they had to atone for what they'd created. They left you at our aunt's and came back home to deal with me."

I stared at him for a very long time. My entire life, everything I'd ever thought about my parents, my importance to them, Tyler just told me it wasn't true.

"Why don't I remember any of this?" I asked finally. Tyler shrugged.

"Ask our aunt."

I couldn't even get into what he meant by that right then.

"I don't get it. I don't get any of it. I don't get *you*. How are you able to do any of that stuff? Mind control and... and..."

"It's confusing, isn't it?" Tyler grinned. "Let me try to explain something. I'm not the first person to possess this rare gift, Vanessa. Our parents were in a similar predicament to yours. They were in a story of their own." He noted my confusion and paced as he spoke.

"Our mother was a Final Girl. A real Jamie Lee Curtis type. Her story was some silly quiet-kid-takes-revenge-on-the-populars trope, or something. The only catch was, the writer was quite lazy. Didn't tie up their loose ends." He made a face - a mix of disgust and amusement. "Our father? He was Killer."

It didn't make sense. "How can our parents be —"

"Sh-h, I'm in the middle of it, geez. Be patient." He glared at me and I realized I really hadn't missed having a slightly older brother at all.

"Anyways. Somehow, they broke out of the written plot. Fell in *love* with each other. And I dunno every detail, but they ended the story with everyone but the two of them dead. Ma didn't kill Pa, like she was supposed to." He folded his arms and spun to face me. He adjusted his posture to mimic that of a teacher giving a lesson.

"Now, little sister. This is something very important for you to remember. Our parents' 'love' was an abomination. And all that can be born from abomination is abomination." He grinned. "Me."

I wondered sometimes why teenage boys thought saying stuff like that sounds cool. Judging by his corny facial expression, he definitely thought it did. I resisted the urge to roll my eyes.

"Here's the thing. I can't stand plot holes. And retconning drives me up a literal wall. I hate the fact that a fellow story creator allowed our parents to break free like that. Allowed their vision to be altered by the whims of characters a creator is meant to control. You see, Van, we all have a role. Some people create, others follow. And I hate when those lines are blurred."

"So, what are you saying? Everyone in the world has a 'story' being written for them by a maniac like you?" I asked.

Tyler laughed and shook his head.

"If only. No, no, I only know of one other person like me, though I hope there are more. And I can only guess why anyone else does it: to entertain. To create *purpose*."

"What happened to our parents?" I was getting impatient. "Why did they never call me, or come see me? Where are they now?" Even before Tyler replied, I knew the answer.

"Dead. Duh." Tyler folded his arms and leaned against a tree with a sigh. "Dead, as they were meant to be."

"You killed them," I whispered, and he shook his head.

"Nah, I wouldn't do that. I'm not a monster, Vanessa, they're our parents… were."

"So, what then?" My voice shook, and I willed myself not to breakdown.

"Vanny, Mom was meant to *kill Dad*. That was how their story was written. All I did was have her finish it." He grinned. "With a little tweak of my own. A deadly stalemate—no winners. It was actually pretty cool, one of my better artistic choices. Oh, and the *emotion!* So good, I almost felt bad for killing 'em off."

"After they were gone," Tyler continued. "I wanted to find you. You made such a good protagonist in my stories, and you were the only one that really appreciated them. By the time I found you, I'd gotten significantly stronger. I had lived on my own and perfected my craft for years. We were older, which meant my stories had to grow up, too. I didn't want to find you and not be able to give you a good story. That's so embarrassing!" Tyler fake shivered. "By the time I found you in good old Logan — that's what the town used to be called — I had figured out how to pull anything within a certain radius into my stories. I commandeered Logan, and have been using it as my little puppet stage ever since." He gestured toward the red sky with a broad grin. "This pretty dome keeps everything quiet on set, but you figured that out already, didn't you?"

"And the cloths?" My voice was hoarse and wavered like never before.

Tyler waved me off.

"A little token from our childhood. Just a souvenir I thought would be a cute addition." He frowned a bit. "Probably shouldn't have added it. Looks like it jogged your memory and took you out of my story. Ruined the immersion, such a pity."

I couldn't respond. I couldn't bring myself to. Rage like I never had before coursed through my body and I couldn't let it out. Not yet.

And it wasn't just rage. I felt an overwhelming, all-consuming guilt in every part of my body. Tyler had done all of this, killed all these people, because of me.

"Why did you do all this, Tyler?" I asked quietly, my hands balled into fists at my sides. "What's your motive?" Some nervous, selfish part of me wanted, no, *needed* confirmation that all of this wasn't my fault. That Tyler would take responsibility. And he did, though it didn't relieve my own guilt.

He laughed, a sharp, cruel laugh.

"Vanessa, come on. *My motive?* What a juvenile term for my

magnificent actions!" He took a step forward, shaking his head. "My 'motive' is more than just a motive. It's not just the reason I kill. It's my purpose. My divine calling. My being as a gift directly from God to the rest of this mundane world! Vanessa, I'm more than just a storyteller. I'm a *creator*. I built you. I built all of this!"

"You're not God," I interjected, and I silently cursed myself for allowing my voice to shake. "You didn't build anything. All you did was make a mess out of what was already here."

"Oh, whatever. I made a story. I gave this stupid town, our stupid parents, and you, my stupid little sister, purpose. That's beyond creation. How many people would kill to have their purpose outlined for them like I've done for all these people? Like I did for you?"

"Yeah, I'm sure the world would love to be at the mercy of an annoying, monologuing seventeen-year-old."

He rolled his eyes. "You can take as many jabs at me as you want. We both know how you really feel."

I raised an eyebrow. "How I really feel?"

Tyler nodded and paced a short path across the forest floor again. "I know you've been denying yourself this whole time, but you can't hide it from me. I know all about you." He turned to me with a wink. "Call it twin-telepathy."

"What are you talking about?"

"You're having fun."

I never knew such simple words could send such a crackle of rage up my spine, but there we were.

"I mean, you even admitted it," Tyler continued. "What, you think I didn't hear you back at the house? I've given you a gift, this lovely story, and you're having more fun than you ever have. That was the whole point of this!" He threw his hands in the air, having the nerve to look exasperated. "This story was a gift to you, Vanessa! Everything I've done was in service to my baby sister."

My blood ran cold. "What do you mean?"

He grinned, and he looks more sinister than any Killer I'd ever seen. "It's just as I said. Vanessa, when I came to see you after our parents' long overdue demise, there was only one character trait I could find in you. Boredom! I mean, you looked positively miserable, drifting around this dull town. I felt sad for you. No friends, practically alone in that old house with our aunt, drab attire—"

"Are you just going to insult me this whole time?"

"Shut up, I'm building to something. Anyways, it reminded me of when we were kids." He picked at his nails, reminiscing. "You never had much interest in regular things when we were young. You didn't play with dolls or cars, and you barely watched any of those educational cartoons our parents put on. There was one thing that would hold your attention." He glanced up, grinning still. "My stories. Well, not just my stories. You liked the ones about princes and talking animals that our parents would read you, but it was nothing compared to when I would tell you stories. So, when I saw you again, I gave you a gift. Helped you out with your lame life. What better way than to give you another story?"

I couldn't speak for a second. If Tyler was telling the truth, if he really did all of this as some sort of twisted service to me, that meant that it *was* all my fault. Everything.

Mack. Rosette. Laine. Jo. Marco. Kian. *Kian*.

"What about this sounded like a good gift to you?" I managed to ask, my voice a dull whisper.

He folded his arms, a small pout on his very punchable face. "Well, it would have been better had you not messed things up. Your theory was right the first time, Vanessa." Tyler pouted. "You did mess something up when you took that cloth off of Rosette's face. At first, when I started the story and killed Mack, you didn't seem all that interested. So I thought I'd immerse you further and give you a bigger role. I had you find Rosette. I expected from there that involving you would make you open your eyes, spice up your life for a bit. But then..." Tyler's jaw twitched. "Then you went a bit... rogue. You see, you were *supposed* to scream, or panic, or something, then call the police, answer some questions at the station as unhelpfully as possible, and leave. But instead, you picked up the cloth. *You picked up the cloth. Who does that?*"

"Maybe the same type of person whose idea of a gift is killing a bunch of high schoolers," I hissed. I was tired of people judging me for taking the cloth.

"In any case," Tyler waved dismissively. "I have no idea how you did it. I didn't script that." He folded his arms, his brow furrowing. "And after that? I couldn't keep you on script. I mean, for one, you kept trying to throw yourself into Killer's arms. It was pathetic, if I'm being honest. Watching *my* sister try to get herself killed like some stupid B-list victim? When I worked *so hard*?" He shook his head. "It pissed me off. I tried to steer Killer away from you, but you were so insistent. Insistent to the point you started saving my victims! That was simply the last straw. You wanted to screw up my story so bad, I gave you a better role."

"Final Girl."

Tyler grinned, nodding. "Isn't it neat, Sidney Prescott?" He chuckled, so amused with himself and his Scream reference. "It took you a little too long to accept it. Another thing that was pathetic to watch — your self-deprecation. Honestly, have some confidence!"

"You influenced my other victims, too. Pulling the carefully crafted wool from their eyes. They weren't like you, though. They're all utter sheep to my command. No matter what they knew, they'd do what I wanted them to."

I caught something. Something he'd said confirmed a suspicion I'd toyed with for a while. *They weren't like me?* "Wait, shut up for a second."

He rolled his eyes. "Can you stop interrupting?"

"Nuh-uh. Something just hit me. You really can't control

me, can you?" I looked up at him, his unamused expression fading into slight surprise, then annoyance.

"I can."

"No, you can't. That's why I'm able to go "off-script" like you said, right?"

His face melted into a scowl. "I can control you, Vanessa. Maybe not... directly... but I control everything around you. Isn't that the same?"

I thought about that for a second. "But, you don't."

"What?"

"You don't," I repeated. "You can't. Not when I interfere." It made more and more sense. "That's why I can save the others, right? That's why you haven't killed Kian, or Laine, or Jo. Because you can't do anything when I get involved."

"That's not true," Tyler growled. "I can control them. You don't have any power, Vanessa. Sure, you're able to save them every once in a while. But come on, you really think you can hold your own against me?" He laughed, a bitter, harsh laugh. "You can only run, Vanessa. And you can only drag your little friends along behind you. They sure as hell can't run forever."

"My god, Tyler. You're so annoying!" I exclaimed. "Why are you speaking like a superhero-movie villain? It's really embarrassing!"

He stared for a second, blinking a bit. "What—"

"And the monologuing, oh my lord. Do you ever shut up? Has being a freak all these years given you the inability to speak like a normal person?"

"Excuse me—"

"And you have a serious creativity problem. I mean, this marvellous story you 'created?' It's like a complete rip-off of every slasher film from the eighties."

His eyes bugged out of his head. "What?" He sputtered. "No, it isn't! It's so different, and better, actually!"

"Are you joking?" I raised my eyebrows. "The plot is so basic. I mean, where's the twist? The originality?" I shook my head, ignoring the building rage on his face. "The only reason any of this was less mind-numbing than the rest of my life is because *I made it that way.* This would be a complete flop if I wasn't such an interesting character."

I meant that, honestly. And I didn't stop there.

"And it doesn't make any sense, either. Take the Volvo, for example. How many times has that thing been irreversibly damaged? Yet it still runs? Plot hole."

He looked physically wounded. "Bro, that's not even a plot hole, that's a sturdy model—"

"And Killer. I *stabbed* him. I watched him bleed out, Tyler. No pulse. Yet he is alive and well! Not a single life threatening wound left on Marco. Does that make sense to you? No. Plot hole."

"That's a part of the mystery of it—"

"My injuries, too. I busted my ankle jumping out of that window. Next day? Healed. Plot hole. My burn marks are fresh, and I *don't even feel them.* Plot hole. Partly McCloudy? Not a plot hole, but stupid enough to mention. Naming everything in the town after Kian's family? I mean, come on!"

I basically shouted my complaints at this point and paced around and gesturing wildly to drive my point home.

"Seriously, Tyler, this was *weak.* You say you wanted to give me a gift, yet all I've received is some uninspired, half-baked *loser's* attempt at a slasher film."

"Lame."

"Boring."

"*Booooo.*"

There was a long, frigid silence as Tyler stared at me.

"That's how you really feel, Vanessa?" he asked quietly.

I nodded. "Yeah, it is. You suck, dude."

CRACK!

The noise was so loud, so sudden. I whipped my head to see where it came from. Just above that fated forest sign was a line. A sharp, jagged, black line that cut through the red of the sky like a —

CRACK!

"What the.." Tyler muttered. He stalked over to the sign, fists clenched. Every step he took toward it made another splinter in the red. "What is this…?"

Another crack.

"How are you doing that?" he accused, whipping his head toward me.

"I'm… I'm not," I mumbled honestly.

Another loud break in the sky and a chunk of red came crashing down, revealing the inky black, midnight sky behind it.

"No, no, no!" Tyler rushed to the fallen piece, trying to pick it up, but it disintegrated in his hands, spilling through his fingers like crimson sand. He cursed, loud and dramatic, as I looked on. Then, all at once, like a plate had dropped, the sky shattered.

Shards of red came raining down like hail, exploding on the trees and showering sand down on us. Tyler lost it, desperately scraping sand into his hands and trying to put it back together again. I felt the sand float around and a wave of relief crashed over my shoulders, as if I'd just been saved.

As if it was all over.

"You ruined it!" Tyler screamed. "You ruined everything, as usual!" He was genuinely tweaking at this point, grabbing at his hair and howling about how I was the worst, blah, blah, blah…

"It's done," I whispered, staring at the sand coating the forest. If the Veil was broken, if Tyler was freaking out like this, that had to mean something. It had to mean I had ended it. This absolute dream turned unbearable nightmare had ended with a sandstorm.

"It's done, right?"

"Oh, yeah. Yeah, you made sure of that, Vanessa!" He

shouted. "All that work, hours and hours of writing, story building! Ruined! Down the freaking drain!"

"My bad?"

Honestly, I'm not sure why I said that.

"Ness!" a voice behind me said.

Kian.

I spun around, and there he was, covered in sand and looking haggard. He rushed over to me and gripped my shoulders. "Are you okay? You ran out so fast, we got worried."

"Kian, I'm okay, but I told you to stay put." I had to think quickly. With Tyler right there, ticked off as he was, who knew what he'd do to Kian? I had no time to act because Kian hugged me.

"Ki, just wait a sec—"

"Don't run off like that again," he scolded. "You're hurt. You scared the crap out of all of us. Laine and Jo are running around town looking for you."

"Hold on!" I tugged myself from his grasp and turned to face Tyler, ready to confront whatever the next trick up his sleeve was.

But his next trick was a disappearing act.

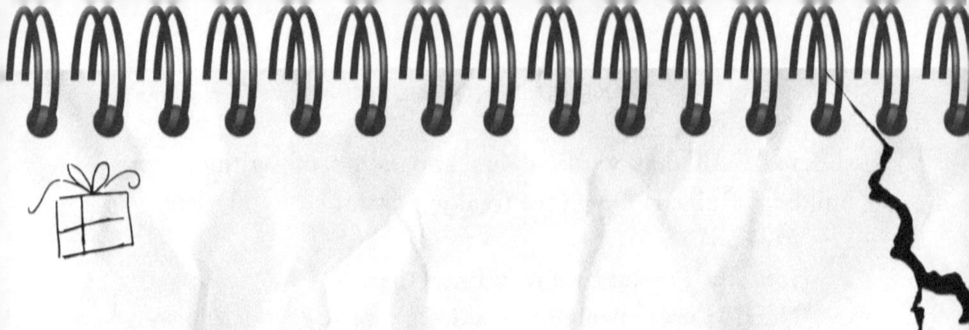

WE SEARCHED the forest for twenty minutes, but Ness wouldn't tell me what, or, rather, who, we were looking for.

She was obviously annoyed and wouldn't explain what was wrong, or even why she was out here in the first place.

"All this red is—"

"The Veil. Broken," Ness mumbled as she continued to search.

My eyes probably bugged out of my head. "*The Veil broke? How? How did you do it? How can you say that so casually?*"

"Can you focus?"

"Can you?" I grabbed her shoulder, stopping her frantic search of the bushes. "Ness. What are we looking for?"

She studied my face for a while, like she was trying to find what she was looking for in my eyes. I felt her tense up under my hand, and she pulled away.

"Never mind," she whispered.

There was something behind her eyes that I couldn't quite place.

"Never mind, I'll find it later."

I wasn't going to pry any further. We had bigger, well, other fish to fry. I took her hand, and we ran from the forest.

Everything had a thin layer of sand on it. The red dust contrasted with the usual green of the forest.

By the time we got back into town, all the townsfolk were outside, dusted in red and looking beyond confused. While my eyes swept the citizens, Ness squeezed my hand and pointed at a nearby shop.

The tea shop, which used to be named Wilson's Leaves, was now called Witch's Brew. An admittedly edgy name for a place like Wilsonville, but...well, it wasn't Wilsonville anymore. Everywhere I looked, places that used to be named after my family were named something else entirely. But the thing that caught my eye the most was a sign hanging off of the tea shop. It read:

Logan's finest tea shop! Leaves from all over the world!

Logan. That's where we were. My town's name was Logan.

"Logan," Ness whispered beside me. "That's almost as lame as Wilsonville."

Before I could reply, Laine and Jo came running toward us.

"What the hell happened?" Laine called.

Ness looked back and forth, her eyes landing on the red cops wandering just steps from us. They looked far too distracted to even notice the wanted "killers" within arm's reach. The cops and everyone else were drifting as if they had just been released from an endless dream, which, I guess, they had.

While Ness explained to Laine and Jo - even less than she explained to me- I nudged her arm.

"No more hypnosis-thing," I murmured, motioning toward the people still filling the streets. "Can you feel it?"

"I can," Jo spoke up. "They all look..."

"Freed," Ness finished.

We watched in silence as people shook the dust from their hair, brushed it from their children's faces, and just sort of stood around. Some people were smiling, others looked incredibly relieved.

We doubted they knew what had happened. They probably didn't know that they had been controlled for the past several weeks, but they all seemed to know they were free from it.

"Let's not stick around," Ness murmured.

We jogged back to the school, dodging police officers who seemed to come back to their senses. As we ran through Logan, my eyes traced around the place. The fruit stands had all rotted. The same with everything in the grocery store, by the smell of it. The grass on every normally pristine lawn was long overgrown, the entire town draped in wear and tear.

Neglect.

We had all been running around in a realm that didn't exist and neglected the real world. Now it had caught up to us.

We got back to the school and climbed through the window we broke earlier and jogged back to the nurse's office.

"Okay. What is the plan?" Laine asked, looking out the window. "'Cause the patrol cars are out, and I think they're still looking for us."

"Really?" Jo hopped up to see for herself. "That's messed up. I kinda thought when the movie ended, everyone would like, forget everything that happened?"

"Same, honestly," Ness murmured. "I guess that wouldn't make sense. Rosette and Mack really are dead."

Everyone went quiet again. We'd spent this entire time reminding ourselves that we were in a movie, but was it? Two kids had actually died. It wasn't a movie to them.

"So, what now?" I asked slowly. "Marco is still in custody, and the police still think we killed Rosette and Mack."

"But mostly me," Ness said. She tugged at the bandages protecting her arms. "Remember? The police are convinced I encouraged all of you to go along with it while I killed people. Marco could take it back, but that would just leave all the murders pinned on him. There's no way for him to get out of it."

"But what do we *do*?" Jo pressed. Ness sighed, letting go of the bandages.

"The only thing we can do. Most of the officers are out looking for us, right? So we break him out."

I groaned audibly. Don't get me wrong, I wanted nothing more than to get Marco out of there, but seriously, how many times in one week were we going to break into a police station?

THIS TIME WAS EASIER, though. Ness was right. Most of the officers were either out looking for us, or trying to deal with all the confusion throughout the town. There was only one officer in the station, and it was just a matter of waiting for him to go to the bathroom before we could slip in. My dad took his keys wherever he went, so we snagged some from someone else's desk.

"Over here."

I led the others toward the holding cells in the back. Marco sat there, all alone in one of the three cells the station had. We didn't use those very often here in… *Logan*, so there was no need for more than that.

He stood when he saw us.

"I'm sorry," was the first thing that came out of his mouth. "I'm sorry guys. I didn't mean to tell them that but I couldn't stop myself, and they wouldn't believe me when I was trying to take it back, and—"

"Marc, *relax*," I said, while trying to find the right key for the cell. "We know. Believe us, we know. It's okay."

He let out a small, whimpery noise as I finally got the cell open.

"I took your car," he whispered.

I tensed a bit. "Yeah, I know. Do you know where it is now?"

Marco shook his head. "I don't know. I think your dad was going to take it, but they were holding it in the back lot as evidence or something. It might still be there."

It would have been inappropriate to celebrate like I wanted to when we located my car out back, but I'm sure the others could see the giddy smile I wore.

Once we were all in Ness started. "Okay, we'll drop Laine and Jo off at their houses, then Marco and I will get out of here. Okay Kian?"

"What?!" we all asked in unison.

Ness sighed.

"Marco's got a boatload of evidence against him. He can't get out of this. And he's already started the 'Vanessa made me do it' thing, so if we ever get caught, he'd get off easier if we lean into that. There's no evidence against the three of you, so there's no reason for you all to come with us."

"No way." I shook my head. She was not gonna do this savior thing, not after everything we've been through.

"Absolutely not. I'm not letting the both of you leave without me."

"Are you being serious?" Ness turned to face me. "Don't argue."

"No, Ness, Kian is right," Jo piped up from the backseat. "I killed, too. I know it was, like, retconned, but no way am I letting the two of you take the blame when I was just as much a part of it as Marco."

"You *don't need to be,*" Ness said, furrowing her brows. "You can stay here and live your life without becoming a fugitive, Jo!"

"Hell no. I'm going with you," Jo said firmly, with more assertion than I've literally ever seen her have.

Even Ness shrunk back a bit, a little shocked.

"And you'll need my car," I murmured. "So I'm going, too."

"Are you joking—"

"I'm not."

I turned to look at Ness, searching her face. "If you're going, I'm going. We're all in this, we're all accused, evidence or not. And from the way you looked in the forest, I'm guessing there's another reason you're running away, too."

She flinched a bit, like I'd caught her in something. I wasn't stupid. I knew what she was looking for. At least I had an idea. The Veil breaking like that after all the time we spent trying to end every? So easy?

No, something was up, and it had to do with Ness, and whoever that Person had been.

"I don't believe this all is over," Laine whispered from the back. We all turned to look at her, and she had a look in her eyes I'd never seen before.

"It isn't is it, Ness? If that's the case, then we're not done. Whatever put us through all of that, whatever had our lives on the line for all that time, I'm not letting it go until it's really over. So put this car in drive, Kian, and let's go. And don't say another word until you're ready to explain everything, Ness."

That was intense, even for Laine. But we all felt it. She was right. We talked a big game about being in this together, but that wasn't all of it.

There was something vengeful stirring in the car, for Mack and Rosette, but also for us. Against Plot, against Person, against the town, even against Ness a little. We were all quiet for several seconds before Ness spoke.

"I need to pick up some things before we go."

TIP FOR AN IDIOT #12: STAY OUT OF TROUBLE

We got to my aunt's house, and all the lights were off. There was a cop car in the driveway, and Kian and I quickly walked past once we confirmed the cop inside was fast asleep. I unlocked the door, and we climbed the stairs to my room.

Clothes, a bag of hunting supplies, Bear. That's what I wanted to grab. Yes, Bear included.

Don't judge. I've had Bear since I can remember.

I'm pretty sure I came to my aunt's house with him. And while I'm not really keen on keeping anything to do with my childhood with Tyler, it didn't feel right to leave Bear all by himself. Well, my aunt would be there.

So all by himself.

My aunt was in the kitchen when we got downstairs. The news was on the TV in the other room, Partly McCloudy on the screen looked dazed, the name "Christine Thunder" showed up on a little bar in front of her. She said something about the sand covering the town, that usual blinding beam smile no longer present on her face.

"Christine Thunder. So her real name is ridiculous, too," I murmured to myself. I wasn't nervous for a second. The

chances of my aunt turning us in were low. It was actually concerning, but, whatever.

"Vanessa."

I walked to her and leaned against the counter. She was cutting fruit, and I watched her hands as they sliced methodically.

How old was my aunt? I had no idea, but I thought she was at the age where her hands might have shaken at least a little, but they didn't. Now that I looked at them, her hands didn't look all that old at all.

"We aren't coming back," I said quietly.

"I know," she replied.

Silence.

"Auntie—"

"I'm sorry I couldn't keep you out of all this, Vanessa." My aunt stopped cutting, but she didn't look at me. "I made a promise, and I couldn't keep it. I thought I could."

I wanted her to explain, but she didn't. She turned to me, holding my blue notebook.

"Take this." She pushed it into my hands. "Use it when you need to."

"When I need to?"

"You'll know." Her voice shook a bit, in a way that was almost emotional. I'd never seen her emotional.

"Stand your ground against that lil' boy, Vanessa. Stay out of trouble."

"Police!" someone yelled from the other side of the front door. I gave one last look to my aunt before grabbing Kian's hand and running out the back door.

We peeled off as soon as we got into the Volvo, sirens behind us all the way to the edge of the woods. The place was still dusted in red, and it swirled around us with the gentle breeze that moved through the trees.

I grabbed the notebook, unhooked the pen that stuck out of it, and started to write.

"We need to write a letter explaining our disappearance and our innocence."

"We do?" Laine asked. "Why?"

"Because," Ness replied. "I don't like being lied on. And your parents will want some sort of explanation. Not to mention the off chance that someday we'll be able to explain it all and if people believe us it might mean you guys can come back to Logan someday. That won't happen if we give in to the pressure to confess."

I drafted the letter. Kian made comments over my shoulder.

"Wait, put an exclamation point there. It'll sound friendlier."

"Kian, it's not supposed to sound friendly."

"Oh, right. Okay, let me write something."

Once the letter was somewhat finished, Kian started the car up again.

"Where to?" he asked, glancing toward me. I shrugged.

"Just start driving. First time we take some time to rest, I'll give some directions."

"You're going to explain everything while we drive, Vanessa," Jo said sharply. "Don't even think about leaving a thing out. We're running away with you, so you owe that to us. Do you understand?"

I hesitated. I didn't want to tell them. I didn't want them to know I caused all this. I didn't want them to see me the way I'd begun to see myself. But Jo was right. I owed it to them. And whatever they thought about me afterward, I deserved.

"Okay."

KIAN'S NOTE #12: RE: STAY OUT OF TROUBLE

NESS SPOKE FOR A LONG TIME. I didn't understand a lot of it, but what I did understand made me mad.

Extremely, uncharacteristically, mad.

Tyler, this evil incarnate scum of a human being, did all of this for what? Fun? It took a lot of strength out of me to not explode as Ness spoke.

Jo and Laine shared my rage, I think, but mostly they just looked horrified and sick. Ness looked worse than any of us.

We'd been driving on empty roads for hours, and Ness's voice shook as she spoke. She didn't cry, though.

When she stopped talking, no one said a thing. We stopped at a deserted rest stop and just sort of sat there for a long time.

"Ness," Laine called out. "You've got an evil twin."

We were all quiet again for several seconds before Ness burst out laughing. It was a different, infectious sound, and soon we were all laughing.

"Oh, my God," Ness murmured. "I really do. That's so corny."

"Extremely corny," Jo concurred.

"Embarrassing," Laine commented.

"Pretty cool," Marco and I observed.

And that was the end of it.

We climbed out of the car and raided the empty rest stop, letting any other words swirling through our mind fall into our stomachs with the stale chips we ate. Jo and Ness sat in the car, working on sending the letter we wrote to the police. Marco went to the bathroom, Laine took a nap in the backseat, and I walked around the car, stretching.

I'd grabbed my phone from the glove compartment out of habit, and it started buzzing in my pocket. I pulled it out and checked.

My father.

Everything in me told me not to answer. That he'd somehow be able to track me, find us, and send us all to jail. It wasn't worth the risk. But... I really, really wanted to answer.

It was my *father*.

I hadn't seen him since the fire, and I wanted, no, needed, to know he was really okay. Even if he'd pointed a gun at Ness, even if he believed I was Killer.

I sank to the hard ground behind the car, out of view of the others. I raised the phone to my ear with shaky hands.

"Hello?" I whispered.

"Kian?" my dad said from the other end. "Son?"

"Yeah, yeah, Dad. It's me."

"...Kian—"

"Dad, I know what you're thinking, and I know you're looking for me, but—"

"You aren't coming back, are you?"

My dad's voice was fragile, like it was at the hospital that day. God, it felt like years ago.

I swallow the lump in my throat. "Yeah, Dad. I'm not coming back."

"Are you going to be okay?"

"Yeah," I answered. I heard Jo and Ness arguing in the car, and Laine joined in, yelling at them for waking her up. Marco came stretching out of the rest stop, waving at me. "Yeah, I'm in good hands."

"Vanessa?"

"And others."

My dad was silent for a bit, and the he sighed heavily. "You can always come home, son. Always. Your mother and I are always going to wait for you. You know that, right?"

I choked up for a bit, tears stinging my eyes. "I know."

"Good luck, son."

"Bye, Dad."

ROLL CREDITS

I'M NOT EXACTLY sure where you are, Tyler, but I know you're out there somewhere.

In fact, I've got a few hunches as to where you might be hiding out. Not only that, I know you aren't finished. I want to ask you to leave us alone. I want to *beg* you to leave us alone, but we're cut from the same crimson cloth. You won't stop, and neither will I.

It's like you said, isn't it? All that can be born from abomination is abomination.

Well, that makes two of us.

The End?

LEAVE REVIEW

Help me out & leave a review: https://amzn.to/40pVbpq

Sign up for news and giveaways: https://bit.ly/VanessaSignUp

THE END?

ACKNOWLEDGMENTS

I want to thank my Mom and Dad first and foremost, for supporting me and honestly carrying me through this process.

Thank you for always believing in me and working with me, even when I'm anti.

I also want to thank my siblings for keeping me grounded, my friends for always hyping me up, and my cat for being a cutie patootie.

Thank you to everyone who posted me on their Instagram stories (horrifying, but the support means a lot), thank you to the "we not all fam" groupchat, my english teachers, the school librarians, and Ms. Page.

Thank you to Frank Ocean, Mitski, and MeganTheeStallion. Feel free to collab in my honor. Finally, thank you readers, and get ready, because we'll be seeing a lot more of each other from here on out. Sorry in advance (but not really!)

ABOUT THE AUTHOR

Gabrielle S. Clarke is a high school senior and vice president of her school's Thespian Society. She has been published in the anthology Black Girl, White School: Thriving, Surviving and No, You Can't Touch My Hair and the Thurber House literary journal Flip the Page.

Her debut full-length YA novel, Vanessa Is Not a Victim, blends razor-sharp wit and rebellious spirit to deliver a wickedly fun ride through high school halls fraught with danger and dark comedy. In this thrilling tale, the line between hunter and hunted blurs, keeping readers laughing one moment and gripping their seats the next.

When Gabrielle isn't writing, she enjoys painting, drawing, hanging out with friends, and applying for colleges where she hopes to major in film directing.

instagram.com/gabbycanttalksheswriting

tiktok.com/@gabbycanttalksheswriting

amazon.com/stores/Gabrielle-S.-Clarke/author/B0DJTT348X

ALSO BY GABRIELLE S. CLARKE

Black Girl White School: Thriving, Surviving and No, You Can't Touch My Hair

Flip The Page 2024, Thurber House